*This Body's Not Big
Enough for Both of Us*

ALSO BY EDGAR CANTERO

*Meddling Kids*
*The Supernatural Enhancements*

# This Body's Not Big Enough for Both of Us

A Novel

EDGAR CANTERO

DOUBLEDAY
*New York*

Copyright © 2018 by Edgar Cantero

All rights reserved. Published in the United States by Doubleday, a division of Penguin Random House LLC, New York, and distributed in Canada by Random House of Canada, a division of Penguin Random House Canada Limited, Toronto.

www.doubleday.com

DOUBLEDAY and the portrayal of an anchor with a dolphin are registered trademarks of Penguin Random House LLC.

*Book design by Michael Collica*
*Jacket design by Michael J. Windsor*
*Front-of-jacket images: flames © Anna Panova/Shutterstock; handcuffs © Oleksandr Malysh/Shutterstock; gun © Tedgun/Shutterstock; faces © Jena_Velour/Shutterstock*
*Spine-of-jacket images: flowers © MicroOne/Shutterstock;*
*bullet holes © Nosyrevy/Shutterstock*
*Back-of-jacket images: car © sierrarat/E+/Getty Images; roadrunner*
*© Banaspati99/Shutterstock; skyline © 24Novembers/Shutterstock*

Library of Congress Cataloging-in-Publication Data
Names: Cantero, Edgar, [date] author.
Title: This body's not big enough for both of us : a novel / Edgar Cantero.
Description: First edition. | New York : Doubleday, 2018.
Identifiers: LCCN 2018003301 | ISBN 9780385543965
(hardcover) | ISBN 9780385543972 (ebook)
Subjects: LCSH: Private investigators—Fiction. |
Murder—Investigation—Fiction. | BISAC: FICTION / Satire. | GSAFD:
Black humor (Literature) | Humorous fiction. | Mystery fiction. | Satire.
Classification: LCC PR9155.9.C27 T48 2018 | DDC 823/.92—dc23
LC record available at https://lccn.loc.gov/2018003301

MANUFACTURED IN THE UNITED STATES OF AMERICA

1 3 5 7 9 10 8 6 4 2

First Edition

**An A. Z. Kimrean Adventure**

Elmore Leonard said it's bad style to open a novel with the weather. Well, fuck him—it was a blazing red-hot August morning. The ceiling fan did little more than amuse the flies, many of which wandered up to the highest layer of the office's troposphere to burst into flame and fall spiraling down like wounded Zero fighters. The air was heavy with the smell of sulfur and interbreast sweat. It felt as if El Niño, California, and Satan were conspiring to push the city to the brink of spontaneous combustion.

And then, like a high-heeled coup de grâce, she arrived.

She paused briefly outside the door, her hourglass silhouette cast upon the glass panel with the fresh shiny vinyl letters reading,

**A. KIMREAN**

**Z. KIMREAN**

**PRIVATE EYES**

She knocked first, waited, then tried the handle, and the door surrendered to her touch. She wandered in like a fairy-tale top model into a CGI forest, a flutter of long skirts and flaming red hair kiting behind her, a flock of freckles swarming her eyes like glistening lakes of whoa whoa whoa, okay, wait, wait, wait.

*Kimrean stops, stares dead at Detective Demoines across
the interrogation room table.*

                    DEMOINES
          Sorry, just . . . Can we dial down
          the poetry a notch? The narration's
          way too colorful.

                    KIMREAN
               *(shrugs)*
          My life is colorful.

                    DEMOINES
          Maybe play down the alliteration a
          little.

                    KIMREAN
          "Alliteration a little." You know, your
          life could've been colorful too, Ted,
          but you chose the SFPD. The thrill of
          paperwork and the flashy badges.

                    DEMOINES
          You need a badge to work as a P.I. too.

*Pause.*

                    KIMREAN
          Sure. I was testing you.
                    —

Darkness prevented long descriptive paragraphs. Blind-striped sunlight poured through the large windows across a vast, empty space navigated by intrepid motes of dust. The woman discerned a cleared desk to the right, smelled a bed in an alcove to the back left. In the middle of the room stood a high stool or a very narrow table, dais-wise. Atop sat a chess set in mid-battle.

Through a lateral door on the alcove's side, somebody—the slender, long-limbed ink sketch of somebody—stepped out, preceded by the sound of a flushing toilet, and stopped right upon seeing her. The woman barely made out an eye glistening in the dark, two hands wiping some rumpled clothes, a mouth greeting her.

"Wow, you are hot."

The woman looked away, smoothed her dress, checked her hair, scratched her forearm, did another thirty irrelevant actions meant to summon her cool, and finally resumed speaking. "Are you the private investigator?"

"I can be whatever you want me to be."

She pointed at the door, baffled. "The sign says 'Private Eyes.'"

"And you're so sagacious, I can't believe you're in need of one." The mouth drew a grin as shiny and sharp as a cutlass.

The dame paused for a second while she realigned her expectations with the slim, beaming reality before her. It didn't match her platonic archetype for a private detective. The spartan pay-by-the-week rental office she had anticipated; also the fedora and the white tank top—maybe not the skimpy black waistcoat on top. But she was also expecting a square jaw, coarse stubble, the odd scar, a dark brow: the features of a man of action as defined in her mind by the cover art of some gritty paperback. The face watching her now was oval or ogive shaped. It had the featureless skin of a mannequin and the vigilant look of a small bird. The only visible eye, spotlit by an implausibly accurate stripe of blind-filtered daylight, was a lemony green. And whether the collection of parts added up to a man was still up for debate.

"I'm sorry, are you A. Kimrean or Z. Kimrean?"

The green eye stared back at her, silent. Then the whole figure moved past her to the entrance, leaned out into the landing, looked both ways, and carefully closed the door.

"Are you okay?" the woman asked, scowling at her host's frowsy appearance.

"Oh, yeah," said the other, pointing toward the bathroom. "Much better now."

The same implausible light stripe fell on the right eye now: a gentle orange brown, like ale, peeking through bangs of straw-colored hair.

"Interesting."

—

                              DEMOINES
          No, it's not.


*Kimrean shuts up, clearly offended by the unflattering*
*review.*


                              DEMOINES
          You're recounting your sexy scenarios
          with red-haired women instead of
          explaining your role in this . . .
                    *(reads notes)*
          "Shooting, arson, and destruction of a
          police vehicle."

                    KIMREAN
I'm giving you context. This is
relevant.


                    DEMOINES
How?


                    KIMREAN
It's a fundamental principle of
private investigation. There's no yin
without yang. No violence without
love.


                    DEMOINES
Zooey . . .


                    KIMREAN
I'm serious! You wouldn't know 'cause
you're in the public sector, but it's
a natural constant in my business.
From the moment you rent an office on
Fisherman's Wharf and spell your name
and the words "Private Eye" in vinyl
letters on the glass, only two types
of people will go through that door:
femmes fatales and neckless thugs
coming to pummel your teeth in.


*The detainee sits back, stick-insect legs spread outward,*
*exposing the irrefutable truth. Demoines rubs his face.*

                         DEMOINES
          Can we just skip the redhead and
          start with the shooting?

                         KIMREAN
                 (sighs, frustrated)
          Fine.

                           ——

Elmore Leonard said blah blah blah blah blah. It was a blazing
red-hot August morning. The fan on the ceiling did little to
stir the gunpowder and brick dust suspended in the air while a
long-condemned second of calm died in the clangor of Kimrean
blasting through the wall, an avalanche of plaster and bathroom
tiles pouring onto the bedspread. Green Teeth Murdoc, standing
in the middle of the office, stepped back and fired a new burst
of automatic gunfire into the alcove, the P.I. barely brushing the
mattress before sliding into the narrow gap between the bed and
the wall, taking cover from the bulletstorm.

    A round of ammo or a piece of shrapnel tipped over the bottle
of bourbon on the upside-down carton serving as a bedside table.
Behind the bed, reeking with adrenaline, Kimrean took some
quick, deep breaths and set out to execute their plan for survival.

    Step one: Plug in the extension cord.

    Step two: Yank the bedsheets and search the bundle for the
revolver.

    Fire ceased. A rare, quivering silence took over the room.

    Kimrean found their gun and flipped it in their hands.

    "Is this loaded?"

    They pulled the trigger and fired a bullet into the brick wall.

A new burst of submachine-gun fire immediately zeroed into that same exact square foot, splashing Campbell's soup chunks of brownstone everywhere.

"That was *unbelievably* fucking stupid," Kimrean judged, hands squeezing the revolver, mouth counting down the seconds, chest heaving at the rate of the Uzi fire, which barely muffled the sandpaper voice of Green Teeth Murdoc screaming, *"WHERE'S MY FUCKING MONEY, YOU CHEATING HOLY SHIT OKAY OKAY WAIT WAIT WAIT!"*

—

                    DEMOINES
            (takes a deep breath)
        That's the neckless thug, I suppose.


                    KIMREAN
        Actually, that was Green Teeth Murdoc.
        Qualifies as a villain, but yeah. He
        still counts.


                    DEMOINES
        Okay, forget it. Adrian.


                    KIMREAN
        Yes?


                    DEMOINES
        Take me back five minutes before the
        shooter comes in.

KIMREAN

*("But, Mom!")*

That's where I started!


DEMOINES

Shut up!

—

"Please take a seat . . . over there, I guess."

The femme approached the alcove indicated on the left. A twin bed, unmade, filled up the P.I.'s burrow, guarded by a bare coat stand. Half a bottle of bourbon dozed next to a pair of handcuffs on an upside-down carton beside the pillow. Kimrean pulled up the window blinds, and jeering sunlight poured in to reveal something ever more embarrassing in the sheets.

"There is a gun in your bed," the femme pointed out.

"That's good to know."

She turned to face the desk. It wasn't completely cleared, she could see now: there was a toaster on it.

The P.I. presumptive was now studying the ongoing game of chess on the dais in front of the window. A mischievous smile dawned on their blank face as the left hand pinched a black knight's head and skipped it over enemy lines.

The femme invoked some saliva and stated her purpose. "I am looking for a detective."

"Good job so far. Any idea who's stalking you?"

"No, that's what—" She cut herself off midsentence. "How do you know I'm being stalked?"

In those few lines of dialogue, the detective's countenance

had segued from patent curiosity to absolute tedium. No trace of interest belied that impression during the following speech:

"Young high-class white woman visits cheap private eye; she's neither employed nor married, so this isn't business or family related; it's personal. Your pulse was shaky when you applied your lipstick, but it's steady now: you feel insecure at home; your space was violated. My first choice would be burglary, but victims of burglary become more guarded, whereas you didn't hesitate coming to this neighborhood wearing that gold pendant shaped like a vine leaf. Nonetheless, despite the heat, you opted for a high-collar dress this morning, so I'm leaning toward my second option: harassment." Oxygen was replenished, and the conclusion followed. "Thus, you're being stalked."

All this had spurted out of the mouth like a telex message, while the hands interrogated a couple drawers in the desk and moved a white bishop on the chessboard.

The femme examined her host once again, or rather the assembly of body parts that played said role. The mismatched eyes hardly blinked; the lipless mouth (lips, in fact, so thin and pale as to be considered absent) virtually vanished when it closed. The body was neither muscular nor bony: both those qualities presume volume; the subject here, perched on the desk, looked flat. And yet, as she glanced down the P.I.'s neckline . . . were those breasts inside the tank top?

"You had breakfast?" the good host chimed, hopping off the table and crossing the room toward the embryo of a kitchen next to the coat stand, left hand prodding a black pawn to c5 on the way. The kitchen consisted of one salvaged wood-grain vinyl cupboard and a camping stove connected to a propane canister. The detective retrieved the single item in the cupboard—a box of blueberry Pop-Tarts—and headed back to the desk, right hand pushing the white queen to xc5 and tossing the captured pawn over the shoulder. It clunked somewhere in the dark side of the alcove.

"Yes, I had breakfast," the femme said. "And I am being stalked. For a time now, at nights, I've been feeling someone watching me when I undress."

"Can't imagine why!" the P.I. inserted as a riant exclamation while loading two Pop-Tarts into the toaster.

"And last night, when I was going to bed, I saw somebody peeping through the French windows. I screamed, and he disappeared into the rosebushes."

She stood by for another comment, but the detective's attention was now on the toaster. The lever was down, but the appliance wasn't working.

The brown and green eyes tracked along the power cord slithering across the room and disappearing under the bed. Then they rose to meet hers.

"Terrifying."

The smile was gone. Along with any other sign of human emotion.

The femme wondered whether the voice (cold, slightly coarse) fell within the masculine or feminine spectrum. *Terra nullius,* she concluded.

"So, can you help me?"

"I charge three hundred bucks a day. Half a day in advance."

"Excuse me, I don't mean to be rude, but I need to ask," she began, gathering courage for the indiscretion: "Are you a man?"

"Aww, she's so sweet. I love silly redheads!"

"I beg your pardon?"

"Granted," the orange-brown eye ruled. "As soon as you give me my one fifty."

The voice had again become a mirthless drone, the asymmetrical face inches away from the client's. If only to look away, she went for her purse and pulled out a wallet. By the time awkwardness yielded to common sense and she realized she was giving $150 to a virtual stranger for no apparent reason, she already had the money in her hand. The other's right snatched the notes in an asp-like movement.

"Thanks, you can leave now."

The detective counted the money and slipped the folded notes into the nonexistent space between the pants and the hip.

The femme felt heat in her cheeks. And not from the blazing red-hot August morning. This was her blushing with shame.

"Are you even going to ask my name?"

"Fiona Hearsh," one of the two eyes answered. It would be difficult to assert which one; they were both looking away. One mantis leg topped the other, hands alighted on a knee. Then the eyes noticed the customer was still there. An index finger pointed at her purse. "Your name is embossed in the inside."

"It says 'F. Hearsh.'"

"And Fiona is the most popular *F* name among women of Irish ancestry," the index postulated, alluding to her red hair. "Plus, it means 'vine' in Gaelic." It pointed at her gold pendant.

A fly buzzed between the characters, aware of its comic-relief role.

The grin dawned back in the lipless mouth one last time.

"If you wanna help, we could role-play the facts of the case. Pretend you're going to bed, it's been a long day, you take off your dress, finally get rid of that bra—do you mind if I take pictures?"

Five seconds later, the femme fatale was walking out of the

office and the novel, her scandalized steps echoing down the stairwell.

Kimrean stood up, smoothed out their two-dimensional pants, and leaned outside the door into the shadowy landing. Eventually, the slam of the front door downstairs announced that the client had left the building.

"All clear," Kimrean said. "No need to rein in your halitosis."

At the far end of the landing, the ember of a cigarette twinkled in the dark. It died a moment later, squished on a step.

There was a soft rustle of impending doom, and Green Teeth Murdoc emerged into the penumbra. Light cringed to shine on the gambler's pale lime skin, the breezy pastel suit, the yellow-smeared fingers curled around a submachine gun.

"Brought a friend of mine along," he croaked, beaming a fan-favorite smile.

"Oh, yeah, sure," Kimrean said, yielding the threshold and calmly retreating into the office. "Calling your firearms 'friends.' Completely normal. Lots of men whose father didn't buy their first prostitute do it."

Before that snarky remark had time to garner a reaction, Kimrean slammed the front door in Murdoc's face and lurched through the side door to the bathroom.

Murdoc kicked his way into the apartment, faced left, and opened fire. A full artillery battalion could have hardly made more noise in the 2.6 seconds the gun needed to turn the bathroom door into a sieve.

Then the door opened, and a two-hundred-pound man in a black suit staggered out with an anal plug stuffed in his mouth and three bullets lodged in his chest. He collapsed facefirst on the wooden floor with the seismic force of what the flying fuck wait wait wait!

—

*Detective Demoines riffles through his notes, Kimrean frozen in the middle of mimicking the fall of a speared mammoth.*

> DEMOINES
> Who the hell was that?!

> KIMREAN
> (like, "Obviously.")
> A neckless thug.

> DEMOINES
> Well, when did that one come in?

> KIMREAN
> Oh, he was from the previous batch.

—

It was a blazing red-hot August morning, strewn with the black-and-white imagery of ineffective ceiling fans and self-igniting houseflies. And then, like an untimely snowstorm, they arrived, their Ikea Dombås wardrobe silhouettes barely fitting the glass panel with the fresh shiny vinyl letters reading,

**A. KIMREAN**

**Z. KIMREAN**

**PRIVATE EYES**

The two neckless thugs squeezed through the doorway into the zebra-lit office, sun highlighting their Hasidic gun-smuggler suits, the baseball bat apiece, the square mugs so easy to picture against a height-measurement screen—somewhere in the vicinity of the 6'8" line.

A lithe human figure slumbered at the desk, two feet in imitation Converse on the table offering the visitors their worn white soles.

"Mr. Kimrean."

The body stirred. A hand lifted the brim of a fedora.

"Almost."

"Mr. Murdoc sent us," the same thug spoke, or perhaps the other. His voice was like the ubiquitous public announcement before a street riot is quelled. "He is distressed about the outcome of the poker game last Monday."

"Well, that's because Mr. Murdoc is like a carpenter who misplaces his tools," Kimrean said, sitting up, a stray right hand stealthily sliding toward the drawer on that side of the desk. The green and brown eyes checked for a reaction from the audience. "A saw loser . . . Really? Do I need to explain this one?"

"Mr. Murdoc's concerned there was cheating at his table," the thug resumed. "He wishes to see you about it."

The way he held up the bat and stroked the barrel made the addition of a time adverb unnecessary. Kimrean nodded, making sure to show undivided attention while their right hand felt its way around the contents of the drawer.

The other thug, already tagged "Gravel" in Kimrean's mental notes to distinguish him from his brother, "Rock," poked around the detective's quarters.

"Any chance you keep your winnings around here?"

"Sadly, no. I already drank, smoked, and fucked those,"

Kimrean informed. "By which I mean, I used the money to buy bourbon, weed, and the services of a pretty ladyboy I met in Little Saigon. She just left. Should've seen her."

By that time, neither Kimrean's eyes, nor Rock's, nor Gravel's, could any longer ignore the fuss of the P.I.'s rogue right hand fumbling behind the desk. All the characters exchanged looks. A very uncomfortable silence somehow wedged its way into the already tense scene.

"Sorry," Kimrean apologized, sincerely. "Do you guys see my revolver somewhere?"

The thugs actually took the trouble to survey the room, as far as the dramatic lighting allowed. They returned to Kimrean, shaking their heads.

"Is there any problem?" one of them wondered.

"No, it's nothing," Kimrean answered, extracting from the right top drawer what everyone in the room unsynchronizedly identified as a large anal plug. "Except now I'm wondering what the ladyboy had inside her when she walked out."

There was another compulsory pause for unsettling mental pictures, and then Kimrean stood up, wiggling the sex toy in their hand.

"No problem! I'll just give this a quick rinse, in case Mr. Murdoc wants to use it in our tête-à-tête, and we'll be on our way."

The thugs felt way too uncomfortable to do anything but watch as the zany sleuth crossed the room toward the bathroom, stopped by the door, sent them a charming smile, and then relinquished any form of composure to run the hell out of there.

It was a six-foot leap to the bathroom window over the toilet, but the first thug still caught the lower half of the P.I. squirming through the opening. Kimrean failed to get a grip on the waste pipe outside before being dragged back in.

The good thing about skirmishes in narrow spaces: they favor the smaller skirmisher. When Rock yanked Kimrean back inside, flinging them across the ten-by-six-foot bathroom, their in-flight puppet body slammed the door on the incoming second thug before hitting the tiled corner at the other end and landing in the shower pan. After which Kimrean's first action was to pull the curtain closed.

"Privacy! Privacy!"

Rock tore it open, just in time to get a jet of scalding hot water to his face before Kimrean leaped onto his back, hoping to knock him down, failing, but managing to rodeo on him for a few glorious seconds and crash him against the door, slamming it once again on the other thug's face. That was a short-lived victory before Rock grabbed them by the neck, smashed them into the mirror cabinet, and haymakered them off the sink back to the shower corner.

Kimrean was still scrambling upright, broken tiles falling off the wall, when Rock gripped his bat and tried to hammer down with a vertical strike, but the tip of the bat knocked the curtain rod over the target. He attempted a power hit instead and capped his partner's face with the backswing as Gravel tried to join in the fun for a third time.

"Sorry!" he roared over his shoulder, and then faced the cowering freak fumbling under the fallen curtain again. He switched hands, measured the distance, watched for any obstacles, swung the bat . . .

And Kimrean whacked his shin with the curtain rod, destabilizing him, and hatched triumphantly from the canvas bundle, spraying half a can of long-lasting deodorant into his eyes and yelling, *"Strike threeeeeee!"*

That was enough to make Rock drop the bat and roll back,

opening a metaphorical window for Kimrean to leap over him and reach the literal window, but the thug reacted in time and slammed Kimrean's head on the toilet, then staggered up and repeatedly—banged—the seat—on—the little—bastard's—head—"Dear—Mister—Lysol—Fresh—Pine—my—ass"—until one of Kimrean's hands located a shard from the broken mirror and jammed it into the guy's thigh. Rock rolled over, his scream of pain cut short as Kimrean jammed the anal plug into his mouth.

"Oh, *now* you wish you let me give it a rinse, don't you?"

The door crashed open. Gravel, blood trickling out of his new tooth gap, glared down at the melee on the floor.

The slippery little clown met his gaze from under the sink, frozen in the middle of a chokehold on his terrified, latex-stuffed partner.

"I can explain," the clown said. "What was I supposed to do? You're never home!"

Gravel lurched in, slipped on the baseball bat, fell forward, and landed on top of them like a sack of rocks, head lopping off a large section of the sink on the way down.

The showerhead was still spraying hot water, the only noise on the sound track for a moment.

Kimrean took a minute to check the vitals of everybody in the room. The thug on top of them was unconscious. The thug beneath, still gagged and half choked and reeking of Chill Ocean fragrance, was on his way there. Kimrean made sure to hold his hand all along, shushing into his ear, until his heartbeat plateaued into a comfortable coma.

And then there was a knock on the front door.

Careful not to disrupt the momentary peace, Kimrean slipped out of that particular manwich, turned off the water, replaced their hat, queried a piece of mirror, wiped off the dust and a little blood from his cheekbone, and then flushed the toilet and scurried out of the bathroom.

Outside, the femme fatale was still letting her eyes adjust to the dark.

"Wow, you are hot," Kimrean said.

—

DEMOINES
Wait--that whole bit was a flashback?


KIMREAN
Uh-huh.


DEMOINES
Inside your statement? Which is itself
a flashback? A flashback within a
flashback?


KIMREAN
     (impatient)
Yes! Jesus Christ, Ted, do you need a
graphic or what? "Oh, this Christopher
Nolan shit's so confusing, give me
linear narrative, I'm a hundred years
old!"


DEMOINES
Right! Right! So the femme fatale
comes in . . .
     (thinks)
She wasn't all that fatale, was she?

                    KIMREAN
     I know. I defused her. Shall I skip
     through her part?


                    DEMOINES
     Yes, please.


                        —


The femme approached half a bottle of liquor next to some
handcuffs on an upside-down carton. "There is a gun in your
bed," she pointed out the ongoing game of chess any idea who's
stalking you blueberry Pop-Tarts queen to xc5 into the toaster
three hundred bucks, "Thanks, you can leave, Fiona Hearsh."

Meanwhile, in the paltry bathroom, the neckless thug known
as Rock bobbed up from his short lapse into unconsciousness to
an unconfessable taste at the back of his throat. His jaw hurt. His
associate lay facedown on top of him, knocked out. Beyond his
body, far above, the bottom of the fractured sink looked like the
unreachable dominion of angels.

His right arm was bent behind his own back. Every cramped
muscle from the shoulder down moaned loudly while he freed it,
but he took pleasure in that pain. Pain meant anger. Anger meant
will. He grudgingly pushed his partner off toward the toilet and
heaved himself up, careful not to cut his palms on the broken
glass. The stab wound to his thigh sent out a tortured distress
signal, but he gulped down the scream.

As Gravel drowsily stirred back to life, Rock cracked his ten
knuckles and stood before the door whence the clown's voice
could be heard. Vengeance awaited behind that door. Sweet,
cathartic vengeance.

Then, within the next second, the door exploded open, banging his head, and Kimrean dashed in and dove into the shower. And in the second after that one, a bullet wave pierced the door and sank into Rock's vital organs.

Inertia allowed him to open the door and stagger out, his senses again shutting down one by one. Taste was the last to go and, as he plummeted forward, it informed him that he had forgotten to remove the plug from his mouth.

Kimrean reached to close the door as the body outside hit the floor like a mass-extinction event.

The celebration, however, had to be postponed at the sight of the enormous shoes that had just appeared behind the door, blocking the way to the window.

Gravel hoisted the P.I. by the throat, held them at full arm's length. Kimrean didn't have time to come up with a flattering comment on the thug's new face before the guy covered the length of the room in one stride and whammed them into the shower, two feet in the air, then swept them across the wall and crashed them again into the southeast corner. The whole wall trembled with the shock: inches from the shower, it was likely rotten and damp. It would make a nice visual memory, Gravel thought, to knock that freaky lollipop head clean through the plaster.

Before he could throw the punch, though, another roaring burst of gunfire came from the main room. Bullet holes blossomed into the corner, on either side of Kimrean's waist, two slugs actually grazing their waistcoat and belt, one sinking into Gravel's abdomen.

"Fuck!" he cried, tumbling back. "Boss! I'm back here!"

It was useless: the shooting continued, bullet holes popping all over the wall and sweeping back toward the door, while both the thug and the detective lay down, covering their heads from the flying debris, Kimrean trying to make conversation through the burst.

"He seems like a great employer."

The thunder stopped, and Kimrean listened to the footsteps in the office and immediately grabbed the baseball bat and used it to wedge the door shut right before Murdoc twisted the handle from the other side.

That was the south exit blocked. West was the bathroom window, its promising view blocked again by Gravel, pressing his newest wound with one hand, gripping a mirror shard in the other, growling out of a bloodied mouth.

Kimrean measured the distance to the window, subtracted it from the length of the room, guessed the resistance left in the bullet-ridden partition wall behind them. It would have to be east.

A long-condemned second of calm died in the clangor of Kimrean blasting through the wall, an avalanche of plaster—

—

DEMOINES
Hey, that's familiar.


KIMREAN
Yeah, isn't this cool? I lived the
whole thing sequentially and it was
way less exciting.

—

—*unbelievably* fucking stupid," Kimrean judged, hands squeezing the revolver, mouth counting down the seconds, chest heaving at the rate of the Uzi fire, which barely muffled out the sandpaper voice of Green Teeth Murdoc screaming, *"WHERE'S MY FUCKING MONEY, YOU CHEATING, LYING, LITTLE DANGLY SHIIIIIT?!"*

A slow stream of bourbon from the tipped bottle was flowing west along the groove between two floorboards, past the kitchenette and nearing the bathroom whence Gravel now emerged.

"Where is she?! *Where?!*"

"Behind the bed; he's got a gun!" Murdoc said.

"Cover me!" Gravel shouted. Kimrean felt the incoming T-rex footsteps shaking the floor. "I'm gonna tear her limb for—"

Kimrean fired three rounds under the bed; one or two hit the incoming thug and sent him crashing to the floor like a tripping wildebeest in a stampede. He stayed there, crying in agony, while the nth wave of bullets hit the alcove, forcing Kimrean to retreat to the back wall and hold the fort just a few seconds more now.

Three. Two. One.

The plugged-in toaster on the desk went *ka-chunk*, ejecting a couple blueberry Pop-Tarts. They barely stopped at the zenith of their trajectory before gunfire blew them both into subatomic matter.

In that nanosecond of distraction, Kimrean popped up and fired the fifth round at Green Teeth Murdoc. It hit him in the shoulder. The modified Uzi dropped with a defeated clank that was the signal for Kimrean to jump out of the trench, grab the handcuffs, kick the Uzi out of the equation toward the lifeless, neckless thug by the door, and connect a cross sucker punch to Murdoc's cheekbone.

The villain fell to one knee, the sharp pain from the bullet wound effectively numbed by the ringing in his ears. It started to fade out only after the detective had clicked the cuffs on his wrists.

"Please don't scratch them up," Kimrean admonished. "They bear very fond memories."

Unappreciative of quips, Murdoc attempted a left uppercut that didn't connect, but the right that was bound to follow did. Kimrean flew backward, felt the revolver leaving their hand—in that order—and landed on their back, vertebrae slamming on the woodwork, and from that angle watched with reasonable horror as the bad guy dove after them to elbow their skull through the floor. The detective rolled over to dodge the blow and, in the absence of the revolver, seized the next best thing: the toaster's power cord.

There was little Murdoc could do in handcuffs to stop the cord from wrapping around his neck. The first strangling yank pulled them together: villain on top using one hand to grind the detective into the floor and the other to keep the cord from fully choking him, Kimrean on bottom wincing at the close-up of the face that had contributed so much to its owner's legendary street rep.

Until the safety switch of a submachine gun spoke.

*The* submachine gun. Murdoc's Uzi. Held point-blank to Kimrean's head by the supposedly lifeless Rock, who wasn't so lifeless after all.

"Oh no," Kimrean admonished. "You lost your plug. Now I have to spank you."

"Don't shoot!" Murdoc warned, anticipating a rage response from his henchman. "I want him alive when we harvest his organs for payment."

He sat up astride Kimrean's crotch, cuffed hands struggling and failing to reach his own side pocket.

"Cigarette," he ordered, taking the Uzi from his henchman.

"I won that money fair and square, Mudsy," Kimrean said, pitying the cruiserweight thug who could barely stand reaching into his blood-caked suit for a smoke. "Why not just let it go?"

"You cheated!" Murdoc hissed. "We checked the tapes. You had an ace in your waistcoat pocket." He leaned forward to receive the cigarette in his mouth, then waited for the light. "I. Never. Lose."

Kimrean made sure to take a deep breath before the next speech.

"Miss Watson was on a draw looking for the king of spades in my hand, Mr. Windsor had the queen, and Professor Sweeney always bluffs with queens or higher, but she just called your twenty. You went all in with a 1.3 percent chance of double aces and kings at best, 6.7 percent just aces, 10.3 percent kings on seven."

Rock, holding out a lit match, blinked twice at the line, unusually long for a fight scene. Murdoc ignored the flame and loomed over Kimrean again.

"What's that supposed to mean?"

The brown and green eyes looked away from his face, revolted. The frail throat almost rebelled at the smell. The lipless mouth smirked, grateful for that perfectly timed villain question.

"It means I never needed the ace."

Which Kimrean proved by showing the ace was still in their waistcoat pocket and bringing it to Murdoc's eyes. All of it in one-twelfth of a second.

In fact, the edge of the card sliced Murdoc's cornea.

Just as the villain jerked back, Kimrean's left hand gripped the cord and flailed the toaster against the neckless thug's head, the burning match flying out of his grasp. Murdoc leaned forward again, ready to unload the Uzi point-blank into Kimrean's brain, while Kimrean swung the toaster again into the air. Over the ceiling fan.

The cord got caught in the rotating blades, winding Murdoc up by the neck, lifting him just as the still-burning match landed in the stream of bourbon on the floor.

—

DEMOINES
The bourbon from . . . Oh, right.
   (beat)
Did you even know it would land there?

KIMREAN
I don't know what I'm doing half the
time. I just hope the other guy does.

—

It was a blazing red-hot August morning.

The ceiling fan did its best to hoist a full-grown, chain-smoking, midlevel gang lord upward and counterclockwise.

A Milky Way of toxic saliva droplets trailed off the nine-inch tongue wrung out of his mouth.

His clenched finger strangled the Uzi's trigger, bullets pulsing out of the barrel drawing a perfect logarithmic spiral.

Rock staggered back toward the door, into the predicted trajectory of a bullet.

The sixth round clicked inside the chamber of the forgotten revolver that Gravel had retrieved near the window.

Blue flames ran up the stream of alcohol across the room, flowing right under the propane canister in the kitchenette, and

A. Z. Kimrean, sprinting ahead of the flames, gazed over the chessboard on the way to the window and, as they passed, moved a black pawn to c3.

"Oooh yeah! Let's see you get out of that one."

And then time resumed, and Murdoc completed a full revolution on the fan, and an Uzi bullet went right into Rock's skull, and Gravel aimed the revolver at the charging private eye, and the propane bottle exploded, and Kimrean rammed against the revolver and the thug and the window behind him and crashed through it, inches ahead of the deflagration trailing them out into the blue sky.

In the time it took to free fall down three stories, wind slapping their faces at 9.81 m/s$^2$, Kimrean clambered on the thug, all the way screaming, "My turn on top, *baaaaaaaaaaaaabe!*"

Three hundred thirty-five pounds of combined weight dropped on the roof of the police car that had just parked in front of the building, sinking its blaring siren and flashing lights beneath the dashboard, where the neckless thug stayed, while Kimrean bounced off the flesh-and-broken-bones sack, flipped six times in the air, and landed faceup on the road two steps away from the incoming Powell-Hyde cable car whose driver jammed on the brakes until sparks welded the brake pad to the wheel and pulled the juggernaut to a full stop just as the front right wheel was literally rolling on top of a strand of Kimrean's hair.

Two policemen crawled out of the cruiser, shaking the broken glass from their eyes. The thug lay buried in the hood, fused with the engine. Smoke and no flames billowed out of the third-floor window.

On the pavement, Kimrean stared dead at the underside of the cable car and at a slice of morning sky beyond, mentally roll-calling all four limbs spread on the asphalt and checking on a wallowing—but still intact—spinal cord.

And then they burst into maniac laughter.

ADRIAN KIMREAN     ZOOEY KIMREAN

IN

# THIS BODY'S NOT BIG ENOUGH FOR BOTH OF US

a novel by
**EDGAR CANTERO**

# 1

Carlyle smashed the receiver on the phone, bit down on a cigar, whatted away some guy who had just knocked on his door, did something else that deputy police chiefs do, though in an unnecessarily violent manner, and rounded on the other person in the room.

"What's the word from Mojave?"

The other person was Lieutenant Greggs, homicide detective.

"We left him a message. Still no word," she said from her corner near the file cabinet. Then, looking up from the linoleum: "Sir, they're our best chance."

"We're the San Francisco Police Department," Carlyle grunted. "We do not outsource."

"Precisely because we're the police, there are things we can't do. They can."

Carlyle Hindenburged into his chair, chugging out black smoke like a coal refinery. He knew Greggs believed in Dirty Harry types: passionately homicidal cops who skip over the chain of command and bend rules for the greater good. She saw these lone wolves as a necessary stopgap for an imperfect system. Maybe she had dreamed of being the first lone wolf on the force since Harry Callahan minted the role, but the truth was she believed in that kind of officer only in theory; she knew the difficulties it posed to try to be one, especially for a first-generation African American woman. It was obvious to her that white males were given much more leeway: when she tried the same approach to police work it took only three days to earn her first disciplinary action, with Carlyle doing the whole *I'll take your badge and weapon* routine in that very office. To this day she still indulged in the odd reckless behavior or merited a reprimand for breaking the occasional rapist's arm in more pieces than could be fixed, but no one considered her a rogue officer. And unlike the white male lone wolves, she was a parent too, so facing gunmen without backup or a suspension without pay was no laughing matter. But she still believed in creative workarounds to the rules, or she wouldn't be in Carlyle's office right now.

Carlyle squished the cigar in his ashtray, or somewhere in its suburbs.

"Where's that wonder duo now?"

"Demoines is taking their statement," Greggs said. She considered adding something else at that point but she bit her lip. It was better to wait.

Carlyle interlaced his sausagy fingers and leaned back in his chair, framed by the bright city skyline behind his desk like a late-night talk show host. To his right, a map of the Bay Area hung voodooed by a hundred colored pins. The pins were part of a case closed in 1975, but they were kept there to reinforce the impression that a lot of work got done in that office. Carlyle himself stayed fat, hypertensive, and divorced for the same purpose.

"All right," he puffed, slapping some indiscriminate object on his desk. "Let's go see them."

Greggs reined in a victory gesture. The hardest part—towing Carlyle out of his office—had been accomplished.

———

They stepped out into the bullpen, spread out under cigarette fog and fluorescent lights. Jacketless cops pulled their feet off their desks or hurried through personal phone calls as the party of two walked past their cubicles, Carlyle filling both lanes of the hallway and forcing the mail boys to take alternate routes. The low-tar air teemed with analog phone rings and yapping typewriters.

At an intersection, they caught sight of Detective Ted Demoines, from the Narcotic and Vice Division. He did not see them, but the guy behind him did. At first glance, Carlyle dismissed him as a lingering detainee from some raid at the harbor on the night shift: nothing to shock a veteran officer, although there was something about that skinny, overexplicit body that made the chief scowl. Perhaps it was his bearing, or the way he moved like an emaciated marionette. On instinct, Carlyle checked the ceiling for the operator's strings. His clothes (somehow not enough to fully dress the wearer) were all in black and white: tight pants, a tank top, and a silly little waistcoat, open. His hair reminded Carlyle of hay, and his face of a carnival in Venice. He seemed to be speaking to Demoines, complaining about some handcuffs (his wrists were not cuffed), when he halted upon seeing Greggs—more accurately, the head stopped first, then the rest of the body followed—and immediately changed directions to greet her.

"Gre-e-e-eggs!"

He hugged her like French people hug on train platforms. Greggs didn't seem off-put; she patted the marionette's back like she would an overexcited dog.

"Hello, Zooey, hello." Then she pushed him away a little, as if to reckon how much he had grown, but she only said, in a different tone, "Adrian."

"Lieutenant," the marionette replied, solemnly. "How's the kid?"

"Fine. Thanks for faking interest."

"The handcuffs on Green Teeth Murdoc—they're mine, I want them back!" he whined, pointing at Demoines, who had joined them.

"I'll tell the morgue," Greggs promised. "We need to talk. Care to come into my office?"

Carlyle noticed the marionette registering him out of the corner of its eye—a furtive golden-brown eye, half hidden behind a sideswept bang. The rest of the mannequin didn't speak to or acknowledge him, but that spying pupil made him feel exposed, naked. Something neither he nor anyone on that floor cared to imagine.

He followed Greggs and Demoines and the marionette into a smaller office than his own. A few Himalayas of case files and manila envelopes stood tall in the perimeter of the room. An overpopulated corkboard on one wall and several swarms of sticky notes here and there gave the impression that even more work got done here, which incidentally was also true. The lieutenant started vacating furniture; the marionette seized the first available seat.

"We missed you," said Greggs. "So nice of you to come see us."

"I know," the marionette said, mouth wide open like one of Jim Henson's Muppets. "I could've come earlier, but I was in a ladyboy all week." There was a pause for laughs, but Greggs wasn't listening, Demoines barely needed to suppress a chuckle, and Carlyle had nothing to suppress. The marionette sat staring at the last with strangely disjointed eyes, legs obscenely spread apart. "I meant to say I was having sex with her. Not that she'd swallowed me whole. *(Pointing at Carlyle's belly.)* As you seem capable of doing."

Carlyle scratched his middle chin, then queried Greggs, who had finished emptying seats, and Demoines. The latter had nestled in a corner, arms crossed, and would say nothing. He was blond, a Quebecker, and exasperatingly timid.

"So?" the chief prompted. "Do the P.I.s come after the drag queen's routine or what?"

There was a sort of Mexican standoff of dodgy stares. Greggs's and Demoines's seemed to drift toward the marionette, who now appeared to be wildly interested in the fluvial system of veins in his arm.

The synaptic spark made Carlyle wince. "No way. This Tinker Bell is a P.I.?"

The Tinker Bell in question bent in a silent Harpo Marx laugh.

"Sir, he's got experience—tons of it," Greggs jumped in. "He's run his own practice in North Beach for quite some time."

"Four days," the marionette refined, brimming with pride.

"He had others before this one," Demoines assisted.

"Where were you four days ago?" Carlyle inquired.

"Green Teeth Murdoc's poker night."

"And before that?"

"Claymoore."

"Claymoore, as in Claymoore Psychiatric Hospital?"

The marionette nodded its big, lolling head.

The chief fell silent. It was only eleven a.m., and already he was regretting not being hit by a trolley on the way to work.

"Okay. Where's the other one?"

Greggs bit her lip again.

DEMOINES: *(Pointing at the marionette.)* It's . . . *(Beat.)* It's him as well.

GREGGS: Her.

DEMOINES: Them.

Now the marionette looked bored.

Carlyle sat in silence for a while and then rose and snapped his fingers.

"Outside. Now."

They left the P.I. wrapped like a boa constrictor around the rotating desk chair; they could still see him/her/them through the window.

Carlyle closed the door and shot a .44 Magnum index finger at his subordinates: "Forget that PC bullshit and someone tell me who the fuck that clown is."

Greggs volunteered for the first round. "Sir, it's . . . Look, you know how a fetus grows in the mother's womb? Sometimes, if two blastocytes merge—"

"What the fuck are you talking about, Lieutenant?!"

"Wait, Chief, it's easier than that," Demoines interceded, waving the conversation back to a civil volume. "You know about conjoined twins? Babies joined at the torso, or two bodies splitting out of one pair of legs?"

"Road show freaks," Carlyle summed up.

"Yeah, in Dust Bowl–era lingo, but yes," Demoines conceded. "Okay, now picture conjoined twins that share every part of one body. Not only one torso, but one head, two arms, two legs . . . But they're still two people."

He gestured toward the window like a zoo guide pointing at the aquarium. Inside, the marionette sat idly feeling their earlobe with a stapler while studying the conspiracy mural on Greggs's corkboard.

Carlyle suggested, "So, he's got split personality?"

"No," Greggs refuted. "Split personality is a psychiatric disorder, and as a matter of fact, virtually every studied case has been ruled a hoax. Kimrean doesn't have split personality; they *are* two people. It's called genetic chimerism: looks like one individual, but it's actually a mosaic organism made up of two people's cells, each with its own DNA. Two siblings. In one body."

Carlyle watched the fish in the aquarium. A soft undulation of ribs could be discerned under the armpits. He got the uncanny impression that the scant clothes didn't actually hide anything, that beneath them the marionette would be all smooth like a Barbie. Or a Ken.

"In a man's body, or a woman's?"

"Well . . ." Greggs began, and hesitated again, this time almost splicing her lip open.

"Both," Demoines said. "They're brother and sister."

Carlyle turned from the glass, dragging a hand over the scalp that several mornings like this one had contributed to despoil.

Demoines went on, if only to shorten the pain: "The funny thing about Kimrean is that most genetic chimeras are not proportional. It happens throughout the animal kingdom: your arm or your pancreas may actually belong to a twin brother who fused with you before the embryo stage. You, Greggs, me—any of us here could be a mosaic, and we wouldn't know. For practical, psychological, legal purposes, we are only one person: the one who owns the brain, the one who is self-aware. But Kimrean is a bit of an oddity."

"You don't say," the chief retorted.

Greggs tagged herself back in: "In Kimrean, their brain is shared as well. Each sibling owns a half. They both have self-awareness, a voice, and control over their body."

"Relatively speaking," Demoines said. "It's . . . like having a pilot and a copilot."

"More like two pilots fighting for the throttle."

"As far as we know, Adrian holds the left hemisphere, the analytic brain. He has an IQ over one eighty, photographic memory, encyclopedic culture . . . He's the internet with Asperger's syndrome."

"Zooey is the right hemisphere, the creative brain. She paints, writes, composes, plays several instruments . . . She's also hyperactive, a nymphomaniac, and an addict to every substance she's tried once."

Beyond the glass, Carlyle watched the subject, or subjects, pushing off the floor and spinning on Greggs's chair like a top, arms and legs spread out. After nine or ten full spins, they collapsed on the floor, toppling a couple of Doric columns of case files on their way down.

When Carlyle finished massaging his brow, he was six months older than the last time he'd spoken.

"We are about to close the biggest joint narcotics op in twenty years. We are working with another sixteen law enforcement agencies. We've got the executed son of a drug lord, an impending gangland world war . . . not to mention an undercover officer sitting like a duck in the middle of Pearl Harbor. And your solution is to bring in this . . . *(Points at the glass.)* These . . . This pair of screwballs?"

A few nearby paper pushers who were distractedly eavesdropping on the conversation gravely pondered the question.

"Actually, we want to bring in Adrian," Demoines pointed out. "Zooey just comes in the package."

Greggs stepped forward: "Sir, I know they seem . . ." She stopped, restarted: "Okay, *are*—they *are* weird. But I know them, Mojave knows them, half this department knows them. They're the best. And their . . . singularity, so to speak, is an advantage.

Lyon badly needs a detective, but he'll want no business with anyone remotely seeming to represent the law. And you know the P.I.s in the Bay Area—trench coats, suspenders, they walk into a bar and people ask them how's the new Dick Tracy film going. A.Z. doesn't have that issue. His—I mean, their—appearance, their demeanor, everything about them is so unconventional, the last thing anyone thinks is that they're a private eye."

"Private *eyes*," Demoines fixed. "The grammar's a little tricky."

An officer interrupted to announce a phone call for Lieutenant Greggs. She sneaked into a cubicle; Carlyle and Demoines stood by, gazing at the aquarium.

"You really want to use this nutjob," Carlyle said. It was not a question, more like a vain attempt to persuade himself.

"Sir, had I known they were back in business, I would've called them myself. They're a gift from above. Quite literally—there's a wrecked cruiser outside that can bear witness to that."

"Of all the P.I.s in the Bay Area . . ."

"Chief, do you have any brothers or sisters?" Demoines actually waited for an answer; Carlyle passed. "I am the fourth of five. Let me tell you: God, or Mother Nature, or whatever there is, didn't create siblings to keep us company. It did to make us compete and succeed at each other's expense. Adrian Kimrean has spent all his life, from the very first minute, since *before* the first minute, competing against Zooey. Fighting for a body of his own, for a life of his own. They are both compelled to be the best at everything they do."

"But . . . why P.I.s?" Carlyle moaned.

"I'm not sure. Adrian sees it as a purely intellectual craft. And Zooey likes the aesthetic cliché, I guess."

"I hate clichés," Police Deputy Chief Carlyle grunted, scratching his big belly and biting on a hapless doughnut that was grazing near the water cooler. "No way am I bringing that clown into this mess."

"Sir." It was Greggs, pulling a handset from the phone in the next cubicle. "Mojave."

Carlyle snatched the receiver from her. "Danny. Good work, son. Listen to me, you give the signal, I can pull you out of there in one hour, okay? Soon as—"

He cut himself off, as if something unexpected or viscous was pouring out of the handset. Out of focus, Greggs gave Demoines a conspiratorial nod.

"Danny, you're not thinking clearly," Carlyle said.

It was the last full sentence he would be able to squeeze into the conversation. He babbled a couple promises, said good-bye, and handed the phone back to Greggs. He laid a hand on the aquarium glass.

"He wants him," he mumbled. "Them."

On the other side, the grinning marionette waved.


All three cops marched back into Greggs's office, hands in their pockets.

"Okay," the chief said, brushing up on his apologetic tone. "Your agents here told me you're a regular sleuth. Two sleuths, as it happens."

"A sleuth and his comedy sidekick, all in one," Kimrean rephrased, neutral.

"Yes, I heard it's a little . . . complex."

The heterochromatic eyes were still unsettling, but somehow he knew to address the golden-brown one. The green one, half veiled by the bangs, gazed in the same direction, shone just as brightly, but somehow seemed permanently distracted.

"I apologize about the language before. The Tinker Bell thing, I mean."

"Oh, it's okay. I don't think much of that PC bullshit either. I too am a bit of a fat, white-privileged, dick-dangling, baby-dipping douchebag that way."

Greggs, ever the mediator, stepped between Kimrean and the chief before the joke even landed; there was barely any time for turmoil to build up.

"Okay, point made, Zooey. Siddown," she begged, pushing the contenders apart—those who could be parted, that is.

"It wasn't me," Zooey proclaimed naively. "But I agree with everything he said."

"Adrian, Zooey," Demoines roll-called. "Maybe we started on the wrong foot here. This is Deputy Chief Llewelyn Carlyle. He needs a favor."

"I'm not doing anything for the deputy chief," Kimrean said. "At best, I'll do it for Danny Mojave."

That successfully cooled down the tempers. In fact, it flash-froze the room. Carlyle checked Greggs, Demoines, then the brown eye, then the green one, then anything inert in the office that might provide an answer.

"How does he know about Mojave?" he barked. "Only three people outside this room know about him!"

"Plus anyone that walks into this office and notices that the fourth guy from the right in Greggs's graduation photo on her desk is the same guy on the board in that picture with Victor Lyon, supreme ruler of the San Carnal drug cartel," Kimrean inserted, pointing at the walls on each side. "In other words, you guys managed to plant a narc in the home of the evil lord who runs San Carnal. The Ciudad Juárez this side of the border. The city where Sudanese war refugees once refused to stay because it didn't feel safe. Good job. Anyone called dibs on Danny's condo yet?"

"You been to San Carnal lately?" asked Demoines.

"Naaah," Kimrean bleated. "Not my kind of town. All glass towers and synthetic lawns. Even the trash cans come in rose gold. It's like the golf of cities: only appealing to the wealthy and easily challenged."

"Would . . . you like to go?"

"You couldn't drag me there pulling me by my nose hair," they said, without a hint of irony. "Is that all? Cool; as soon as I get my handcuffs I'll be on my way."

Greggs prodded them back to the chair as she approached the corkboard, ready to give the lecture.

"You're right: we did plant Danny Mojave in the Lyon's org—and he bloomed. Started undercover among Lyon's men at the harbor and now he's practically the old man's right hand. He's become the fulcrum of this state-level op to topple the cartel and the whole kleptocracy running San Carnal. We're weeding out the city. We share intel with DEA, FBI, you name it—but Danny's still our man. Last spring, Lyon assigned him to his youngest son, Mikey, who's in line to inherit a third of the family business. Part of the old man's legacy will be this alliance with the Red Chrysanthemum Clan—the Japanese yakuza that's spreading in the south, running the local gangs out of L.A."

"I know all that."

"Okay, this you may not know: as of this week that alliance is falling apart." Greggs pointed at some photos brimming off the periphery of the board. They showed a parking lot in the desert, cordoned off with black-and-yellow tape. "Mikey committed a bit of a diplomatic faux pas."

"Do you usually collect over a hundred bullet casings in a faux pas scene?"

"Sadly, it's not infrequent for San Carnal. Mikey lost one soldier in the shoot-out: Cuban gunslinger by the name of Tomás Hilfiger. He was left wounded at the scene, died in the hospital."

"Heh. Tommy Hilfiger? That's one off my to-do list," Kimrean said.

"Danny was there when it happened; according to him, it was all a misunderstanding. The Japanese didn't speak good English."

"Damn immigrants, coming over here and stealing our crime syndicates."

"Danny was confident that talks between both clans would resume . . . until this happened."

She handed Kimrean a last photograph, one that still hadn't made it to the board. It had been taken at a crime scene with a phone camera. The man in it bore an evident resemblance to Victor Lyon. Only younger, with higher cheekbones and a broken nose, a burst lip, and an extra orifice in his face. The body lay in a pool of blood, ruining a leopard rug. The right hand rested on the chest, fingers wrapped around the stem of a red flower.

"Mikey Lyon," Greggs captioned. "Beaten up and shot in his father's residence, Villa Leona."

"Breaking and entering plus homicide in San Carnal?" Kimrean exclaimed. "There *must* be a mistake."

"The problem," Greggs resumed, "is that before we find out who did it—"

"The Japanese," said Kimrean.

"Yeah, well, before we know that—"

"You know, 'cause I just told you: the Japanese."

"Before we can *confirm* that," Greggs italicized, "Lyon is going to retaliate like this was a declaration of war."

"It was!" Kimrean shouted. "And guess who from!"

"It wasn't the Japanese."

That was Carlyle's line, straight from the back row. He was sitting on the radiator, back against the window. Those had been his first words since the exposition began.

Kimrean read the silent agreement in the room, then ventured, "I'm assuming that's not based off the ruling of the local police inquiry."

"San Carnal Police is Lyon's third arm. Or his fourth," Demoines said. "The whole department is coming down with him."

"Then how do you know . . ." Kimrean began, but those five words were enough. They smirked, lipless mouth skewed toward the right side of their face. "No shit. You have a mole inside the yakuza too?"

"Not us—that one's LAPD, but yes," Greggs explained. "We're pooling resources, you see."

"But their mole could be wrong; there could be rogue soldiers operating on each side," Kimrean argued, sounding out everyone in the room. "But you don't believe that. You believe it, but you rather wouldn't. Because if it's the yakuza, they just started a gang war."

No one needed to answer.

Suddenly Kimrean went off in their seat.

"Well, fuck them! You guys said it—another day in San Carnal—who gives a paragliding shit? It's an artificial oasis for people with broken moral compasses! It's *Sin City* in Technicolor, it's Biff Tannen's 1985, it's the Sodom and Gomorrah of California—and I'm saying this from San Fran-fucking-cisco! It's a money Laundromat, an evil interior designer's sandbox, a playground for coked-up mortgage brokers and semen-choked spring breakers scripted by Bret Easton Ellis, ruled by John Grisham villains, roamed by SUV-driving Ayn Rand cultists, and sponsored by kingpins, sex traffickers, and sports execs with their chipped trophy wives who home in from all over the country attracted by this beacon of phallic skyscrapers, pubescent prostitutes, and glittery toilets! Christ—I am a multiple-drug-addict hypersexual felon and it repulses *me*!"

The audience waited respectfully for Kimrean to collapse back in the chair, panting away what was left of their fury. After that, Greggs stepped in and picked up the thread.

"This situation you so graphically described, Zooey, will continue after a gang war. Best-case scenario, one side wipes out the other, buys the bureaucrats cheap, and it's another year in Gangsta's Paradise."

"The casualties of that war would be us," the chief said, with unsurprising empathy. "For two years, twelve counties and five state agencies have cooperated to bring down the cartel—gathering evidence, tapping phones, building cases against every gun, every punk, every corrupt public servant. We are on the brink of cutting off all of the hydra's heads at once."

"The hydra would just grow twice as many heads—not a good analogy," Kimrean judged.

"Gang war doesn't help, and you know it," Greggs insisted. "Even if every cartel soldier went to jail for pulling a trigger, they'll take all the blame; they have to, or they die. Unless we take down the bosses, all bosses at once, it's all in vain."

"That's what it will be," Kimrean said, "unless the San Carnal coroner rules that Lyon's son tripped and landed on a bullet on the floor."

"We're not counting on the coroner," Demoines said. "We're counting on you."

There was no automatic reply to that.

Greggs added, "Lyon trusts very few people, but Danny is one of them. Danny can convince him that the Red Chrysanthemum didn't kill his son, but he'll need proof."

"Otherwise, Lyon will go to war with the Red Mums, and he'll lose," Demoines predicted. "The man thinks himself stronger than he is: too many enemies. He will fall. And Danny will fall with him."

"Pull him out of there," Adrian urged, coldly.

"He doesn't want us to. He's been there for a year and a half, he's way too invested. He thinks he can stop this war."

"He's wrong. It's not his call to make."

"He just made it anyway," Greggs said. "He called ten minutes ago. He wants you, Adrian."


Kimrean stayed silent, their stray gaze flown out the window. Flat geometric rooftops shone dazzling white against a deep blue, almost indigo sky.

The left hand was twiddling with some paper clips on the desk. The right one distractedly lurched toward Greggs.

"Cuffs," Kimrean whispered, so soft that Carlyle had to lean closer.

Greggs sighed, went to pick up the phone: "I'll tell forensics to bring them."

"Not mine," the marionette grunted through a slit mouth, both eyes fixed on the window, left hand sneakily pulled to join the right one. "Yours. Now, before Zooey finds out."

# 2

Zooey found out on the Bayshore Highway on-ramp, as they were joining the southbound lane. For the first minutes they managed to distract her with a Rubik's Cube, which thanks to the nonintervention of Adrian (whose personal record stood at 10.3 seconds, 13.9 blindfolded) kept her busy while she was being cuffed, escorted to the underground garage, and seated next to the car seat in the back of Greggs's Toyota. That was when Demoines bartered her the Rubik's Cube for his PlayStation Portable, which kept her fully engrossed while they rolled out into Franklin Street and headed for the expressway. They had nearly made it out of the city when a spray of water hitting her window made Zooey look away from the screen and wave at some children playing around a gushing fire hydrant. She went on to make a lewd comment at a Victoria's Secret billboard, and then, alerted by the high number of ad boards around the junction, she noticed they were leaving town. That was when she checked their recent memory and realized she had been tricked.

From that moment on, she spent the whole trip kicking in protest and singing atrocious road songs about San Carnal, not all of them entirely improvised, until they stole off the highway and passed the solitary road sign of State Route 325, pushing into the unmitigated desert of Gran South County.

Often called "America's Namibia"—a nickname that Namibians deeply resent—Gran South County is an eight-hundred-thousand-acre expanse of rocks and sand that forty-niners refused to inhabit and coyotes, vipers, and scorpions alone call home with a fair amount of resignation. Only lower life-forms than those, such as land speculators, had learned to appreciate the territory for the gift of God it was, remembering the Old Testament's tendency to oversell arid regions, and accepted the gift by sending a caravan of construction trucks to the spot of the last recorded human settling in the area—one which Spanish explorers had vacated shortly after its foundation, leaving behind their old and sick—and there they dug wells, rolled out lawns, and erected a city grid of concrete and plastic profusely strewn with palm-flanked avenues and roads of sun-whitened asphalt and houses with swimming pools where bad porn is filmed and interiors lavishly decorated by brain-damaged designers whose use and abuse of spiral stairs, aluminum, and zebra skin made any sane observer advocate for a Guantánamo Bay for aesthetic offenders.

While traversing the desert that kindly separated San Carnal from civilization, Zooey had a brief relapse into the song-improvising stage. The air cooler didn't work: Greggs drove with the windows down, Demoines had loosened his necktie, and Kimrean, their dragonfly shape somehow spread all over the backseat, howled some new lyrics to the theme from *New York, New York*.

*Start spreading the AIDS,*
*I'm headed your way!*
*Kids rush outside to greet me back—and sell me crack!*
*Teenagers wave at me on their way to school*
*In makeup and pumps, and ask to carpool,*
*And pay me with their behinds,*
*Condoms declined,*
*Fresh anal tears*
*Currency here,*
*in San Carnal!*

She finished with a drum solo, hardly devalued by the presence of handcuffs or the absence of instrument, and crashed back in their seat, waiting for her ovation.

Greggs flipped a curl of her hair. Demoines just shrugged and talked to the mirror.

"Okay, I gotta ask: So you've been six months locked away in the men's ward in Claymoore . . . and the first thing you buy yourself when you get out is a ladyboy?"

"Yes!" Zooey said impatiently. "I looked over the menu, and that's what I felt like having! Why does everybody have a problem with that? You, the arresting officer, those old ladies on the bus!"

"Why do you hate San Carnal anyway?" Greggs jumped in. "You're a pervert."

"I'm not a pervert. I'm a hedonist. There's a difference."

No expansion was offered to that argument, and no one requested it.

The silver-gray Toyota went on swallowing dashes of yellow line, like a mighty boring Pac-Man.

ZOOEY: I'm thirsty.

DEMOINES: We're almost at the exchange point.

GREGGS: There should be water in the glove compartment.

ZOOEY: It's okay, found something. *(Pulls a feeding bottle from the car seat's cupholder.)*

GREGGS: What—no! Zooey! That's my—

*(Zooey is already squeezing the bottle six inches above her open mouth. She swallows, loudly smacking her lips like a cartoon cat.)*

ZOOEY: Sorry, you were saying?

GREGGS: Nothing.

ZOOEY: Okay. *(Watching Greggs, licking her lips again.)* You were born in South Africa, right? Where would that be—Lower Orange River?

GREGGS: Shut up!

Demoines was keeping his eyes on the side mirror, his reflection covering a grin with his hand.

Kimrean leaned forward, showing their cuffed wrists.

"Seriously now, you can take these off. I'm not going to jump out of the car."

Nobody pretended to listen, not even for a second.

"Guys? Come on, I know where we're going, and I understand why we're going."

"You asked for the cuffs," Demoines said.

"No, *I* didn't," said Zooey.

Greggs checked the mirror: the heterochromatic face smiled a pencil-lined smile.

"It hurts you know me so little, Ted. I *know* we have to do this. For Danny. Which one of us do you think is worried about Danny?"

"Not you," Demoines bet.

"Of course me! Do you think Adrian cares about Danny, or you, or anyone? He doesn't. I am the one who cares. I'm a people person."

"You don't *care* about people," Greggs intervened. "You're attracted to people. The loyal one is Adrian."

"Yeah, keep talking about me like I'm not here, bitches."

Greggs turned back to the road. The most frustrating thing about A. Z. Kimrean was not that they were two people, but that both of them were among the most intractable people she had ever met.

In a random point of the desert, perhaps to mark the historical spot where some frontier settlers were forced to resort to cannibalism in the 1800s, a candid soul had erected a gas station and diner for their art school project on streamline moderne. Greggs pulled over at the sleeping neon sign and sneaked the Toyota among the large ruminant eighteen-wheelers in the parking lot.

All four got out of the vehicle, squinting at the sun-reflecting sand. Kimrean once more stretched their cuffed hands like a beggar, although their expression wasn't as much a supplication as an invitation to kiss their derriere. The detectives tried to ignore them.

Adrian commented, "So you guys want to take me into a crowded restaurant in cuffs, then let me walk out with one of Lyon's top men?"

The wind set a cloud of dust on them. Greggs fished the key out of her pants and tried not to acknowledge the orange-brown eye as she unlocked the cuffs.

It was peak lunchtime in the diner—a place that had recently expanded from trailer truck stop to modest roadside tourist trap by virtue of one flattering review that everyone had failed to read in the sarcastic spirit that was intended. Two different VW Camper enthusiast couples, along with two old ladies on the toll-free route to Vegas, completed a cast of background extras made up mostly of lonely men in denim. Greggs and Demoines avoided the booths by the large panoramic window looking onto the parking lot and picked an inconspicuous table near the counter, far from the corners. Greggs ordered coffee. Demoines checked his watch.

"We're late. Danny will be here in ten."

Greggs confirmed it and looked down at Kimrean, who was already sitting. "Can we trust you'll stay?"

"Sure." Kimrean looked up from the menu. "You're taking the car with you, aren't you?"

"That's the spirit."

"I'll need money for the coffee."

"Danny will pay for it." She read the P.I. for the last time, her jacket folded under her arm and a well-rehearsed mother look on her face. "Please try and behave, will you?"

"I'll be fine, Mom. Go take care of your real toddler."

"Bye, A.Z.," said Demoines. It was the shortest form to embrace both Kimreans on a first-name basis.

The bell over the door jingled them good-bye.

As soon as they were gone, Kimrean intercepted a waitress in violet uniform and perm.

"Forget the coffee—I'll have the steak, blue rare; chili cheese fries; and a beer." Adrian gave the waitress a quick scan, then added, "What happened to the girl who used to work here?"

"Oh, she's fine," she said, laying a place mat on the table. "Her surgery went well, I'm told. But I'm not sure they're holding the spot for her."

"Don't take it for granted, you're just a stopgap. They should've given you your own uniform by now; this one's not your size, the blouse is mended up, and you're too cheerful for a Cecilia,"

Adrian said, pointing at the embroidered name. "You want her job, work for it, Frenchy."

The waitress hesitated for a minute, fact-checked the story, then said, "Thank you?" and she hurried back to the kitchen.

Kimrean tucked the napkin under their tank top and passed the time studying the desserts.


Outside the air-conditioned capsule of the diner, the desert bustled with the voices of busy insects and happy cheering vermin frying in the sun. Every now and then a big dumb rolling tumbleweed crossed like a bouncing beach ball between them on its migratory route for the coast.

Then a Firestone tire scraped the living earth off the continent as it burst on-screen, obliterating the microfauna. The coarse sound of scorched rubber faded into the lower, softer sabertooth purr of a V-8 engine while the dust storm slowly scattered to unveil the calm horizon mirrored on a shiny metal bumper, then the sky gleaming off the azure bodywork and yellow racing stripe of a 1969 Camaro Z28.

The engine shut off, a metal *click* opened the door, and a pair of black leather dress boots stepped down with a crunch of ground dirt.

A couple of truckers in the diner excused one brain cell apiece from their sandwiches as the doorbell announced the newcomer. They both noticed the shirt open at the neck, the curly hair, the sideburns, the sunglasses, the hat—all in black. Without appearing to have recognized anyone, the man walked across the restaurant, past the inviting window tables and the noteworthy collection of state car plates, and stopped in front of the weakest-looking patron, like any troublemaker in the school cafeteria.

Kimrean ignored him for another two spoonfuls of strawberry pie, until the brown and green eyes granted him a second of combined attention.

"I'm eating here. Can't you put a hairnet on that chest?"

Danny Mojave removed his sunglasses. The eyes and brows below didn't spoil the overall black motif.

"Ade. Glad to see you too."

"Glad to see you three," Zooey sang, raising their voice pitch to identify herself. There was whipped cream on their nose.

"I'm ready when you guys are."

"Get the check," A.Z. instructed, relocating the last of the dessert from their face to a napkin. "And an iced latte for the road."

The landscape for the rest of the trip offered as few sidenotes as the first half. Danny drove with the patient air of Muhammad waiting for the proverbial mountain to pop up on the horizon. Kimrean sat back with their feet on the dashboard and a cigarette between their teeth, head tilted toward the open window, wind flapping their blond hair like the national flag of Bhutan. California dashed past them, roaring like Hurricane Irene.

"So. I heard you took a sabbatical," Danny icebroke. "Where did you stay?"

"Pennhurst Asylum, then Claymoore."

"Nice?"

"Ritzy. In Claymoore I was even allowed to shave my legs. With tweezers."

Zooey was trying on Danny's hat. Mojave took the chance for a full body shot.

"You look good."

"Yeah, yeah. Easy on the compliments; I don't want to ruin

your seats." Kimrean examined him back. "You don't look bad yourself. For someone who's been undercover for eighteen months, carries a gun under his jacket and another one on his ankle."

Danny conceded a sporting smirk. "Anything else?"

"Not much, except that you beat off twice a day, and you should have that rib checked out." Adrian waited until Mojave looked in his direction again to explain. "You winced when you got in the car. Could be a fracture; you should get an X-ray."

Danny felt his right side with his left hand, not hiding the discomfort. "And the beating off?"

"Everybody beats off twice a day," Zooey said. "Don't they?"

Danny almost laughed. Zooey had a knack for brightening up the mood. Adrian delved into business while the spirits were light.

"How deep in shit are you?"

"Chin-deep. And sinking," Danny answered. The smirk showed how seriously jokingly serious he was. "What do you know about Victor Lyon?"

"Not much," Kimrean said. "AKA 'the Lyon,' sixty-six, white, born poor in southern Florida, where he started flirting with gangs. Worked his way from zero to protégé of street legend Fat Jim. After the latter's death, he fled to California to escape the Miami-Dade police. He pops up in Los Angeles with a humble opiate start-up, then he orchestrates and executes the simultaneous extermination of three rival families in one night—the infamous Hostile Takeover of '74. He kept a low profile while his territory spread through Southern California. He began buying property here in San Carnal, where he married Evita Durango, Miss Guatemala 1982. His heroin empire weathered the crack epidemic of the eighties and meth in the nineties. In recent years, his influence has declined in L.A., but he still owns the Mexico border. He doubled down in San Carnal through several abusive deals with other cartels and the occasional blitzkrieg against young upstarts. After divorcing Miss Guatemala, he married Elizabeth Omahira, British-born merchant attorney in the Cayman Islands, twenty-five years his junior. Three children, zero grandchildren, Catholic, Lakers fan, triple bypass in 1996."

"Yup, not much indeed," Danny evaluated. "You missed the daughter from his second marriage; she'll turn twelve this year."

"I was counting her; I wasn't counting the son that died on your watch. Tell me about the others."

"The eldest is Xander Lyon. He's the apple that fell closest to the tree. Raised in the streets, educated at Stanford; the wisdom of a fifty-year-old and the energy of thirty-three."

"Energy and diplomacy are a rare combination. What does he think of his father's deals with the Red Mums?"

"If he opposes the alliance, he's too smart to share. His entourage is just as discreet; he surrounds himself with the best. When he's not doing business in Mexico he's fortified in his penthouse on the thirty-seventh floor of the family hotel on Palm Avenue. He's married and separated; she lives in Santa Monica."

"*Bor*-ing."

"Frankie is the second born; I've only met him a few times. He handles some of the cartel's legal businesses in San Carnal; his henchmen are a squad of accountants who do most of the work. He just shakes hands, buys drinks, and entertains the VIPs at his club on Palm Boulevard."

"Is there any place in San Carnal whose name doesn't contain the word *Palm*?"

"Not that I know of. Frankie is the black sheep of the Lyons. Thirty-one years old, bad student, terrible gangster; his father keeps him away from the tough work and he doesn't care. He's nice enough, but bland. He can't find his place. Middle kid syndrome, you know."

Adrian and Zooey consulted with each other, then stared at Danny inquiringly.

"Okay, maybe you *don't* know," he concluded. "Anyway, Mikey, the third son, was more involved. Twenty-seven, graduated from Princeton two years ago, but I don't think he spent much time in the library. Very interested in the family business, but too much hubris. His father saw in him the same kind of reckless soldier he'd been during the Takeover days; the kid's idea of diplomacy was two gorillas with shotguns and a sack of grenades. Officially, Mikey was in charge of the military arm of the cartel, but in practice, he was limited to territorial disputes. His lieutenants knew they answered to the father, not the son. This was cause for frequent family drama. Deep down Mikey was just a moody teenager—add armed, coked up, and always one tequila shot away from full-blown psychosis. He'd been antagonizing his father ever since he divorced his mom, but the Lyon still hoped to see him mature. He loved Mikey. Putting me in his inner circle was a proof of trust. That is, of not trusting his son, but trusting me."

"Great call," Kimrean rated. "What did you do—leave him watching a *SpongeBob* DVD while you talked boys on the phone with your girlfriends?"

"He got hit in the pool house," Danny related, a hint of exhaustion in his voice now. "That used to be Mikey's lodgings. I thought I could leave him alone for a minute. It's Villa Leona, for God's sake—must be the safest hundred acres in the county: CCTV, armed guards, dogs. I sneaked out for a smoke. This was Monday night—Tuesday, really, after midnight. In the main building, everyone was asleep. Then I heard the gunshots."

"How many?"

"Two."

"How far apart?"

"Close. One second. Me and half a dozen guys ran to the pool house. Mikey was dead on the floor with a red flower on his chest. The window was open. The dogs tracked a scent, but they lost it near the fence on the north side."

"Where had you been smoking?"

"On the north side."

"And you didn't see anyone?"

"No. That part of the garden is in the dark."

"Cameras?"

"There's only one on that fence; it's easy to dodge."

"Dogs?"

"They don't patrol that side; Mikey complained they pissed on his azaleas."

Adrian closed their eyes. "For the safest hundred acres in the county, I know of French vaginas that are harder to sneak into."

"Yes, we realized that. We'd gotten lazy; no one thought anyone in San Carnal would be crazy enough to try this."

"Weapon?"

"Nine millimeter, probably Mikey's."

"'Probably'? How long does it take to match a gun?"

"We don't have the gun. Mikey kept a Beretta in the pool house; we can't find it."

"Hmm." In Kimrean's personal argot, *hmm* could mean anything in the range from *Very interesting* to *I just remembered a particular photo shoot in* GQ *with girls in lingerie holding fishing rods.* "Tell me about the flower; I couldn't see it properly in the picture. Your phone camera sucks."

"It was a chrysanthemum. Red."

"You can identify a chrysanthemum at a glance?"

"Well . . ." There was a second of hesitation. "No, but someone said it was."

"Surely one of Victor Lyon's in-house henchmen slash botanists."

"Whatever; we kept the flower—the Lyon put it in a vase. You'll see it in a minute," Danny promised. It was beginning to dawn on him that he might have cried wolf too early. "Maybe it wasn't a chrysanthemum."

"Nah, I'm messing with you; it probably was. How about motive—the shoot-out with the Japanese? What happened there?"

Danny lit up a cigarette. Kimrean noticed the slightest tremor in the cop's hand when it wasn't gripping the wheel.

"That happened the night before, Monday after midnight. An exchange gone wrong. A trade in neutral land."

"What makes you all think the diner we just left is in neutral land?"

Danny cut himself off, this time definitely impressed.

"I recognized the parking lot from the pictures on Greggs's board," Adrian expanded briefly. "And the panoramic window looking onto the parking lot is brand new—it still had the sticky labels on."

"It's far enough from everywhere, but it's still in Gran South County Sheriff's territory. That guarantees that whatever happens there will be swept under the carpet," Danny explained. "It was a routine deal; I've done this many times with Xander. But this time they sent Mikey. Xander was abroad for the week attending some meetings."

"Thanks, hadn't heard that euphemism for 'banging my mistress' since 1992. Why did Daddy trust Mikey?"

"Good faith. The kid had been begging for a chance; he was given one. It was a mistake. Mikey showed up high, acting out.

He strutted into the diner for a burger while we waited, flashing his piece around. When the Japanese arrived, they were intimidated. They don't speak good English; Mikey's hypergesturing didn't help. He got impatient, they got impatient. He insisted on counting the money. Stupid paranoid kept saying they were ambushing us. Suddenly one of his Cuban thugs, Hilfiger, spotted a sniper on top of a truck, and Mikey opened fire."

"Was it a real sniper?"

"Yes, but we drew first blood—under gangland law, it was our fault. From that moment on, every decision we took was bad: we lost Hilfiger, started shooting toward the restaurant; we hit a civilian, blew her tit off. We made the *Chronicle* front page."

"Any more casualties? Apart from Hilfiger and your rib and an extra's tit?"

"Not on our side. I didn't see any on theirs either. I wasn't even aiming to kill." He put the cigarette back in his mouth; it'd been burned to ashes long ago. "This is not my trade."

"You should leave," Adrian advised. Zooey added, "Can I come with you?"

"I'm not quitting now. Not after eighteen months. I'm not letting this whole op go to hell because a spoiled brat screwed up an exchange. I need to fix this. You two have work to do."

"I could have solved this case from Claymoore: it was Chrysanthemum-san, in the pool house, with the nine millimeter. Greggs and Demoines and Carlyle are wrong: the yakuza just declared war on you."

"Don't tell that to Lyon. Don't even mention Japan. Don't mention I mentioned Japan."

"But it *is* Japan."

"Say anything else."

"I'm a P.I.—I don't get to randomly pick who the murderer is. That's the screenwriter's job."

"Adrian, forget about the war—if you come in and tell the Lyon that the Red Chrysanthemum killed his son because an operation I was supervising went awry, I won't live long enough to drop you at the station," Danny stated. Not as distressed as the line called for, but close enough. "I can convince him it wasn't the Japanese, but I can't pull the story out of my ass; I need to bring an expert. And you're the best P.I. I know."

"But you don't need a P.I., you just need a pretender."

"Well, you're *also* the best pretender I know," Danny said, facing both.

Kimrean gazed out the window. A wall of slate clouds approached from the north.

"Just say anything to stall him," Danny instructed. "Tell him there's reasonable doubt, tell him anything to distract him, but don't fuck up. And be tactful. He's the king of San Carnal, and he just lost a son; Villa Leona is a house in mourning."

# 3

A Nubian nymph tucked her bikini bottoms, capered along the diving board, bounced off into the air, and dove smoothly into the cyan swimming pool imbued with blissful laughter and solar glares. A beach ball bounced between rainbow-nailed hands, black- and blond- and pink-haired heads spraying water in slow motion toward the deck chairs where female bodies endured the sun like sinuous dunes and the vaults of pagodas of ancient cities along the Silk Road. Butterflies danced to slow reggae, and the mustachioed barista from *The Love Boat* shook a margarita while listening to the security guards' frequency on his earpiece as they ordered the gates to close after Danny, who was now walking up the path from the garage, talking to himself.

"My cover is Daniel Monzón, but everyone calls me Danny for short," he explained. This was common practice among undercover agents: an easy way to prevent an acquaintance from ruining the whole operation with a *Hey, Danny*. "I think we can stick to our real story, you and me: you're a P.I., you helped me out of a couple tough spots—something like that. Just don't mention that we met when I arrested you for drunk-driving a Porsche from the backseat. Deal?"

He waited for Kimrean's usual non-apology apology for that particular incident—by arguing that the llama was taking up the driver's seat—but it didn't happen. Danny stopped and turned to find he was speaking to nobody.

Back by the swimming pool, Kimrean, mouth open, arms hanging bloodless on each side, stood under the tropical heat in full Stendhal syndrome before the spectacle of naiads sunbathing, rinsing their hair, cavorting around like characters in a Bouguereau rendition of a Roger Moore 007 scene. A Venus on the left climbed out of the water, long curly black hair dripping estrogens; by the deck chairs, a random soft body part wobbled nimbly under the inertia of a turn toward the camera. A giggling fairy in a pink bikini ran past Kimrean like a gazelle, brushing the P.I.'s elbow, and Kimrean felt that exchange of ions trigger a chain reaction extending like spidery lightning up their arm, flowing down their chest, and igniting their lower abdomen.

Danny Mojave snatched them from Arcadia, pulling them by an ear.

"We've got work to do, Zooey."

"I'm on it," she said, heels dragging through the lawn. "I'll need saliva samples from all those suspects."

"I thought you hated San Carnal."

"Oh, I hate it—all the institutionalized sexist frivolity. But I'm all for the authentic everyday sexist frivolity of true, hardworking San Carnalians."

They returned to the path, and Danny released Kimrean when he was sure Adrian had taken over. "Just try and behave in there, okay? Apart from being a drug lord and all that, the Lyon is a pretty traditional guy; I don't want to shock him. I'll introduce you as Adrian; let's pretend Zooey isn't there for a while."

"I've been trying that most of my life," Adrian replied. "It doesn't work."

On the main building porch—a humble entrance to what zoomed out to be a four-story villa—a seven-foot-five Mexican, looking like the kind of man who spends twelve hours a day working out at the gym (or just working there, as an elevator counterweight), skipped the greetings and proceeded to frisk them. Kimrean obligingly spread both legs and arms with no objection: their revolver was still somewhere in the San Francisco office, and their handcuffs were in the morgue. At least they had borrowed a new hat. Without one, both Adrian and Zooey felt naked.

"Speak only when spoken to," Danny resumed, as they entered a shady, narrow anteroom with a statue of a mounted conquistador and a bead-curtained door. Danny knocked on the doorframe. "On second thought, maybe give him your condolences. He buried his son yesterday."

"What do you say to a Lyon who's lost a relative? Hakuna matata?"

The beads rattled softly under an AC breeze. Adrian glared back at Danny.

"What? I told you ignoring her is useless."

A maid pulled the curtain open.


Victor Lyon was pretty much like any other cartel boss Kimrean had met: big, white-haired, megalomaniacal, and convinced that every decision he made regarding money, ethics, or fashion was inherently right. The pulp-inspiring street legend of the 1970s was somewhere in there, buried deep under the businessman, the family man, the general. He resembled a lion the way lions are depicted on coins—vigilant, not bloodthirsty. He appeared to be sixty years old and sixty days from his next heart attack.

They found the man sitting in an Emmanuelle wicker throne, clad in a black kimono, pink feet in sandals resting on a matching stool. Danny and Kimrean stood by, waiting for the Lyon to finish grumbling into the wireless phone. The room was rich in indoor plants and hunting trophies. Another bodyguard stood in a corner, successfully mimicking the taxidermied empty stares.

Kimrean had already scanned the contents of the room twice and was already assigning names to individual flies buzzing around by the time the boss finally ended the conference with a Spanish swearword and hung up.

"Rodrigo Villahermosa," he recounted for Danny. "He's ready to assist us in battle for thirty percent, plus the districts of Barro and Arellana. But it's okay if we don't agree to his conditions; he can get fifty percent from the Red Mums when it's all set anyway. The greedy swine!" He slapped the phone off the side table. "There used to be loyalty."

From the same table he picked up a cigar, snipped the cap off with a guillotine, and lit it up. The first drag produced a cloud of white smoke like the verdict of a papal conclave. He sat back and used the cigar to point at Kimrean.

"Who's the girl?"

Danny felt his prepared introductory words committing suicide on the tip of his tongue. He checked on Kimrean, green eye glinting behind the blond bangs. For a second of madness he even considered correcting the old man. In the end, though, sanity prevailed.

"Mr. Lyon, this is Zooey Kimrean. She's the private eye I told you about."

"I don't need private eyes, I need an army," the Lyon epigrammed. He spoke like the emperors of old, powerful and weary. "My son is underground. It's been three days. It's time for cannons, not detectives."

"With Zooey's help, we might not need the cannons."

"Goddammit, Danny, can't you see this is war?! Michael's dead—a red flower was on the body! What more proof do you—"

Zooey took a ripe pear from a bowl of fruit on the table, rubbed it on her waistcoat, and champed into it with delight. She stopped munching as soon as she realized that both Mr. Lyon and Danny had shut up.

"What? I waf hungry." She pointed at the bowl. "That'f what it'f there for, ifn't it?"

A fly (possibly Jennifer) traversed the scene in a slow flight, punctuating the pause.

"Mr. Lyon," Danny tried to reroute, "all I want is to contain the damage. Zooey here is a genius. Give her five minutes. If we missed anything, she'll find it. If there is proof of a third party involved, we can salvage the alliance; your work will not have been in vain. If the signs point to the Red Mums, you'll have your confirmation to strike back."

He sounded both tough and servile. The kind of person all the Mr. Lyons in the world can't get enough of.

"I don't need any more confirmations," he persevered, clearly for the sake of appearance.

"And Zooey doesn't need more than a glance at the pool house," Danny replied.

Zooey was holding the pear core in her hand, longing for a waste bin.

The Lyon gripped his cane and hoisted himself off the chair with a tired sigh. "It's the Mums, Danny."

"I hope you're wrong, Mr. Lyon," Danny said, with not a hint of victory in his voice.

They exited through the back door and took the scenic route around the pool, Danny holding Kimrean's hand just in case. Mr. Lyon, leading the party and slowing it down a little, paid as much attention to the women laughing and splashing in the water as he would to goldfish or ducks. The girlscape had long been there for his son Mikey's enjoyment rather than his own; he had therefore considered it improper to send the decorations home while the boy's memory was still fresh. Of course, the news of a murder just a few yards away, not to mention the wake and the funeral that followed, had dampened the mood in Villa Leona, but the girls seemed to have overcome their distress and put aside their concerns for just a little increase in their pay. That was professionalism.

On the way to the pool house, a considerable hike from both the main building and the pool, Danny told Kimrean how San Carnal police had swept the room and examined the corpse. It was implied how brief their involvement had been: Mr. Lyon had always taken care of his own security, and extending an invitation to the local authorities had been a mere formality. The autopsy had been equally swift and superficial.

"There were obvious signs of struggle: he had bruises on his face, a broken arm. The CSI's theory, and mine, is that Mikey caught the murderer when he sneaked in through the bedroom window. They fought, and once Mikey pulled out his nine millimeter, the intruder disarmed him and shot him. Then he took the Beretta with him, so as not to leave prints. Only the red chrysanthemum on the body."

Beyond the swimming pool and a paddle tennis court that the garden path circumvented stood the overgrown bungalow, which could have comfortably lodged the families of a dozen Irish coal miners but had instead served as Mikey Lyon's quarters. A guard patrolling the garden hurried to unlock the front door as soon as he saw the old man approaching.

"This is where it happened," the boss showed, crossing the brief foyer. Danny followed him to the center of the sitcom-sized living room.

Kimrean stopped on the threshold. Visible from there were the fireplace, the media center, the open kitchen in the back. The fireplace was unpolished stone; everything else, mahogany and bamboo. A hollow wooden elephant played the cocktail cabinet role. On the mantelpiece, a single red flower in a vase sighed at its own reflection in the mirror.

"We found Mikey faceup here," Danny said, pointing at a sharply defined disinfected area on the leopard rug. "The only door was locked from the inside; the bedroom window was open."

Adrian said, "It wasn't the Japanese. Let's go."

He turned around and left. He had not walked six feet into the room.

Lyon grunted like an English bulldog at someone who just pretended to throw a ball for him. Danny babbled an apology to him and ran after Kimrean.

He caught them by the wrist on the garden path.

"Zooey, Jesus Christ, you didn't even—"

"I'm not Zooey," Adrian whispered angrily, shaking Danny's hand off. "Don't ever do that again. Ever."

"What? Do what?"

"Shit, I don't even know if I want to know if you know that room is bugged."

Danny mouthed a random question word, more due to the convoluted form of that line than to its implications.

"Okay, you don't know," Adrian sentenced. "There's a scuff mark on the floor near the entrance from when someone dragged the phone stand to access the socket on the wall behind it; there's dust on the socket cover, but the screws are all shiny, because someone removed the screws to hide a transmitter inside—FBI field manual. Also, the framed picture of nine-year-old Mikey and his mom on the stand has a bent corner from the time someone hid a microphone on the frame. You will find at least two more mikes, I'm guessing in the kitchen and either behind the mirror over the mantelpiece or in the philodendron. That room has been bugged for at least a week."

Danny strove to digest all that information compressed into twelve seconds, then muttered, "But . . . who the . . . ?"

"Oh, I don't know, let's see. Who would care to eavesdrop on Mikey Lyon's business? Can't think of anyone, except for the 'twelve counties and five state agencies cooperating to bring down the cartel,'" he quoted. "Each one throwing their own mikes and moles and territorial piss marks in the bad guys' yard! Brilliant coordination as usual!"

"Shit," Danny wheezed through gritting teeth. "Week before last, the health department came to inspect the place for molds, said some bullshit about new regulations. We had painters working on the ceiling. They were being watched most of the time, but—"

"But while they weren't being watched they turned the house into Dr. Dre's studio."

"The company seemed legit; I checked them out, even drove by their office downtown."

"Danny!"

The Lyon was catching up with them, hindered by his cane.

"What the hell—you in cahoots with this woman to take the blame off the Mums? Are you—"

Kimrean stepped between them with a wide, fake, conciliatory smile: "It's done, sir. It wasn't the Red Mums."

"But—"

"Mr. Lyon, that flower you found on the victim is not a chrysanthemum: it's a rare species of rose native to northern Mexico, used only in ornamentation and the preparation of oils. Chrysanthemums are strongly symbolic flowers in China and Japan, where they have been the standard of the Imperial Yamato dynasty for fifteen hundred years; to a Japanese, replacing it with any other flower is like the White House substituting the bald eagle with a penguin. What that Mexican rose there is telling you is 'Greetings from the South.'"

All characters waited for oxygen to flow back between them, Danny and Mr. Lyon gaping at the detective's ever off-putting, yet calmly reassuring, expression.

"'Greetings from the South,'" the old man echoed. And he scowled a little deeper upon asking, "Villahermosa?"

"I'll let you boys talk," Kimrean suggested, and they disappeared around the corner.


Kimrean marched over the lawn following the left flank of the bungalow, away from the pool mermaids and toward the colloquy of cockatoos dwelling in the thickest area of the garden. A man was pruning a crape myrtle by the far side of the building, which was fringed by flowery shrubs. Adrian pointed at the sprinklers.

"¿A qué hora las azaleas?"

"A las nueve."

He thanked him and stepped into the bushes. It was a small jungle in the six-foot-wide strip allotted, the highest twigs reaching well over the P.I.'s hat. Adrian stood in front of the bedroom window and peeked inside. The sill was almost level with his eyes.

He knelt down and started combing the earth for what was left of the footprints after the stampede of criminal investigators. He examined the base of the wall (brown brick over a stone plinth), the brickwork, the mortar between the brickwork like streets clogged by lichen. He ran a fingertip along one of the streets and licked it. He fished his cigarette pack out of his waistcoat, and from the pack he extracted his Detective Kit™: it consisted of a magnifying glass (just the lens), a razor, tweezers, and an empty vial for samples. With the razor he started scratching the edge of the plinth, ten inches above the garden floor.

Myriad insects patrolling and pollinating and eating the jungle assimilated the detective like any other worker.

"What are you doing?"

It was a feminine voice, genuinely interested. Kimrean sprung up, twirled on their feet, expecting to face one of the naiads from the swimming pool. Then they corrected the angle of vision by a few degrees downward.

Her bikini was strawberry-and-cream colored, retro, closer to a vault jumper's top. She wore her black hair short and sunglasses like big, bedazzled insect eyes. She stood four feet, eight inches.

Adrian didn't say anything, so Zooey inserted a friendly "Hey."

The girl nonchalantly took a sip from her Vanilla Coke. A few yards farther, on a sunny patch among the peach trees, a deck chair and an open Harry Potter book lay out of focus.

"Are you looking into Mikey's murder?" she inquired.

"Uh-huh," answered Zooey, while Adrian seemed busy groping

a cluster of flowers. "It's a commission, really; I'm not personally interested."

"Me neither," said the little girl.

She waited to see if that caused any effect, but the stranger was apparently too engrossed fondling the azaleas. For a second there it seemed like the conversation had been extinguished.

She commented, if only to defibrillate it: "Police didn't seem to care a lot either, did they?"

Adrian eyed her again over the fluffy white blossoms. "Why don't you go play with your little friends by the swimming pool?"

"I'm not allowed there. They say it's awkward." She scoffed. "Who wants to look at their prostitute-filled swimming pool and feel dirty or anything, right?"

That did cause some effect, enough to attract Zooey's attention. Adrian's was forced to follow, so he gave the girl almost two full seconds' worth of analysis.

"Okay, lemme see: high zygomatic bone, British accent, attitude . . . You must be the Lyon's daughter from his current marriage."

"Also, I'm eleven, so why else would I be here?" she said. "That wasn't too impressive."

Adrian lost interest and returned to the wilderness, nose inches from the ground, seemingly counting the fallen petals.

The girl followed them from a safe distance. Red-nailed bare toes curled on the fresh grass.

"If you're a cop, shouldn't you be wearing a visible ID?"

"If you're eleven, shouldn't you be busy exploring your own body or something?"

"Done that," she replied, and pointed at the ground the stranger was now fine-raking. "I also checked under that window for footprints."

The stranger rose up to full height and stepped out of the bushes, a brown-orange eye piercing the girl from above like an icicle shot straight through the heart.

"These are your footprints?!"

"No, not those," she promised. "I never stood there."

Adrian puffed out, then went back to work, grumbling between his teeth. "The fuck you following footprints for if you don't care who killed him."

"I was bored," she answered, not noticing the absence of a question mark at the end of the previous line.

The stranger stopped again, on one knee, and removed their hat to flip their hair. The other eye—green—was now scanning her in full. Not just the surface. This one felt like a sunbeam while you're drying out on the riverbank.

"My dad is a mobster, there are thugs in the garden and prostitutes in the pool," she said with a shrug. "Not a very child-friendly environment."

The stranger was paying attention to her now—maybe not full attention, but most of it. One hand scratched the other.

"There are worse places."

The odd face loosened up a little. You could almost get a hint of front teeth spying behind the hair-thin lips.

The girl removed her sunglasses. Big dark eyes transformed her face from rubber-stamp pop art icon to actual eleven-year-old girl.

"I'm Ursula. You?"

A breeze blew at every character's hair.

"Zooey."

Adrian called time's up and pulled Zooey back into the underbrush. The girl lowered her hand, which the stranger had not shaken.

"You're a private detective?"

"Yup."

"From San Francisco?"

"Indeed."

"I love it there. I wish I could go."

"I wish you were there already."

"Are you going to interrogate me?"

"Yeah, because you need encouragement to talk."

"I might have seen something."

"You weren't here when he was killed."

"How do you know?"

Kimrean was now on tiptoes, spider-fingers scuttling onto the highest blossoms.

"How do you know?" the girl repeated.

Adrian breathed in a lungful of patience.

"Your tan. Your knees are darkest: you've been wearing long socks and a skirt until recently and you're catching up now; you only got here for your brother's funeral. I'm guessing you're in a five-star summer boarding school for troubled children in Northern California. I'd say . . . Gillian Towers?"

"Cool." She grinned. "Not brother—half brother. But I'm flattered you noticed my legs. And you know a lot about troubled children institutions. You been to Gillian Towers?"

Kimrean stepped out to her again for the ultimatum.

"Okay, kid, look—I've seen your routine. You're a tattered child whose life spent in crime-paid luxury torn between your drug lord dad and money-laundering mom has smacked too many life lessons into you too quickly, forcing you to grow a carapace of protective sass under which a soft heart yearns for love—all really sad and sweet and food for thought. Now fuck off before I tell your daddy his little angel smokes pot."

With that he started putting away his Detective Kit™.

The barefooted child on the lawn finished processing the speech and could only object, "I don't smoke pot."

"Yeah, you do, but you don't know it," Kimrean overruled. "Whoever you're pinching your tobacco from, news flash: plain tobacco doesn't smell that good." They pocketed the sample vial and rounded on the child for the grace shot: "Impressed now, Shania?"

They abandoned the scene to join whoever was calling for them. A shaken-not-stirred Danny Mojave came running around the corner.

DANNY: Ayzee. *(Noticing the kid; softer.)* I hope you know what you're doing; they're talking total war on Villahermosa back there.

ADRIAN: Would you guys win a war against Villahermosa?

DANNY: Uh . . . yeah, probably.

ADRIAN: Then I'd say I'm doing fine. Give me your cell phone.

The kid approached, insect sunglasses back on her eyes.

"Daniel, can you drive me to the mall?"

"What? No, sorry, girl. I'm working. Maybe later."

She looked down and turned around, making sure to display her disappointment for an invisible audience.

ADRIAN: Phone me, please?

DANNY: *(Confidential.)* You found something?

ADRIAN: Yeah, the kid smokes pot.

DANNY: *(Falters, frowns.)* Okay, now I know who's stealing my cigarettes. And about the murder?

ADRIAN: Not much. The killer's shoe size, height, and build.

DANNY: We know: size eight and a half; that makes him around five-eight. Heavy.

ADRIAN: Smaller. He didn't disturb too many flowers and had to tiptoe to see through the window.

DANNY: So, he has big feet?

ADRIAN: Big shoes, actually. There's not much pressure on the toes.

DANNY: *(Visualizing.)* Okay. So, what does that tell us?

Kimrean exhaled like either Adrian or Zooey thought they were smoking.

ADRIAN: Considering height and build, I could go with female, but in the present circumstances . . . I'd say Asian male.

DANNY: But the flower came from Mexico.

ADRIAN: Are you dense? I made that up. Do you think I know every flower in America? I only mentioned Mexico to buy you time. Phone.

DANNY: *(Unpockets it, unlocks it.)* Here. Remember you cannot call home base fro—

ZOOEY: HEEEY, Mr. Lyon!

The man was just hobbling up to them, out of breath, his pink face sporting the discombobulated expression that was becoming his staple in this chapter.

"What's going on here?"

"We're done!" Kimrean stated gleefully. "There's really nothing left to do; your cops are very efficient, worth every cent you pay them. Uh, with your taxes, I mean. Danny darling, I'll wait for you in the car."

Mr. Lyon attempted to insert another line, but he was interrupted by the little girl joining back in:

"Papa, can someone drive me to town?"

"No, they can't!" the old man snapped at her. "These people are working—they're not here to attend to your whims!"

Kimrean heard the argument fade into the background while they strode up to the north side, cell phone in hand.

The estate was vast; it took them two and a half minutes on a straight line to reach the outer fence. At this latitude, the word *garden* was being clearly overstretched; the setting was a pine-wood, if not wild, not tame either. Adrian located the cameras along the tall iron fence, too slow moving and poorly spaced. He ambled toward the right, holding Danny's phone out in front of them like a compass, and stopped by a small clearing under a couple tall, easy-to-climb eucalypti. Adrian checked the network on the phone. Then he knelt down, examined the ground, and took a pinch of dirt to his nostrils.

There was nothing else to do. He trekked back to the path and then took the long way around the swimming pool, so that Zooey wouldn't get distracted.

They resurfaced near the entrance, in sight of the sentries posted at the front gate, and Zooey waved at them cheerfully while Adrian opened the shotgun door to Danny's blue Camaro, parked under a vine-walled pergola.

As soon as they shut the door, they noticed the marijuana scent.

"No way."

They lifted the polyester car cover that lay in a bundle on the backseat, and Ursula Lyon stuck her head out.

"What are you—"

"Give me a break, okay? I just want a ride to town; it's on your way!"

"Are you crazy?! Get out of the f—"

"Quiet!" she shushed, and ducked back under the cover.

The speed of the following events surprised even Kimrean themselves: Danny opened the driver's door, plumped in, and before he had time to receive the distress signals from Adrian's face he blurted out the next rant:

"I can't believe this, the Effing-B-I! I'm gonna phone Chief Carlyle and tell him to tell them where to plant their bugs. Nice fucking teamwork!"

At this point he noticed Adrian's face—just as Adrian was diving it into his palm.

"What?" Danny asked. "What?!"

"Wow." Ursula emerged, little head sticking between the front seats like any kid passenger who was about to throw up in the car. "Shit. Okay. I know I shouldn't have heard that."

She looked like a child who just caught Santa taking off his padded red suit in an alley behind the Toys"R"Us. Or one who walked in on her own parents banging. Or walked in on her parents banging in Santa suits in an alley behind the Toys"R"Us. She confronted Danny.

"So . . . you're a cop?"

Danny sat jaw-dropped, neatly listening to every sphincter in his body saying, *Well, it was nice working here!*

"Brilliant!" Adrian judged. "I mean, absolutely brilliant! One line, and you managed to catch an eleven-year-old up with the plot! Shit, there are Disney Classics harder to follow!"

Nobody talked for the next three or four minutes. They just sat there inside the yellow-striped pony car under the pergola while the sentries stood by the open gate and two other watchmen radioed each other, wondering what the holdup was; Danny soaked in cold sweat, Ursula still assimilating the revelation, Adrian searching for something to kick angrily, and Zooey pondering the best way to ask permission for a quick dip in the swimming pool and perhaps a piña colada.

"Okay," Ursula said at last, breathing in. "First things first: you're not gonna kill me, are you?"

"Damn, I wish I'd thought of that," Adrian groaned.

"Ursula, listen," Danny started, but Ursula cut him off before he could muster the words.

"Relax," she said. "I won't rat you out. Even if I didn't like you, I wouldn't be able to live with my conscience."

That soothed the tension a little. Three out of four people in the car took a deep breath.

"Although," Ursula reprised after that, "I would appreciate some compensation."

"Excuse me?" Danny said. "We're negotiating now?"

"Wouldn't you?"

"Okay. Let's make it easy then: you don't tell your dad I'm police, I don't tell him you smoke pot."

"You're kidding, right? I'm terrified of my father, but even I know that's trading Baltic Avenue for Boardwalk."

"What for what?"

"Like in Monopoly? Baltic Avenue is cheap and—"

"Will you shut the fuck up?!" Kimrean interrupted. "Jesus, I'm just realizing how annoying it is to have someone gloating about every smart thing they say! *(To Danny, concerned.)* Do I sound like that?"

"Adrian, what are we going to do?!" Danny begged.

A beige-suited goon with a radio in one hand and the other hovering over his hip stepped under the pergola. As though he'd heard the clapboard go, Danny slipped back into character, torqued the key in the ignition, and lowered his window.

"I'm driving the P.I. to the station and taking the kid to the mall. No need to bother the old man."

The goon nodded and let the car roll out the gates, radioing for the page break.

# 4

Take the neon palaver, the plastic luxury, and the smell of bottled air and pine freshener common to all of San Carnal, and multiply by ten. That's San Carnal's mall right there.

Danny Mojave, Ursula Lyon, and A. Z. Kimrean occupied a stool-like table in front of a Taco Bell on the second-floor balcony in the atrium. Kimrean was wolfing down a Mission burrito with chorizo, pineapple, and sauerkraut. Ursula was drawing circles with a straw on the foamy surface of a chocolate milkshake. Incredibly annoying ambient music consisting of instrumental versions of '60s and '70s pop hits plagued the silence, masking a layer of subliminal messages playing on the PA system: *Buy skiing gear now. Eat doughnuts. Fear foreigners.*

"So what's gonna happen to me?"

It was Ursula's first attempt at an icebreaker. She sat on her stool like she was outside the principal's office, thoughts in her head literally weighing her down.

Danny squished his third Newport on an eco-friendly paper ashtray. He had aged five years in the last thirty minutes. Fruit flies stared at him in amazement.

"Nothing, Ursula. What do you think is gonna happen?"

"When they arrest my father, are they gonna take me?"

"No. Of course not. You haven't done anything."

"My dad is a gangster. Isn't there a law that says if you know someone is committing a crime and you don't speak out, that's a crime too? I saw it on *Law & Order.*"

"Yes, but you're eleven. You are not supposed to be aware of everything going on in your home."

"I'm supposed to be stupid because I'm eleven? I know what's going on."

Adrian jumped in, not caring or noticing that his mouth was full: "If you're so perceptive, why didn't you speak out?"

Ursula made a silent statement of disgust at Kimrean's manners, then answered: "It's one thing to notice other kids don't have armed chauffeurs with prison tattoos; it's another thing to be ready to send your parents to jail for it."

Danny joined in on the disgust bus: "How can you eat in a moment like this?"

"I'm wondering myself," Adrian admitted, before his left hand chucked the remainder of the burrito in his mouth.

"Okay, I'm not going to jail," Ursula resumed. "Then what? You guys kick in the door and you arrest my dad and my mom back in Grand Cayman and you take the house and the cars and the bank accounts. What happens to me?"

Mojave shrugged, avoiding eye contact. Something in his voice undermined the pretension of indifference.

"I don't know, kiddo. Not my job. I'm not staying long enough to find out."

Ursula seemed to appreciate the honesty. She then turned to Kimrean: "What is your job?"

"I make sure it's the cops who kick in your door."

Ursula made sure to read between the lines. "Then it's true. There's gonna be a war."

Danny removed his sunglasses. Fifty thousand watts' worth of fluorescent light stabbed his eyes. He rubbed the bridge of his nose. He had almost forgotten about the war.

"It's not a hundred percent sure yet," he said.

"Just in case, don't order sushi for dinner," Adrian advised. Zooey pointed at the milkshake. "Are you gonna finish that?"

"Yes, I am."

"Nah, you hardly tried it." *(Pulls the glass closer.)*

"I'm working on it!" *(Pulls it back.)*

"Not fast enough."

*(She takes one of the two straws and starts sucking; Ursula immediately takes the other one and sucks as hard as she can. The liquid descends rapidly as Zooey and Ursula drink, foreheads touching, eyes on each other, cheeks caved in like they're trying to create an absolute vacuum in their mouths.)*

*(Ursula ends up exploding in a laugh, spraying chocolate all over Zooey and the table.)*

"Aw, damn!" cried Zooey, making a big show of wiping her face. "'Ursula used milk spout! It's super effective!'"

Danny shifted to shoulder off Ursula's boisterous laughter while he made a phone call.

After Taco Bell they went to the Rampage store on the first floor, and Ursula tried on a lot of clothes while Danny talked on the phone and Kimrean studied the security measures for purely professional reasons. Shrilling teenagers flocked around the clothes racks, popping fifteen-megaton gum bubbles and lying to each other with the keenness of authors raving on each other's book jackets.

Danny hung up, crossed back through the tag detectors, and planted a foot on the bench next to Kimrean, whose hands were playing with a three-inch-wide leather belt with pink lollipops drawn between the spikes. Precisely then, Ursula blasted out of a fitting room in a neon-rimmed black shirt and glossy tights. She spun once before Zooey and raised the sunglasses she'd borrowed from Danny.

"Well?"

"Cool! Lose the leg warmers; no need to go full Jennifer Beals."

"Who?"

"Forget it. Keep the shirt, try it with the shorts again and these shoes," she advised, handing her a pair of Panzer-sized sneakers in colors only bees could perceive properly. "Platform sneakers need to be brought back; it's up to cool people like us."

Ursula took the shoes and pranced back into the fitting room.

"You're good with kids," Danny commented.

"I hate kids," Adrian snarled. "They should keep them in incubators until . . . How old are you?"

"Thirty-three."

"Until their thirty-fourth birthday."

"I'm being summoned back to Xander's penthouse."

"Okay, drop me at the train station. I'll tell Carlyle you send love."

"What am I supposed to do, Ade?" His voice had dropped a full octave. "About the kid."

"Who cares about her? She doesn't alter your mission. She just slunk out of Fort Narc and so far no one cared, did they?"

Ursula ta-daed back before their eyes, her noodle legs looking like Hellboy's right fist, ending in heavy-armored sneakers.

"*Wow!*" Zooey hollered. "Give this girl a battle-ax and a rideable white bear—she's my new favorite manga heroine!"

"There's a supercool bra back there," Ursula pointed. "You should try it on; matches one of your eyes."

"Nah, I'm not allowed bras. I have to wear an elastic band to hide what little I got."

"Ursula," Danny squeezed in, with a sad party-pooper accent. "We gotta go."

"Now? I'm not done here!"

"I have to work, and I have to get you home before your father notices you're gone."

"Sure, any time now," she grumbled. "He wouldn't miss me unless I took the safe with me."

"I'm serious, Ursula. Go get changed, we're leaving."

Ursula pouted, legs shifting to a more confrontational stance that incidentally suited a model on the catwalk.

"You know what's the first thing I'll tell my dad when I get back?"

"Oh, come on!" Danny cried. "You're blackmailing me now?"

"Ugly word. I liked 'negotiating' better."

"It's not a negotiation when it's my life on one end!"

"Your life?!" Ursula fought back. "My life will be over in a matter of weeks! What will I have left when you take my parents? Witness protection? Foster care? This could be my last shopping day till adulthood!"

Some other teenager was now looking in her direction, offended to be outshrieked. Danny lowered his voice.

"Ursula, I understand your frustration. But I need to think in the short term now: you just sneaked out from home, and I can't babysit you. What am I supposed to do?"

The kid grabbed Kimrean's arm: "I can stay with Zooey!"

ZOOEY: Yeah!

DANNY: No!

ADRIAN: No!

Ursula frowned.

"Are you like bipolar or something?"

"One: bipolars don't usually turn detectives; they're naturally gifted stockbrokers," Kimrean lectured. "And two: I don't have time to play Mary Poppins; I need to go back to San Francisco."

"Cool! Let's go to San Francisco, I need to buy books!"

DANNY: We're in a mall. Isn't there a bookstore here?

ZOOEY & URSULA: Pfft. Please.

Danny's phone buzzed again in his pocket; he rejected the call.

"I can go and come back on the six fifteen train," Ursula argued. "I've done it before! Someone will pick me up at the station."

"I can't look after her," Adrian dug in.

"I don't need to be looked after; I can be on my own!"

"Danny!"

Danny's hand was still in his pocket, daring his phone to ring again. He looked Kimrean in the eyes. It was like searching for someone in a multitude.

"Danny, I can do this," Zooey said. "Trust me."

He pulled out the hand from his pocket. The keys to the Camaro dangled in it, hovering over Zooey's palm.

"Zooey, listen to me," Danny admonished, in the tone he reserved for discussing heist arrangements. "He drives. Do you hear me? *He* drives."

"Yeah yeah yeah, I hear you," said the green eye, joyfully accepting the keys. "No problem."

Danny turned to Ursula, his unprotected eyes flinching at the color blast. "I am not paying for those clothes."

"I'll cover the shoes, you pay for the shirt and the bra," Zooey said, fishing the $150 they kept from the femme fatale that morning. "Believe me, I know a sound investment when I see it."

—

Twenty minutes later, Adrian sat at the wheel, Ursula Lyon co-pilot, while two Rampage bags oohed and aahed in the backseat, gaping at the brave new world outside the mall. The Camaro zoomed along the road like a yellow-striped zipper splitting the Gran South desert in two.

Ursula spent a part of the trip dialing through music radio stations until Adrian barked at her and she finally switched it off. Currently, Adrian was considering how to switch off Ursula.

"I had a Nicki Minaj phase too, but I'm getting over it. Same with Katy Perry; it's a little too shallow. But 'Roar' hits me every time—I'm only human, right? Lately I've been listening to Lorde a lot. Do you like her?"

She turned to Kimrean, their gargoyle profile outlined against the blue sky.

"You would love her," she added.

Kimrean's lips had faded away long ago, lost in the frugality of features of their smooth, pale face. The brown eye was fixed on the road, the green one veiled by blond hair.

"I play drums too," Ursula said. "I dreamed of forming an indie duet with my doubles partner in the Caymans, but we've kinda grown apart. I play soccer now. We're lining up a team at Gillian."

Ahead, the yellow road lines kept crashing into the car, merging with the hood's stripes.

"I also play with dolls. I remove their heads and replace them with those of cats I hunt in the backyard."

She checked the gargoyle again. It didn't appreciate her grin.

Her attention then alighted on Kimrean's chest.

"Can I ask you a candid question?"

"Yes, please. The level of sophistication so far is killing me."

"Were you . . . Like, I mean, not judging or anything—completely safe space here, okay? But were you born a woman?"

Two utility poles elapsed.

"I'm not fully born yet," Adrian answered.

Ursula unhooked her seat belt and shifted in her seat, confronting the driver.

"Okay, I know I can do this. There was this really cool girl in there called Zooey a while ago. I want her back."

She stared at the gargoyle, waiting for a reaction.

Not immediately, but in their due time, lips kindled up like a small blue flame on the featureless face. Kimrean swept their hair to the other side and grinned at her, and Ursula grinned back.

"You know, you can be a real jerk sometimes," said the child.

"Tell me about it. I spend twenty-four seven with that jerk." One hand unclasped from the steering wheel to frisk the waistcoat for cigarettes. "Don't tell Danny about this, okay? I'm not supposed to drive; apparently, I have trouble focus—*look! Roadrunner!*"

She sprang onto her seat, half her body leaning out the window, gazing in awe at the dumbfounded ground cuckoo that was foraging for critters on the side of the road. She lingered on it until it disappeared in the distance, then she sat back down again, glowing with glee, noticed Ursula holding the steering wheel and calmly relieved her from duty with a customary thank you, all of this at 90 mph.

Ursula exhaled a long-held breath, too wide-eyed for cuteness, then crept back onto her seat and fastened her belt.

"The thing about the cats and the dolls—that was a joke, right?" Zooey asked.

"Yeah."

"Good. 'Cause I don't tolerate violence against dolls."

Ursula chuckled, and a blue sign splattered with buzzard excrement signaled the end of Gran South County.

—

Four p.m. Sunshine flowed onto San Francisco's Columbus Avenue, a stray shaft piercing the second-floor window of City Lights Bookstore, the one in the poetry room, and splashing on page sixty-four of the botany manual that A. Z. Kimrean was flipping through, curled up on a wicker armchair. Ursula sat in lotus on the carpet, reading from a pile of paperbacks. They were the only three customers in the room.

Ursula cleared her throat and reread the poem she'd been studying, aloud this time.

> *The guy from Sicily's taken a bullet,*
> *And now he has to tear his good shirt up for a*
>     *tourniquet—meanwhile*
> *He's bleeding all over the radio*
> *While I drive and try to find a decent music station.*
> *And the little girl lies in the backseat,*
> *Raindrops skiing down her window*
> *against the glitchy skyline.*

Zooey listened carefully, then resolved: "I'd fuck him."

The narrow stairway squeaked, foretelling the arrival of a visitor. Lieutenant Greggs glanced over the scene, her jacket folded under her arm and a deli coffee in her hand.

"This is nice," she said, sitting on the armchair across from Kimrean, on the other side of a coffee table where the unpopular books lay in shame. "Can we do this fast? I have to go back to work."

"This is work," Adrian said, not granting her a look from either eye. "I just thought if anyone happened to recognize Danny's car, they'd better not see it parked in front of the police station."

"Danny let you borrow his car?"

Kimrean momentarily bobbed up from their book. "Surprise—some people do trust me."

Greggs lowered her voice, aware of the kid who was sitting on the floor, leafing through the restored text edition of *Naked Lunch*.

"Demoines checked about the bug. It was the FBI, ten days ago. They swear they didn't know we had a man inside."

"Makes sense. Why would the FBI know things? It's easier to kick the door in and ask."

"I requested the recording from Monday night, but—"

"Confidential."

"Right. To be fair, I think there's something about privacy in the Fourth Amendment. I can get a judge to—"

"Forget it, no state judge wants to antagonize the FBI. I'll just go to the source."

"What do you expect to hear in the audio? Anything short of 'Hi, Mikey Lyon, I'm not related to the Red Chrysanthemum but take this anyway, *bang bang*' is no use to us."

"True, although that was kind of implied in the absence of a red chrysanthemum in the scene."

"The flower's not a chrysanthemum? Then what is it?"

"A red rose. A red herring. Who knows." Adrian closed the book, left it on the coffee table where it so comfortably belonged, and untangled their legs. "The yakuza have been in Southern California awhile. Do they even have a history of leaving flowers on their kills? Is that a thing?" Greggs searched her mental files for a second, but Adrian couldn't wait that long. "I don't recall them doing it. Maybe the flower was just there. The Lyons have a big garden."

"So it's not the yakuza?"

"Sadly, everything else points to them."

They both sighed. Greggs's sight line wandered toward the little girl, if only not to look at Kimrean directly, like spies meeting in a Parisian café.

"There's something else pointing to the Japanese," Greggs said. "Demoines got it from our colleagues in the bureau. Are you familiar with the name Yu Osoisubame?"

"AKA 'the Phantom Ninja.' Japanese hit man, stealth expert, nineteen jobs confirmed. Yes, it rings a bell."

"He's in California. Landed in LAX Monday afternoon, hours before Mikey's killing. Looks like the yakuza might have outsourced to Jesus Jefferson Christ, that girl is Victor Lyon's daughter!"

"About time you noticed."

"What is she doing here?"

"So far? Making censors shake their heads and early reviewers tag the plot as #problematic," Adrian summarized. "May I say, if the guy who killed Mikey Lyon calls himself a ninja, he's been relaxing his standards. I've seen tropical storms go through the Caribbean more discreetly."

"Maybe you have too high standards. Have you ever seen a real ninja work?"

"Isn't the whole point of ninjas not being seen? Anyway, he left tracks. I'll tell you more when I get access to a lab."

"Give me what you got; I'll hand it to forensics."

"Sure, and by the time we have the results, Japan and California will have been reconciled by the continental drift. I'll take care of it." Adrian rose and Zooey snapped their fingers. "Ursy? Kiss Auntie Greggs good-bye; we're leaving."

"Wait, Ayzee," Greggs whispered, concerned. "Seriously: the kid. What's up with that?"

"Nothing's on. We're babysitting. At times, Danny trusts us

too much," Adrian judged, and Zooey added, "Can you pay for her books? I'm tapped out after the shoes. And throw in a puppy-eyed Ginsberg postcard."

Five p.m. A.Z. knocked on a corrugated metal door while Ursula Lyon leaned over a rusty rail on a catwalk that ran around an abandoned lumber mill outside Oakland. The path and the stairs up to this landing were once smothered in luxurious, not always wild vegetation; now, facing north from the balcony, oil derricks nodded against the brown-and-gray sky like giant robot cranes drinking from puddles of crude. The western wind carried the barks of lonesome dogs and heavy machinery.

Ursula stroked the flaking yellow rail and the yellow leaves of a potted plant. "Who are we visiting?"

"Can't you just wait literally five seconds?" Adrian said over his shoulder.

Zooey then spoke over hers: "You'll see, you're gonna love her."

Metal bolts slid within the door, and it clanked open. Ursula saw two boots, a fireproof apron, a wrench large enough to jam the cogs of a battleship, and a wicker hat. Under the hat she later noticed the face of a woman, some fifty years old—most of them sunny and windy.

A grass-blade of a grin unbalanced the perfect symmetry of her jaw.

"The prodigal children return."

Zooey hugged her like a theme park Snow White. "Gwe-e-e-e-en!"

"Zooey, Zooey, Zooey," the woman soothed her. "What took you so long?" Her voice was chipped, the way of a porcelain teacup.

"I would've come sooner; Dickhead wouldn't let me!"

"Yeah, yeah. That excuse is getting old."

"I called right after they released me!" Kimrean said, ushering themselves in.

"I know, I got your message. I could've picked you up."

"You wouldn't have taken me where I wanted."

The lady was about to close the door when Ursula squeezed through, apologizing. The hostess's face returned to its default expression—that of a slightly shocked English governess.

"Whose child is this?"

"I don't know! All she does is follow me and say, 'Please give me more pixie dust—I've got money this time.'"

The child eyerollingly ignored the joke and stuck out a hand. "I'm Ursula."

"Gwen," the lady said, shaking her hand. She was courteous but not condescending, a treatment children welcome as unusual. Her bearing reminded Ursula of one of those women who are sometimes interviewed on TV, with a caption pointing out to younger audiences that they are magical and did great things in the past, like Julie Andrews or Madonna. Her waist was set high, and she had the kind of stance that said, *I was a sexy blonde once,* but also the wrinkled forehead and the glint of an intelligence never patronized by Bridget Jones or Carrie Bradshaw that added, *And luckily, I got over it.*

Gwen's den was a wide, diaphanous, rusty mezzanine inside the lumber mill. Large interior windows overlooked the derelict machines, asleep like the contents of pyramids, their dreams suspended in the sunrays pouring in through the skylight. On the outer wall, a smaller window surveyed the bay. Plants chitchatted everywhere, gathered around the different workspaces the area was divided into. One of those workspaces turned out to be a kitchen—Ursula had been misled by the gas canisters and the computer on the countertop.

"Will you have some coffee?"

"I will!" Zooey cried from another point of interest in the loft, where she had gone to greet the caged budgerigars.

Gwen queried Ursula; she shrugged her shoulders four feet above the floor. "Yeah, why not."

They all sat on stools around a card table shrouded in a vintage flowery oilcloth, and Gwen poured a coffee whose atomic weight granted it a position in the lanthanides section of the periodic table.

"She's not from the place I wouldn't have taken you to, is she?" Gwen asked, pointing at the kid.

"Oh, no, she came later!" Zooey reassured her. She had not yet sat down, nor did she plan to; she just held the cup in her hand and kept abusing exclamation signs. "I've got a new office!"

"Really."

"And a new case!"

"Really? Femme fatale or teeth-pummeling thug?"

"Both!" Zooey said, in ecstasy. "But those came and went; I'm into something better now. Remember Danny Mojave?"

"SFPD? Curly hair, really cute? Wasn't he the one you helped raid that sex slave trafficking auction?"

"Yeah—actually I only wandered in to use their ATM. Anyway, I'm working with him. We're gonna stop a gang war!"

"Ooh. How are you gonna do that?"

"I was getting there." Adrian landed the cup and produced a seemingly empty vial from their pocket. "Can I use your microscope?"

"I feared this would be a business visit."

"Business and party all around—that's me, Mom!" And with

that and a kiss on the lady's forehead, they capered toward the laboratory, far on the other end of the mezzanine.

Ursula watched them go while she took her first sip of coffee. She was interrupted by her throat constricting fast, an iron-willed signal saying, *No way.*

Gwen lit herself a cigarette and slid the sugar toward her.

"Thank you." She poured five spoonfuls into her cup.

On the fridge, inside a radio, very little clones of the Runaways were singing.

"Are you really her mom?" Ursula inquired.

Gwen waved off the idea like a cheap compliment. "No, I'm not. But 'mother figure' is a mouthful. You're Zooey's friend?"

"Uh . . . I guess. For the last three hours." Then she made sure that Kimrean and the lab were far enough, and lowered her voice: "What is wrong with her?"

"With her? Nothing." Gwen took a gulp of her coffee and for a moment she smirked at some memory attached to the oilcloth. "Nothing at all."

"But she has these super weird mood swings," Ursula said, spying on the nimble marionette perched on a high stool, vulturing over the microscope. "This isn't that PMS thing everyone talks about, right?"

That made Gwen laugh. It was a good laugh, for someone who didn't seem naturally inclined for it. "No, it's not."

"Does she have split personality or something?"

"Not at all. They have a whole separate personality apiece, each perfectly defined. Adrian and Zooey."

"Adrian is . . . like, the jerk?"

Gwen smirked again. "Yeah, you could say that. Let's just say he's her brother."

Ursula mouthed the word, astonished. Gwen opted for following the thread to the end.

"I used to be their doctor. One of them. I do research now. But I've been following their case since it fell in my hands."

"What do you mean, 'one of them'?"

"Well, I wasn't the first person to diagnose them. They spent their whole childhood in institutions, tried different foster homes . . . Their real family abandoned them long ago. None of the doctors who treated them could figure out why this 'schizophrenic hermaphrodite' was always shouting to himself and needed his right hand to hold down his left. I was the one who told them apart. I listened to both, took DNA samples, and proved to the world that they were two different people. In biology, we call them chimeric twins. More specifically, Quain cenoencephalic chimera syndrome. Named after its discoverer, Gwyneth Temperance Quain." She pointed at herself with a flourish; then she returned her attention to the laboratory. "Ayzee is the only known occurrence."

Kimrean was watching some piece of lab equipment work (a centrifugator), slapping their knees and cheering at it as a child would to a toy hippodrome.

"So . . ." Ursula resumed. "She's not a girl?"

"One half is." Gwen gulped down the rest of her coffee. "Adrian is a little on the antisocial side; you must be patient with him."

"Hey, Gwen!" Kimrean called. "Check this out."

Gwen put out her cigarette and stood up: "But he's charming when he's having fun."

She and Ursula hiked toward the laboratory—another workspace consisting of classic chemistry equipment and a few modern machines that felt awkwardly out of place. The wooden furniture was weathered as if it had been salvaged from the streets during a Minnesotan winter. Kimrean yielded the microscope to the doctor. All Ursula could see with her naked eye was a white, green, and black speck on the slide under the lens.

"Mold," Gwen determined, leaning over the eyepiece. "Dead mold. It's been sprayed with fungicide."

"No, someone stepped on it. Sample comes from a wall in a garden; there was mold all over the foot of the wall, except for the part that was under the toes of whoever climbed up."

"Then that someone was carrying fungicide on their soles," Gwen resolved. "Some kind of floor disinfectant, maybe. Industrial cleaner?"

"I thought of that—no bleach."

"Check for phenol."

"I'm on it. You're out of iron chloride."

"I'll add it to my shopping list."

Ursula tried pinning her eyes to the microscope, but Adrian took the slide before she could see anything. With keenly meticulous fingers, he managed to split the speck of a sample in two, picked one of the halves with some pincers and dropped it in a test tube of water. Into another tube he dissolved a pinch of yellow powder. Carefully, he put two drops of the second solution into the first.

He stoppered the tube, shook it vigorously, and brought it to the lamp.

"Red is positive," Gwen reminded him.

"I got purple," Adrian said.

Gwen pouted, then turned toward the library and relieved a shelf of a giant-sized volume, multicolor Post-its sticking out between the pages. She queried the index, then a numbered table, and came up with the verdict. "Chlorophenol."

Adrian jogged back to the kitchen area and googled some key words on the computer. A few clicks later he read for his audience, who were just coming after him: "'Ortho-benzo-para-chlorophenol, used as an active ingredient in top-range disinfectants.' Commercial brands recommend it for"—two more clicks—"operating rooms, sterile chambers, vet clinics."

Ursula said, "So the killer is a doctor?"

"No," said Adrian and Gwen in unison. Then Gwen expanded: "Hospital personnel don't wear street shoes on duty."

Kimrean's left hand idly alighted on Ursula's head, ruffling her hair.

"Well, it will mean something. Thanks, Gwen. By the way, I'm gonna need some you-know-what."

"You leaving already?" Gwen said.

"Some what?" Ursula asked.

Adrian shushed her, then answered Gwen: "I've got a case to solve. And I gotta drive Little Miss Daisy here to the train station."

"I'm eleven!" Ursula shouted after Kimrean when they left for the lab again. "Can you stop using prehistoric pop references when you talk about me?"

Gwen had moved toward a side cupboard near the kitchen that had been a school locker in a previous life. Ursula peeked while the doctor pulled out a small case and checked the syringes inside.

"What's that?"

"Diarctorol," Gwen answered. "A psychoactive drug derived from amphetamine. It stimulates the left hemisphere, which in Ayzee relaxes the right one. In other words, it puts Zooey to sleep, so that Adrian has more room to operate."

Ursula did not like that picture.

"Does Zooey know about this?"

"They know the same things—they share a brain. But it's one thing to know and another thing to be aware of knowing."

She closed the locker as Kimrean jogged back to them, pocketing the vial from their Detective Kit™. On passing Ursula, they fixed both eyes on her and gave her a silent one-dimensional smile while their right hand took the case from Gwen and the left scratched their belly.

"Come back soon," Gwen said. She then turned to Ursula: "You too, if you like."

"We will," Kimrean promised, planting a little kiss on the doctor's cheek. "Bye, Mom."

They popped back onto the catwalk, the sun already falling beneath the toxic smog.

Six p.m. A.Z. and Ursula sat on one of the red benches on platform nine in the Caltrain station under Fourth and King Streets.

ZOOEY: . . . so it's very important to stay hydrated and always buy from a trusted dealer, because one day you meet a nice old hippie lady on Haight Street and you think, "Oh, she's all organic and everything, what could go wrong?" so you drop some of her homemade acid and next thing you know you're in the back of a van with a cow and three rednecks en route to blow up a power station, and they're all talking about ditching the cow but you won't have it 'cause that cow saved your life, goddamn it, so you and the cow run across the border and you end up in an STD clinic in northern Mexico, and there, my friend, they do things to you I do not wish upon my worst enemy. *(Pause.)* Well, okay, I do wish them on Pitbull—but no one else!

Ursula was leaning on the edge of the bench, hugging her bag of purchases from City Lights.

"What's acid?"

The PA system announced the imminent arrival of the 6:15 Express Caltrain to San Carnal.

"Oh," Zooey said, sincerely disappointed. "That's your train."

"Yup." Ursula nodded. "Back to my monitored, goon-patrolled desert fortress."

"Sounds like Dick Cheney's favorite home decor magazine."

Ursula didn't laugh. "At least you'll get rid of me for a while," she said.

"Hey," Zooey complained. "That hurt."

"Not your brother."

"Don't worry about him; he's in his thinking corner."

"Really?" She pulled off a tiny smile. "Can you tell what he's thinking?"

Zooey's sight line strayed for a second.

"He's . . . calculating how different leg injuries would affect an Asian male's average footprint depth and stride length."

"You can read his thoughts?"

"They're not his alone. It's . . . like sharing a dorm room. You can mind your own business, but you're hearing the other guy all the time; at any point you can turn and see what he's doing. He has a more accurate way to explain it, but not nearly as graphic."

The hurtling train prevented the conversation from continuing, clanking and puffing like a mad fire-breathing red dragon. It slowed down just as angrily to an exhausted, resentful stop.

A door opened right in front of their bench. It took all of Ursula's will to stand up.

"Will I see you again?" she asked.

"Sure!" Zooey said. "We're gonna see a lot of each other; you're part of the case now. You're the femme fatale."

"What's that?"

"Femme fatale? It's an archetype: the devious, beautiful woman with a dark past and compromising knowledge, playing other characters like chess pawns and getting the hero into trouble. That's who you are now. Innocent but dangerous."

"But I don't want to cause you trouble."

"Oh, please—trouble is necessary. It's what moves the plot forward. And your presence is a breath of fresh air; this case oozes testosterone. Drug cartel, undercover cops—this would be a sausage factory without you, girl. Don't worry about us, you're doing great. You do you."

She hadn't stood up; she was leaning forward, eyes level with the child's. Ursula smiled, amused, repeating the words *femme fatale* to herself so she could google them later, and sticking a hand out.

"Been a pleasure, Zooey."

They shook hands politely. Ursula turned to the panting train before her, stepped toward it. A couple feet short of the doors, she spun on her heel: "Good-bye, Adrian."

Kimrean's head turned sideways some ten degrees. The lipless mouth was again a straight line, neutral. He didn't say anything.

Ursula climbed onto the train. She chose a seat away from the platform, and she overstretched the ritual of carefully settling her shopping bags and folding her jacket on the seat across from her in order not to have to peek through the window before the car started moving. Which did not take long to happen.

The train left, as impatient and loud as it had come, red dragon shrieks and fiery puffs disappearing into the eastbound tunnel.


Night.

After several hours of silent contemplation at the pubs in North

Beach, A. Z. Kimrean climbed up the Hitchcock-lit stairwell of their building on Fisherman's Wharf and, upon reaching the third-floor landing, noticed the yellow-and-black police tape X-marking the door to their quarters, partially striking out the fresh shiny vinyl letters of their names. With barely a thought apiece, they stooped under the tape, unlocked the door, and repossessed their office.

There was no need to switch the lights on: the cracking sound of debris and bullet casings under their imitation Converse indicated that everything was exactly as they left it. Through the shattered window, the high-power lights of the night-shift stevedores on the docks shone bright enough to confirm the hazy recollections of the fight choreography from that morning. The daily batch of neckless thugs might have made it out alive after all, judging by the absence of chalked silhouettes on the floor—or maybe they had been dragged out by the firemen and died downstairs. In any case, their ghosts would not inconvenience Kimrean for the night. The exploding propane canister had taken out the one kitchen cupboard, but overall it had not worsened the damage inflicted on the rest of the building. Kimrean spent a few minutes flapping the debris off the bedsheets, rearranging their few personal items, and restoring the toaster to its seat on the desk and the chessboard to its dais. The ceiling fan didn't work.

They stood for a while within reach of a cool draft coming through the window, smoking a cigarette and listening to the boat horns from the bay.

Idly, their right hand lifted a white knight to h4.

The left prodded a black pawn to f2.

The telephone rang, somewhere in the bedroom area, under the bed.

Kimrean put out the cigarette and picked up the receiver.

"Your car is in one piece," Adrian said.

"Ayzee! You gotta come back to San Carnal, now!"

*(Removing their hat and placing it on the coat stand.)* "No can do—I just put my jammies on."

"It's Frankie!"

An iris glimmered in the dark like an orange-brown standby light.

"Frankie?"

"The middle Lyon! He's dead, with a red flower on his chest!"

"Don't call the cops!" Adrian shouted into the receiver while they plopped their hat back on their head. "This time the scene is all mine!"

# 5

It was a perfect night for driving aimlessly under the stars. And Kimrean happened to have an aim, which justified doubling the state speed limit. Everything was in their favor.

The case had taken a nasty turn—nasty enough to make Adrian think about it while driving. Adrian always tried hard not to speculate on a case while it was still developing, and he passionately despised detectives who thought in voice-over. He considered it a cheap trick: filling those boring transition scenes between action sequences with inner monologues summing up the events thus far and building airborne castles of hypotheses just to meet page quotas and comply with publishing contracts that assign value to literary works by the ounce. If such paragons of investigative incompetence spent less time sitting on their asses baffled by how strange the mystery was and more time proactively solving it, they might actually catch some criminals and even spare a couple square miles of Amazon rain forest, Kimrean thought while driving, fine-tuning the radio, lighting a cigarette, and scratching their crotch at the same time. All being said, the case was strange. Because—at the risk of stooping to as low a writing standard as posing rhetorical questions in the narrator's voice—what was the point of killing Frankie?

If Mikey Lyon's murder was the declaration of war, Frankie's was redundant. That, or the plateau stage of a blitzkrieg: a war declared, fought, and won in one week.

Those were Adrian's thoughts. During the same interval, Zooey thought that she could murder an egg and bacon bagel, that Jon Stewart looked like he was not naturally good in bed but he was definitely worth teaching, and that someone should just create a wormhole to travel eighty million light-years away, then peek back at Earth with a very big telescope and finally settle whether the T-rex looked like the one in *Jurassic Park* or more like a big angry hen.

Frank Lyon had been the owner of three Latin dance clubs in the city, but they murdered him because of something else. Death surprised him in his office above the Luxuria—a venue for bawdy theme nights on Palm Boulevard, in the cluster of yellow and red lights that is San Carnal's least insalubrious nightlife. Danny Mojave had complied with Kimrean's demands, as expected: at their arrival, there were no police cars to be seen and the club had been closed but not evacuated. Rent-by-the-hour limos vomited wave after wave of squawking boys in Hugo Boss and girls in Elvira the Mistress of Dark's Salvation Army donations onto the sidewalk, feeding a long line of people too loud and drunk and horny to notice they weren't even moving.

Kimrean sneaked the Camaro into the side alley and pulled up in front of the back entrance. Danny Mojave, in a tailored suit jacket over a daringly open-collared shirt, stood in the company of a bigger, less stylish thug in gray and a couple club bouncers in black turtlenecks. He checked the integrity of the car's fender first, then his wristwatch.

"That was fast."

"Your car makes a funny noise at one twenty," Kimrean greeted, striding past him toward the entrance. The yawning red metal door led into a very narrow passageway between cinder block walls; at the other end was another red door; halfway in between both lay a corpse—or rather sat, for the passage was too narrow to fit him obliquely. It was a thick-necked man in track pants and a tank top, possibly another club bouncer. An earbud was still lodged in his right ear; the left one had been displaced by the bullet.

Adrian stood over the body, picturing it the way the man must have stood an hour before, with his back against the right wall. He pointed two fingers at that picture and fired.

"He didn't even hear the killer come in," he enunciated. "He was an obstacle, not the objective."

"His name was Andrew," Danny commented.

Adrian frisked the body. "Was he the only bodyguard?"

"The bodyguard is upstairs. This guy was just here as a precaution; Frankie was the least of our concerns." He rubbed his eyes. "I put him here to keep him out of trouble."

"You're awesome at this protection business."

"Fuck you, Adrian."

"Tell it to Zooey—that's her department."

Kimrean inspected the head wound. Blood covered the guy's ear and jaw.

"Who has a handkerchief?" Adrian asked the audience. The bouncers took a while to check their pockets and shake their heads. "You, take off your tie."

The thug in the gray suit checked Danny first, removed his necktie, handed it to the P.I., and whined when the latter used it to wipe some blood off Andrew's temple. Using their own thumbnail as reference, Kimrean measured the bullet hole: 9mm Parabellum.

"Shouldn't you be wearing gloves for that?" a bouncer asked.

"It's okay, I don't mind getting dirty."

Upon standing up, Adrian noticed the change in Danny's appearance since the previous afternoon—or rather Zooey noticed and nudged Adrian. Their friend had a darker look tonight, uninfluenced by his dark hair, brow, and style. That was all still there, but there was something deeper, trapped under his gangster cover, dimming his skin like a storm darkens the clouds. It was probably just crippling anxiety, Adrian concluded.

"*Andrew* was standing here, the murderer kicked that door open and shot him before he even noticed," Adrian captioned, actually trying to be comforting. "Considering the business he was in, it's about the best way to go."

That ought to do it. He leaped over the stiff and walked the rest of the passageway.

The next room was a storage space for crates of liquor and orphaned sofas; it was so small, Adrian didn't need to stop to inventory it.

"Video," he said, pointing at the CCTV camera on the ceiling.

"Cameras are on rotation; we're checking them," Danny said, hurrying after Kimrean, who was already on to the next room. This one offered several paths; Kimrean picked the one that led farthest away from the booming music on the dance floor. They crossed through an empty kitchen, then climbed two flights of stairs and landed on a new straight corridor with wood-paneled walls and red carpet. In the center lay the bodyguard, facedown, head pointing toward the entrance, right arm stretched forward, a dropped Glock near his hand. Adrian didn't even slow down while narrating:

"The bodyguard hears the first shot, sounds the alarm, then comes this way to investigate, runs into me, and I take him out."

He had already reached the body when he noticed something on the stiff's pants: a couple red droplets that didn't belong there.

"Whoops." *(Checks the door he just came through.)* "Okay, this one did have time to shoot; he nicked my side." *(Points at the door; Danny and his crew turn that way to find the bullet hole in the doorframe, a couple inches below the upper hinge.)* "I must be really tough or really angry, 'cause I didn't falter." *(Kneels down, rubs a finger on the blood drop.)* "The blood print is gravitational; no arterial spurt." *(Licks his finger.)* "A little low on sodium."

He looked up to find Danny and the bouncers staring like cavemen in a David Copperfield show. Kimrean's face split in a smile.

"Just kidding. How am I gonna know that just by tasting his blood?" *(Stands up; to Danny, in confidence.)* "Really, though—he is low in sodium." *(Points at the doorframe.)* "I'll be needing that bullet."

A brief hesitation rippled through the men. Kimrean realized and picked up the sentence again: "Sooo I will recover it myself, 'cause no one else here knows how to do it since none of you are cops." Then they resumed their way, while Zooey smugly sidenoted: "Nice save there."

They went through the last door, and the last room scored a simple "Wow."

Neither the scarlet wall-to-wall carpet nor the crimson fleur-de-lis wallpaper mitigated the bright pool of gore in the middle of the room. Frankie had died a few steps from his desk, the contents of his skull spread partially under it, a single red flower drinking from his red-soaked tuxedo shirt.

"Okay," Kimrean said appreciatively as Danny and the others

joined them. "Point-blank to the head. But it looks like there were punches first. Give me the timeline."

"12:08, George here receives the alarm from the bodyguard and comes this way; he was backstage. 12:12, I get a call. 12:21, I get here."

"So you found this?" Kimrean asked George—the thug whose necktie he had ruined earlier. "How long between getting the alarm and reaching this room?"

"Uh . . . A minute? Maybe two? I couldn't hear well because of the music."

"Let's say two minutes," Adrian settled. "So I barge in, Frankie's standing up here to see what's happening outside . . . and I punch his face!" He pointed at the corpse's chest; the blood on his shirt had to have come from his broken nose. "Then I stop, because . . . because Frankie doesn't hit me back?"

A humming among the bouncers seemed to confirm the hypothesis timidly. It is bad manners to trample over a man's grave—especially before he's lain in it.

"Yeah, I see. I was expecting a street fighter like Mikey, but Frankie's not like that. The first blow stuns him; he freezes. He's scared shitless. *(Pointing at the body's pants.)* On his way, at least. And I'm just standing here, watching him. Must have been awkward. And all the while, the anger's subsiding. And my side wound is beginning to sting. No point in beating him to death. So I finish him."

Kimrean scanned the environs. The room, all in red and black with gold details—the quills on the desk, the frames around the autographed pictures of Univision celebrities—constituted an accurate answer to the old philosophical question: What if two Romanian whorehouse owners had a son who wanted to be an office decorator? It was elliptical in shape, with one door on each side. Like the Oval Office, but with dimmer lights and a minibar. Say the Oval Office during the JFK administration.

"He wouldn't get out the same way he got in," Adrian guessed. "But you didn't run into anyone, of course," he spoke for Tieless George. "When did you seal the exits?"

"I told them to when I got here," Danny said.

Kimrean knelt down to read the body. The middle son of the Lyon family had been elegant, flaccid, and balding—as noteworthy as middle sons usually are in folktales and biblical parables. He would have been handsome for a used car dealer, but just average for a mobster. He had enjoyed a nice straight nose throughout most of his life too.

A distant commotion seemed to unclog the hallway outside. The bouncers instinctively cleared the doorway, through which was bound to enter, judging by the trepidation, either a derailed steam train or a very important member of the Lyon clan. Kimrean barely looked up to confirm it was the latter.

Xander Lyon stormed in, boisterously demanding an explanation, his roar needlessly reinforced by the handcannon in his grip, big enough to pierce the Hoover Dam. Kimrean lingered on the newcomer for a second: he was, at that moment, the spitting image of his dad in the seventies, the smart, aggressive Floridian gangster before he was spoiled by a comfortable throne. Perhaps, in many ways, he was even better than his father at the same age: more expensively dressed, more fashionably discreet, and with a share of Hispanic blood from his mother for extra appeal. He was the soap opera villain who slaps the female lead every week and has all the ladies at the Laundromat murmuring, "He's *so* bad—but *so* handsome!" He was handsome even now, as he stood still, color flushed out of his face, contemplating his younger brother's carcass.

Adrian registered the dilated pupils, the colorless fists, the unsteady pulse. He made a mental note: *Anger, no tears.*

Zooey immediately tagged him: *Latino Marc Anthony.*

Adrian appended to that: *Marc Anthony* is *Latino, you stupid bitch.*

Then he rushed through the body examination before someone's emotions contaminated the scene.

Danny begged Xander to holster the gun, but did not succeed in defusing him.

"Who did this?" the man howled, daring anyone to offer an answer. *"Who did this?!"*

"Someone even angrier than you," Kimrean calmly replied.

Xander turned to them with a movement that probably caused a typhoon near Tokyo.

"And who the fuck is this clown?"

"Xander, this is Kimrean," Danny assisted. "The P.I. your father hired."

"This guy?" Xander eyed the detective, confused. "My father said it was a woman."

Adrian finished the exam and sighed himself up.

"Okay, while you guys go through the Glen or Glenda bit, I'm gonna go down to the club, see if I catch a murderer on the dance floor."

They left through the other door, not bothering to check if anyone followed, but Danny and Tieless George did.

The next room was a green stairwell. Adrian checked upstairs before down.

"The rooftop's closed," George said. "He couldn't go that way."

"He didn't," Adrian confirmed, pointing at a smear of blood on the green wall, halfway to the top landing. "He just hid up there when you were rushing up from downstairs, then he ran downstairs while you were in the office." *(On George's embarrassed look.)* "It's fine, man. If you had run into him, he would have shot you. You were saved by your obliviousness."

They ran downstairs, Adrian driving the others' attention to a new blood droplet on the landing; they were dangerously near the beat of drums now. They bent around two corners, met another camera, pushed a final door, and then a primitive form of proto-music slapped them into submission.

On the black-lit VIP balcony, Cheshire shark grins and mounds of cocaine like the OCD potato art of *Close Encounters* victims shone as bright as airstrip lights, marking the way to the center stage over the rail. Kimrean sighted purple caged dancers, mud wrestlers, tattooed devils, G-stringed Atlases erected like Pillars of Hercules out of a liquid crowd waving in worship of ancient twerk masters summoning cellulite tsunamis.

The pupil in Kimrean's green eye augmented to the rim of its iris.

"Oh boy."

Adrian pulled Zooey away from the rail and hastened downstairs.

"Don't get distracted now, we're looking for *Jesus H. Kirsten Dunst!*" A go-go dancer, fully dressed in jingling bracelets and neon body paint, walked past them on the stairs. "Hey, beautiful, is that the regional costume? Love it! I love San Carnal!"

A chorus of onlookers echoed the cheers, raising their drinks and spraying them all over, while Adrian led them down to the dance floor.

"He would come this way, hide in the multitude. Focus!"

It was disco inferno, though easy on the disco bit. Kimrean dove into the human sea and swam down to the depths, almost crawling an all fours, snaking through the leg forest. Under the

stomping crowds and the frenzied lighting, he read the marks in
the sea bottom: a labyrinth of footprints and joint stubs and ice
cubes and some darker droplets of a liquid, suddenly squashed
by a skyscraper platform shoe with exposed turquoise-nailed toes,
fishnet stockings, sky-blue microdress, TITS.

"Heeey," Zooey grinned up at the repulsed woman looking
down from atop the tits. "So noisy up here—wanna go down
with me?"

"Fuck off, freak."

*(Ducking back.)* "Down, triple idiot!"

"Excuse me?!"

*(Looking up.)* "Not you, self-worshipping twit!"

The woman squawked an even louder, more dramatic *what*
while Adrian dove back, twenty thousand legs under the sea,
trying to pick up the track again. Some three broken glasses
farther on the way to the emergency exits, he found it: a new
solitary droplet of blood.

"Here! I see the bouncers near the exits, so I turn to . . . the
restrooms!"

A pair of feet in four-inch stilettos walked by. Zooey gazed up
like a child at a holiday parade.

"Oooh. Bars look really interesting from this perspective; we
should do this more often. Well, come to think of it, we do end
up down here a lot of times, don't we? *(Peeks under the miniskirt.)*
Oh, looky—wanna interrogate the servant staff? Let me ring the
butler for you."

Adrian jumped to his feet, scattering the bobbing creatures
near the surface, and approached or crashed into a bar counter.
A dazzlingly hairless man sitting there, wearing a tight crew-
neck T-shirt and an eyepatch, stared at the detective in surprise,

along with the mojito-holding woman nestled in his arm. Zooey noticed the attention, or the guy's pecs.

"Hello, sailor."

They locked eyes for a blank second, then Adrian snatched the eyepatch off him. The woman screamed.

"I'm sorry, it's an emergency," Adrian explained to the man, who'd just spilled his drink in the hassle to cover his empty socket. Adrian slapped the eyepatch over the green eye and turned around, but Zooey made it a full 360-degree turn and added: "Don't worry, it's not the least sexy hole I've seen around here."

Adrian pulled them both back before the one-eyed sailor exploded into an atomic mushroom of rage and Nemoed back into a reef of grinding ravers, now heading toward the restrooms queue, right index finger hovering over the vinyl dance floor like a dowsing rod.

"Here . . . here . . . Here!" *(On a new blood droplet.)* "I hesitate, but what am I looking for? The escape route is clear; why do I stop?"

"Hey you, *what the FUCK?!*"

The aftershock of that thunderous scream left an eerie sort of silence bubble amid the drunken laughter, the clinking ice, even the subwoofer's seismic pulse. Adrian, genuinely piqued, dared look in the direction of the cursing, surprised to find that Zooey's hand was already there, making up for the loss of her own eye by braille-reading the human landscape around them. Her hand had gone through six people at the maximum height it reached, which meant crotch-level for most humans, and had now disappeared inside the fly of a football-scholar frat boy, Aryan blue eyes gaping at the little perv browsing inside his lower drawer.

Adrian stood up, calling all hands back to headquarters. An arrogance of college jocks, for lack of an agreed collective noun, was now staring at them.

Even without the mob pressure, the best apology that ever-diplomatic Adrian could come up with was: "As an extenuating circumstance, let's agree you're packing like six hotel towels down there; it could've been hours before I actually did something inappropriate."

One of the females in the pack gasped at the bonus insult, but two others cackled in merriment, whereas the profaned frat boy, as expected, responded with a sledgepunch to the perv's face.

Kimrean swooned backward, their co-op nose now split into a duplex, and fell right into the arms of the one-eyed sailor who was just storming up to them, Red Sea crowd parting at his terrifying look. He tipped Kimrean off him and threw another punch, but Kimrean was too groggy from the first hit to stand for the second and fell down, effectively dodging the fist, which hit one of the college girls instead.

Zooey, lying on the floor trampled by the retaliating pack, lost consciousness with the satisfaction of having started a bar fight that would be discussed in American history textbooks.

# 6

A long yellow morning had just been proclaimed—the kind that follows the swift, sweeping desert dawns and sounds like electric guitars and truck engines. A. Z. Kimrean sat smoking a cigarette on the curb outside the Luxuria, next to their hat, stanching the hemorrhage from their freshly realigned nose with a clump of tissues. Any given Saturday.

The brawl lasted a good two hours before the San Carnal police saw few enough people standing to intervene safely. Once they had taken over, it had been a swift operation: the club had been evacuated and cordoned off, the patrons frisked, and the less white of them arrested. A cluster of police vans and ambulances was still obstructing the westbound traffic on Palm Boulevard. From where they were sitting, Kimrean was now watching the all-black figure of Danny Mojave hatching from the crowd of uniforms and neon vests. Zooey had ample time to appreciate the aesthetic of the back-lit figure walking the length of the block in what the wide shot made feel like slow motion: the guy playing the cop playing the gangster playing the man in control—and carrying a box of doughnuts. Adrian wondered how the cop's cover had held up this long.

A few steps behind him, smoothing his stress-proof suit as he crossed the crime scene tape, came Xander Lyon.

Danny arrived first and peeked at A.Z. over his sunglasses. "You look good," he said.

"You should see the biker's face."

"The one who hit you wasn't a biker."

"I know, but I couldn't retaliate against that one—he was expecting it."

Xander Lyon joined them and extended a hand. Kimrean misinterpreted the gesture and used the hand to help themselves up; Lyon decided to chalk it up as a shake.

"Mr. Kimrean, Danny has told me he called you as soon as he found the body. I want to apologize for my behavior earlier. I am grateful for your coming so quickly."

Everything in that line sounded exquisitely civil. Kimrean nodded, shooing the formalities away.

"I am grateful," Lyon repeated, "yet sorry to have wasted your time. Your job was to confirm that the death of my brother Michael was an act of war. I'm afraid that is beyond doubt now."

"Is it?"

Danny's fingers discreetly breezed Kimrean's hand.

"Yeah, I guess it is," Adrian said.

"My father is devastated, as you can imagine. By his request, I am now in charge of responding to this . . . hostile takeover. Meanwhile, I think we have to let you go."

From the inside of his jacket he produced a thick wallet. Kimrean almost heard the flock of dead presidents inside it gasping for fresh air.

"How much do we owe you?"

"Oh." Kimrean queried Danny, unsure whether to decline the offer or to celebrate that the Federal Reserve was having an open house day. "Well, Danny was really just calling in a favor."

"Oh, no, I won't hear about that. Name a number."

"Okay. How about that of that blonde in the flowery sarong?" Zooey pointed at the photograph inside the wallet. "I wouldn't mind taking her to a horror movie and yawning my way around her shoulders, down Bambalooza Canyon, and into Funny-Name-for-Vagina Valley, if you know what I mean."

Xander Lyon looked up, and in the next sentence his voice frosted the asphalt.

"That's my mother."

A pause, while Kimrean maneuvered out of that one.

"Right. So, should I just call your home and ask for her, or—"

Danny decided to end the sketch at that point by shoving a doughnut into Zooey's mouth, hurriedly telling Xander he would take care of the bill, and dragging Kimrean out of the solecism. Adrian kept an orange-brown eye on the gangster until Danny had pushed them around the corner.

"And you thought he was the smart brother," he commented.

Danny ignored the remark and made them sit down on the curb, facing the glowing sirens.

"The Lyon is not just devastated," he explained. "He's stupefied. Xander is now acting commander in chief and he's just put our lieutenants to DEFCON One. The Japanese are back at the top of our enemy list. Tonight, our boys in L.A. are moving against the Red Mum soldiers on the Westside."

Kimrean bit on the doughnut, squirting banana jelly over two blocks, and meditated aloud. "If the Red Mums are responsible—"

"You doubt that now?"

"*If* they are, what makes you think they're fighting for territory? How come your cartels are at war, yet their dealers are just standing on the corner opposite yours, like nothing's happening? And even if you strike first, who cares if you win a corner? You're sending pawns to fight pawns. Meanwhile, there's a sniper taking out your major pieces."

Danny sat down next to them and lit a cigarette—one of his hand-rolled ones. Kimrean helped themselves to another doughnut to celebrate the chess-themed metaphor.

"You're wasting manpower," Adrian resumed, indifferent to the fact that Zooey had her mouth full. "They killed the youngest brother; they just killed the middle brother. Who would you say is next? Don't think like a cop or a gangster; think like a fable writer."

"The eldest brother."

"Brothers Grimm 101. If my advice is worth a penny, and it's actually worth a little more when adjusted for inflation, your top priority is to protect your remaining pieces. And a free tip: stay away from Xander. Mikey fell all alone; Frankie dragged down two bodyguards; Xander is gonna take his own terra-cotta army to the grave."

Danny coughed, or chuckled, and took off his sunglasses. Apart from his nose being whole, unlike Kimrean's, he too looked like he'd lost a fight in the last few days.

"You're looking at Xander's new head of security," he said. "Effective ten minutes ago."

Kimrean bit on their doughnut and munched in silence.

"Hey, congratulations."

Danny took another drag, and for a while they just sat there on the curb, watching the blinking blue and red lights of police cars in the quiet morning.

Rebellion dawned on Danny after a minute or two. "But we can't just play defense. We need a strategy! They have a strategy!"

"Do they?"

All three locked eyes.

"Do you really believe the guy who just killed Frankie had a plan?" Adrian continued. "The only thing he planned ahead was bringing a flower."

"Well, he did his homework," Danny argued. "He knew the place pretty well—went straight into Frankie's office."

"So did I and I've never been here before."

"And no cameras caught him? And what about Villa Leona? He exploited every breach in our defense!"

"And yet he forgot to pack a gun there," Adrian retorted. "Think about it. He had to take Mikey's *after* finishing him— a nine-millimeter Beretta—the one he used here."

Danny mulled that over and tossed his joint on the asphalt. "Motherfucker. He went to Villa Leona armed with a flower?"

"Like a mime confronting the riot police. The funny thing is this time he had a gun, but he only intended to use it to deal with the potatoes: the guy at the door and the bodyguard in the corridor. When he got to Frankie, he punched him. Same with Mikey. That's your killer's whole strategy: go up to a gangster and start a fistfight. He's got balls, but he's not a planner."

"Except for the chrysanthemum."

"Except it's not a chrysanthemum," Adrian counter-objected. "I looked it up yesterday: it's actually a rare variety of rose called *Erithra lunis*. 'Red moon.' It's native to Canada; there are a few breeders in California."

"What does that mean? The killer ran out of chrysanthemums?"

"Or he only *wants* us to believe it was the Japanese."

"Why? Who wins if the two cartels destroy each other?"

The answer reached them both at the same time, uttered in a perfectly choreographed epiphany: "Villahermosa!"

They parted eyes, watchful of the implications. Danny regretted having put out his last joint. Adrian rubbed his side of their face.

Danny spoke first: "But Villahermosa would send a real assassin to Villa Leona. Not a brawler."

"Maybe they didn't send an assassin," Adrian considered. "Maybe they sent a messenger, a diplomat, and Mikey started a fight. He did the same thing in neutral land's parking lot."

"So we're saying someone just went to talk and things got heated?" Danny asked, skeptical, though in retrospect he believed the late Mikey Lyon more than capable of heating a situation up to that point. "Mikey and someone from Villahermosa meeting in secret? *In the pool cabana at Villa Leona?*"

"I'm suddenly interested in this conversation," Zooey said, joining the dialogue, but Adrian flicked her off again. "Don't mention it to anyone," he advised. "It's useless speculating when we can just find out what happened in that room."

"The wiretap," Danny guessed.

"It won't be too juicy, or the FBI would have shared, but there might be details. Can you remember the name of the company who painted the pool house? The one who had an office here in San Carnal?"

"Yes, but it's just a front; they won't be there."

"Nah, they will be. You said they came two weeks ago. They'll keep the place for another week or so to avoid suspicion."

"Right. It's San Carnal Golden Star Painting Co. East Palm and 10th. Want a ride?"

"No need, my car is right there."

"That's my car," Danny reminded them, hiding his exhaustion behind his glasses.

"Easy, buddy—I'm taking great care of it. It's in pristine condition," Zooey reassured him, grabbing another two doughnuts for the road. She was going to walk away when she remembered something. "Heh. You know, there was this guy whose car I borrowed once, and I called him a week later and told him, 'Your car's in pristine . . .' *(Chortle.)* Only I actually meant—"

"I know—in Pristina, Kosovo."

"Right. Did I tell you that one before? Oh, wait, it was your car, wasn't it?"

"Yeah."

"Right. Good times. Well, see you in a while."

Parking was no trouble on 10th Street, which ran through a quiet neighborhood of Victorian row houses whose only purpose was to trick the tourist into thinking that San Carnal's history predated the invention of the compact disc. San Carnal Golden Star Painting Co.'s headquarters belonged to the kind of diminutive, merely symbolic strip mall space that often serves as a maildrop for money-laundering fronts and ghost companies, and that is only accidentally leased to legitimate professionals who, spurred by a motivational book on the magic of entrepreneurship, invest all their life savings in a Power Balance franchise or a vape shop. Happy to partake in that halfhearted collective pretension of lawful business, A.Z. tucked in their tank top, smacked the dust off their waistcoat, and waltzed into the store in their best impression of a law-abiding citizen ready to keep the gears of the economy turning.

The interior was skimpily lit and as boring as expected. A young man in a fresh sky-blue shirt and a twenty-dollar haircut flashed a standard welcome smile at them and returned his attention to the computer screen. Kimrean's vision hopped along the featured palettes, the pigment swatches, a darkened back room, the unobstructed desk, and the clerk's impeccable manicure.

"I'll be with you in a second," he said.

"No problem." Kimrean grinned. "*Minesweeper* is a bitch on expert."

The man stared red-handed at the visitor. His monitor was facing away from the customers.

". . . But it reflects on your glasses," Kimrean finished his thought. "Sorry for interrupting; you were highly recommended by an old friend who was really satisfied with you guys. A Mr. Lyon—does that ring a bell?"

"Uh . . . yes, I think it does," he said, an eyebrow raised high enough to pose a danger to aviation.

"I'd love to hire the same team."

"Oh, well, I think they're busy today," he said, ceremoniously opening a virgin appointment book, "but if you tell me what needs to be done, I'm sure we can squeeze you in."

"That's nice, but you see, it's a precision job. If I could first speak to them in person . . ."

"I understand, but sadly they just started an office building in Palm Dale so—"

"No." All smiles in the room vanished. "I want you to get your ass off that chair, go into the secret room in the back behind the stucco samples, and tell your partner in there with the minty aftershave that we need to talk."

The clerk adjusted his glasses, took a couple breaths, and tried to squeeze in another full line. "I don't know what you're tal—"

"Go."

"Okay."

He rose, skedaddled to the back room, and pulled open the stucco display. A cyan glow of bored monitors oozed out from the chamber hidden behind it.

After five seconds, Kimrean ran out of patience and followed him inside.

"Keep your seat, thank you," Adrian told the second agent, who had just sprung off his watch post. "A. Z. Kimrean, P.I. I'm working with SFPD on the Lyon case. You can check up with Detective Ted Demoines," he added, flashing the badge they kept in their wallet and that they never really had the chance to brandish, either because most people are stupid enough to grant authority to whoever asserts it first and speaks fast enough, or because the usual visitors at Kimrean's office—femmes fatales and teeth-pummeling thugs—were seldom interested in their qualifications. Which was a shame, considering how hard they had worked for them: Adrian had had to steal almost twelve hours from his summer reading program to get the law school diploma, and Zooey had to seduce a municipal clerk named Brunhilde to persuade her that all the time served in psychiatric wards mingling with sociopaths, pyromaniacs, and sex offenders satisfied the three thousand hours of fieldwork required to get their license. Not even the FBI agent now paid enough attention to the stupid badge to notice it was five years expired.

"I talked to Demoines yesterday," the agent said, offering a hand that Zooey accepted. He was black, square-jawed, and way too caring about his biceps to be wasting away on a stakeout assignment. "Agent Marlow. That is Agent Dawes," he said, re: the store clerk.

"Exulted to meet you," Adrian said. "Who bugged the pool house in Villa Leona?"

"I did," Marlow said.

"Terrible job. Who painted the ceiling?"

"He did."

"That was neat. *(To Marlow.)* I'm sorry, I was hoping it would've been you too and I could praise you for something." He pointed at the surveillance equipment in the room. "Why are you still listening? Nobody lives there anymore."

"We haven't got ears in the rest of the villa," Dawes explained. "This is better than nothing."

The demonstrative pronoun embraced the whole monitor-lit room, the little carnival of standby LEDs, an Empire State of plastic food containers and Styrofoam coffee cups, their dregs well into the process of becoming fossil fuels.

"You guys been here what, a week?" Zooey polled, attention flicking through several areas of interest in the bleak scenery before landing on Agent Marlow's highway-billboard pecs.

"Yeah," Marlow said, noticing the focus and rubbing at a beet stain on his necktie. "We . . . may have relaxed our standards a little."

"But he hasn't," Kimrean pointed out, prize-showing Agent Dawes. "Look at him: all clean-shaven, perfect shirt, zero nose hair. He's a young and dreamy Edward Norton."

Dawes said nothing, but visibly tried to shrink his own body à la Ant-Man and sift through the attention.

Marlow reasoned: "Well, he has to be outside facing the customers."

"Sure, it's the customers of your imaginary paint store he's trying to impress, who else?" Zooey said before Adrian changed the subject. "Whatever. So you guys have the death of Mikey Lyon recorded? Because *that* would be interesting."

"If we were trying to solve that case, yes," Dawes said. "But it's the San Carnal sheriff's turf; there's no official investigation."

Kimrean colonized an office chair.

"I am the official investigation. Play it for me."

Marlow hesitated for a second, as though catching up with the different motifs in the conversation. Then he wheeled himself to the keyboard and loaded a new file.

"This is Tuesday after midnight," he announced. He clicked on play and dialed up the speakers. Humming white noise padded the packed surveillance room. Adrian pushed every unwanted stimuli out of his half of the brain, curled up on their chair, and closed their eyes.

He heard a door slamming, clothes rustling, keys tinkling. He heard someone opening a window.

He heard Mikey Lyon's cold, arrogant voice in secondhand Spanish.

*"No, me ocuparé de ellos. ¿Quién se llevó las pertenencias? (. . .) ¿Ya regresó? (. . .) ¿De las Caimán? (. . .)* Okay. *No, le llamaré mañana."*

"We don't know who he's talking to here," Dawes offered, "but he speaks Spanish with most of his men. We think it's about—"

Kimrean shushed him. "Hilfiger's body, the casualty in the shooting the night before. Don't worry, I got it."

After that there was a stretch of humming breeze. Agent Dawes checked on the P.I.: their right hand seemed to rock slightly, as though surfing the fluctuation of white noise.

Suddenly, there was a commotion: too many steps in too short a time. The same voice pronounced a single word: "You."

What followed was not as much a fight as interference, a

random sequence of static bursts, punctuated by a human puff or a gasp here and there. Dawes and Marlow had heard it several times; it was all too low-fi to evoke a picture.

Then, a gunshot.

Silence. A moan. A gurgle of blood. Then nothing.

Then a second shot.

Adrian raised his hand, to prevent the studio audience from standing up before the end credits. Another twenty seconds' worth of white noise followed, which culminated in a stampede of male voices: the guards finding the corpse. Adrian had enough.

"Captivating." *(To Marlow.)* "Why the minty aftershave, anyway?"

Marlow faltered, the change of topic catching him unprepared again.

"I'm not trying to impress anyone," he said, in a tone that clearly didn't encourage further conversation.

"Not at all. Got any leftover pizza?"

"We don't eat pizza," Dawes said.

"You don't eat pizza in a stakeout," Zooey noted, pointing at the pile of empty food containers, not pizza boxes. "Of course. It's murder on your waist, but we're not trying to impress anyone." She kicked off the wall, singing as she spun on her chair: *"Two bros / Working undercover in the back room of a paint shop / Five feet apart because they're-not-gay!"*

Adrian's hand grabbed the table and brought the chair to a stop. "Just ignore that. Go back to where he says 'You.'"

Marlow, a deep frown settling on his impressive forehead, returned to the computer and clicked on a solitary peak in the audio mountainscape on the screen. Mikey Lyon's voice boomed out of the speakers again: "You."

"That's Yu Osoisubame," Marlow captioned after pressing pause. "The Phantom Ninja."

"No, it's not," Dawes complained. "He says 'you,' in English."

"But he speaks Spanish to most of his people."

"Not his father."

"Fathers use the door," Adrian pointed out. "It's no one from the household, but it's still someone he knows."

He fell silent after that. The FBI resumed the argument:

DAWES: He also speaks English with the Japanese.

MARLOW: The Phantom Ninja is Japanese.

DAWES: But he's never met the Phantom Ninja; he wouldn't see him and say "You." Or "Yu."

MARLOW: Maybe he just saw the Phantom Ninja and said "You" because all the Japanese look alike to him.

DAWES: That's racist.

"Oh, God, I could listen to your sweet bickering all day," Zooey said sincerely, blinking twice the normal amount. "Imagine you guys arguing whether to order beets in your salad."

"I don't like beets," Marlow complained.

"Whatever," Adrian resumed. "Play it again, Sam."

Marlow sighed, resumed the file from the aftermath of "You." Kimrean, legs now stretched out to opposite corners of the spacious phone booth width of the room, narrated as they listened.

"That's Mikey Lyon running for his gun in a drawer. *(Sharp thuds.)* Kick to the shin. Punch to the sternum. *(Clang.)* There's the gun falling. *(Points to a corner of the room; instinctively, Dawes and Marlow follow the P.I.'s index.)* Mikey leans on the armchair. *(Whiplike smack; crash.)* Punch to the jaw, Mikey falls along with the armchair. He has time to stand up. *(Floorboards squeaking.)* He's stumbling. *(Deep intake of air.)* Improvised charge, easy to dodge. *(Crunch, gasp.)* Kick to the shin—broken tibia. *(Thud, thud, crack.)* Two jabs to the face; broken nose. *(Clinking.)* Loose tooth. *(Rustling, groaning, claws scratching on wood.)* They're on the floor now. Tables turn; Mikey's the top. *(Loud whack.)* Mikey's the bottom. They're struggling away from the microphone. *(Adrian's finger pans to the right.)* They're heading for the gun. Mikey has it. *(Wham.)* Mikey lost it."

*(Gunshot.)*

Marlow pushed the volume up to eleven. The following moan sounded like the whole building was in pain.

*(Gurgle of blood.)*

"Did he just say 'Why?'" Marlow realized.

"The bullet's gone through his lung," Kimrean explained. "Now the murderer is showing him why."

*(Breathing.)*

*(Fast, heavy breathing.)*

*(GUNSHOT.)*

Dawes flinched at the sound of the blast.

"Does this tell us anything new?" Marlow polled, dialing down the volume.

"It does to me," Adrian said. "It tells me Danny should cut down on the pot."

"Who?"

"An ear-witness. He told me the two gunshots were a second apart; that's a five-second gap. He was high at the time. Which also explains how he practically bumped into the murderer without seeing him."

"How are five seconds significant?" Marlow asked.

"They are," Dawes said. "It's a trained assassin's mark: a body shot to bring the target down and a cooler, well-placed round to the head."

Kimrean whirled on their chair, addressing Marlow, pointing at Dawes: "And he's a good listener too! What's not to like?" *(Whirls again, now facing Dawes.)* "Only you're mistaken; the second shot is not 'cool.' Listen to the breathing."

Kimrean leaned over to click-select a hill range by the end of the sound file and press play. *Breathing. Fast, heavy breathing.*

"That's Mikey," Dawes ventured.

"No, it can't be," Adrian rebutted. "Mikey's lungs are filled with blood; he wouldn't sound like that. That is our murderer. And he's not panting from physical exertion; he's having an anxiety attack. This guy isn't cool; he's losing his mind. *(Back to Marlow.)* No reliable hit man takes their job to heart like that. This is personal. Mikey didn't say 'Yu'; he said 'You.'"

Marlow nodded, a man convinced by the force of arguments. But the frown was still there.

"What about the flower?"

"Shit poopoo caca feces, always the stupid flower," Kimrean snarled. "It's a decoy. It's not even a chrysanthemum." They lay back, tipped their hat to scratch their hair. "I was expecting some verbal context, but obviously the intruder didn't come to confer. You listened on Mikey for days; did he make any enemies?"

Dawes took a nearby notepad, flipped to a random page, and started reading.

"Wednesday the third, Mikey has a quarrel with one of his lieutenants in L.A.; he accuses him of being soft on his pushers, threatens to cut the guy's balls off and hang them from the rearview mirror of his car. Thursday the fourth, Mikey on the phone with a lawyer in San Carnal; he promises he will steal his car, drive it into the guy's house, and then set it on fire. Thursday the fourth, afternoon, Mikey almost drowns the pool boy because there's a leaf in the water. Should I go on?"

"No, I get the picture."

"But what about Frankie?" Marlow jumped in, visibly more engrossed with the case than he'd been in days. "Wasn't he shot earlier today, with a chrysanthemum on his chest?"

"Not a chrysanthemum."

"Whatever," he insisted, now eager to score a point. "The question is, Mikey and Frankie didn't share many contacts; they hardly saw each other. In fact, Mikey despised Frankie."

"Everyone despised Frankie," Adrian acknowledged. "He lacked guts. In a family of sharks, that made him a pariah. And yet he didn't pose a threat; he didn't feel like a threat; he had only one bodyguard and his club bouncers. Who could hate him so passionately?"

"Maybe it's not the same killer," Dawes suggested.

"Flower," Marlow objected.

"The flower's a decoy, you said it," Dawes argued, pointing at Kimrean. "The first killer uses a flower to blame the Japanese; the second killer uses a flower to blame the first killer."

Kimrean nodded. They did find that interesting.

"Good point," they judged, standing up. "I'll leave now, but you guys have made great progress. Close the shop tonight, go home, have a shower and a good night's sleep." Their left hand pointed at Marlow. "Then *you* go home, change your necktie."

Marlow simply leaned forward and asked, "Has anyone told you before that you are weird AF?"

"Many times. Often right after I bring a crucial clue to their attention or I save their life," Kimrean said from the threshold, and pointed at the surveillance equipment one last time. "Stay tuned, if you will. You may hear some interesting things."

They closed the stucco display behind them and left the shop. They didn't see how Agents Marlow and Dawes were left alone in the back room, one sitting by the computer, the other standing against the wall by the empty salad boxes.

Dawes said, "I thought you liked beets. Why do you always make me order them?"

"Because you like them."

# 7

INT. A. Z. Kimrean's Office—Dusk
An orange sky peeked through the blinds, along with the sound
of waste boats and seagulls heading home for the night. Kimrean
moved the white king's bishop to h5.

"So, an efficient assassin. Who also has personal issues. And
who signs with a red flower but is not with the Red Mums."

They completed a half orbit around the chessboard and peeped
back at the dying day through the broken window. *(Close-up: skin
pores south of mascaraed eyes yawn at the western sun.)*

"Who is it?"

Kimrean twirled on their feet, nudged a black pawn to e3, then
drifted toward the desk to gulp down a mouthful of bourbon
straight from the bottle.

"Victor Lyon?"

They U-turned back to the chessboard.

"Too old. Too tall. Too heavy. Too attached to his children.
And to his cartel. And to his cane. Just shut up."

*(Bxg6.)*

"And if you can spare a moment, try and stop that bishop that's
wreaking havoc in your rear guard. No rush."

*(Takes their hat off, rubs their hair like a golden retriever evicting fleas.)*

"I don't know why I keep playing you. Chess is a game of logic; you're incapable of rational thought."

*(Nd4. Steps on the stairway. A furtive smile slithers across their face.)*

"It's not a game of logic; it's a game of wit. And I'm witty as fuck. I'm the queer Oscar Wilde. And you play me 'cause you have no one else to play."

Someone knocked on the door. A wavy silhouette had crystallized on the glass panel.

"Hello?"

A.Z. watched the door open a crack and the femme fatale peep inside, a flame of Irish hair fending off the shadows.

"Don't you ever turn the lights on?" she wondered.

"Never! It's sexier this way."

She stepped in, for some reason ignoring the broken glass swept into a corner and the bullet acne on the walls. She was wearing a who cares about her clothes, they're just padding words meant to highlight her awkwardness. She breathed in, as deeply as her corset allowed, incidentally appreciating the booze-and-sweat aroma of the Kimricave.

"Have you made any progress with my case? The man who spies on me in my bedroom?"

"Yeeeees, of course not." Kimrean folded their arms. "I haven't given it a thought since you last left this room."

"Okay," she said, surprisingly not surprised by that answer. "Then about the money I paid in advance—"

"Yes, you can give me the rest in a check, if you wish."

The woman froze once more, as disoriented as she should have grown accustomed to be.

"Nonononono wait, kidding kidding kidding!" Zooey exclaimed, stepping forward as the femme stepped back, hands talking at twice the speed of her mouth. "It's a complex case, could take me a few days, I should go to your house and comb your bedroom, might as well go tonight, we could grab something for dinner and it was your maid."

Zooey facepalmed. The femme needed a little more time to react, having to separate all the ramblings from the actual mystery solution at the end. And once that sank in, she responded with only two words, poorly chosen: "What . . . My . . ."

Adrian rose up from their palm.

"Okay, here's what happened: yesterday when you visited you had a little yellow-brown stain on the neck of your dress: it was iodine—very characteristic. The previous night, your maid was stalking you hidden in the rosebushes; you noticed, screamed, she ran away and scraped her fingers on the thorns. The next morning, while helping you lock that vine-leaf necklace you were wearing, she stained your dress with the disinfectant on her fingertips."

A blank lapse followed, perhaps a couple seconds longer than what it had taken Adrian to deliver the exposition.

The femme was simply left to inquire: "If you knew all this from my first visit, why didn't you tell me then?"

The green eye glinted, incapable of lying. "I wanted to see you again."

The femme pulled out a checkbook from her purse, scrawled a few lines, ripped out the check, shoved it into the extended hand opposite, and walked out. Zooey monitored the action, pouting like an abandoned dog. She remained silent after the femme left, listening to the heels fading out down the stairway for good.

Slowly over Zooey's face was cast first a saddened frown, then a threatening snarl.

"You asshole!" she said, crumpling the check into a ball and throwing it to the floor. "I really liked her! She was special!"

"She wasn't special—what are you babbling about? She was literally the first woman to knock on that door. And she was a terrible femme fatale." They retrieved the check and hand-ironed it on the table. "If that's all it takes for you to fall in love, you can just as well wait for the next one. But not now, of course: it's the teeth-pummeling thug's turn."

They were walking toward the living area when they suddenly froze halfway, retraced their steps, exited the office through the open door, and stopped on the landing. Then they reentered the office.

And then Zooey threw a left to their face.

There was a fraction of a second, an aesthetically perfect photo still, during which their feet were off the floor, their eyes were shut down by the punch's shockwave rippling through the face, and Kimrean—detached from the material world, cruising through the ether after a few drops of saliva that flew faster than the body by virtue of their lower mass—was *pure* Kimrean, with no other sensory stimulus than self-inflicted pain—100 percent idealism, perfect poetry.

And then they landed on the floor like a passed-out buffalo.

Immediately, one arm locked its opposite and a leg curled around the other leg and five fingernails dug into the other side's side.

"*You selfish douche!* I wanted to see her!" Zooey bawled. "Why do you always push them away?! Why?!"

Outside, seagulls and rooftops stared bemusedly at the sight of a human worm writhing on the floor of its office, trying to punch itself again, dodging its own fist, and smashing its knuckles on the floorboards. Some seagulls hollered at that.

"Gaaah! *(Shielding their injured left under their arm.)* I push them away?! *I* push them, you demented goat?!"

*(They stumble up, Quasimodoing toward their desk.)*

"Where are you going? Wh—No! Nonononono please wait no no I'll be a good girl I promise I promise I—"

She didn't have a chance. Adrian yanked open the desk, grabbed the case with Gwen's syringes, and spread the contents over the table. The left hand tried to slap the needles off the desk, but the right one saved one just in time; it drove it to the mouth, uncapped it with their teeth, and stabbed it into the left biceps like a wooden stake into Christopher Lee's chest.

Two heartbeats were enough to carry the Diarctorol wave toward the skull and have it break against the brain like a typhoon on an aircraft carrier, flushing the crew off the deck. There was no other metaphor they both could agree on. For Adrian, it was like wings sprouting out of his spine, like the ropes snapping apart between rival ships in the maelstrom in the third *Pirates of the Caribbean* movie, like two white hands grasping each other and their fingers loosening and then slipping away, until the fingertips just kiss each other good-bye for the last time and Zooey gets lost in the quietly violent current toward the calm after the storm.

And Adrian, temporally weakened, accepting the physical pain for the sign of victory it is, listens to the seagulls and the waste boats outside and peacefully drops to the floor, finally alone.

—

Daytime and decent visiting hours had long slipped away when the groaning wooden staircase forewarned the arrival of a new visitor. It was a femme's turn.

Only this time it was a true femme fatale: a deceptive, strong woman forged over fire and cooled in liquid nitrogen, escaping from a turbulent past and ready to dump her baggage on the first samaritan to fall for her charms. An angel of bronze skin and Kuiper Belt black eyes, whose sinusoidal silhouette on the door spelled only one word: *trouble.*

Or would have, had her silhouette been tall enough to jut more than six inches up into the glass panel.

She knocked, triggering a swift response from the dark-dwelling creature inside:

"Yes, I heard about God; no, he doesn't exist; yes, your ancestors were as wrong as you are!"

Two seconds fluttered by. She knocked again.

Kimrean stomped to the door and almost tore it open.

Ursula Lyon dropped her backpack on the floor, spherical droplets of rain still unbroken on her coat shoulders.

"Hi."

Adrian arched an eyebrow, peeped out into the landing, expecting to catch a young unwilling mother or the Easter Bunny hurrying away, then focused back on the little girl.

"How did you know where I live?"

"You said you lived near City Lights; I asked around in the pubs. You know, you leave a vivid impression on bartenders."

"What are you doing here?"

"Somebody wants to kill me."

"Have them call me tomorrow; I'm busy now."

He tried to close the door, but Ursula stuck a fluorescent Rampage shoe in the gap.

"I need protection. I know you all think that since I'm eleven I must be a moron, but I can see the pattern: someone is killing Victor Lyon's children."

"His sons," Adrian corrected.

"How are you so sure?"

"I'm not, but if you keep hiding we'll never find out."

Ursula exhaled, shifted her weight to her other leg. She was wearing *Adventure Time* leggings under denim shorts.

"Can I speak to Zooey?"

Kimrean seemed to check, the brown eye glancing for a moment behind the curtain of hair covering the left side of their face.

"No."

He then checked the window. He raised a foot and retrieved a folded piece of paper from inside his high-top Converse.

"Okay, there are no trains now, so here's what you're going to do." He unfolded a check for $150. "Take this, go get a room at La Bohème—it's a hotel near here on Columbus Ave., all decorated with Beat memorabilia and pictures of Kerouac and Cassady looking all BFF in the bathrooms; you'll love it. Tell the man at the counter you're Adrian Kimrean's guest. Not Zooey—Adrian. Got it?"

Ursula didn't even motion to take the money.

"You can't just send me away. There's a killer on the loose."

"They're as likely to find you here as in a hotel. More likely, as a matter of fact."

"But you can't send me into the streets, at night, all alone!"

"Should've thought about that before leaving your house, at night, all alone!"

"They don't care about me there—they don't know I'm gone! They don't notice me!"

"I so envy them."

"Do you even know how it feels?!" she challenged. "Being there, in a crowded room, and no one actually seeing you?!"

"Yes!" Adrian roared. "I know *exactly* how it feels!"

The rain patter on the window shushed them down like an offended librarian. Ursula took the hint.

"Can I stay here tonight? Please?"

Adrian seemed to wrestle back a cussword caravan. He managed to subdue it and swallow it, washed it down with a deep breath.

At last, he stepped aside. Ursula inhaled as if she were about to raid a lost temple and crossed the threshold.

Teeth-pummeling thugs all over the underworld beamed a carnivorous smile: it was their turn again.


The office lay in undersea darkness, except for the street lighting sneaking through the windows (one whole, one broken), drawing the furniture in pale colors over black like a Mike Mignola frame. Ursula noticed the scorch mark on the kitchen wall over the splintered stump of what must have been a kitchen cupboard.

Kimrean pulled the sheets off the bed, inspected the mattress. He flipped it over, winced, then flipped it over again.

"Try to stay on the white half," he advised, flapping the sheets back on top. "Toilet's over there."

"Yeah, I can see it from here," Ursula said, spying through the P.I.-shaped hole in the wall of the alcove, opening onto the ruins of a bathroom.

"I'm working on your case right now, so it's in your best interest not to disturb me."

With that he resettled to the middle of the room, a few steps away from the spotlighted dais with the chessboard, and stayed there, gaze strayed, lit in waxing first quarter.

Ursula remained expectant for a minute or two before she understood that *that* was Adrian working. Once she did, she sat on the bed and made a point to breathe softly.

At the foot of the bed there was an empty bottle of bourbon and a box of Ritz crackers. Gathered around the coat stand there was a guitar and some dead cans of beer. Out of curiosity, Ursula reached for the guitar and accidentally knocked the cans over.

Kimrean's brown eye shot her a glare that managed to drop the room temperature 10°F. Ursula hurriedly picked up the guitar and placed it against the wall and sat back on the edge of the bed, hands crossed on her lap.

By then, Adrian was lost in his thoughts again. A breeze rocking his hair was the only thing separating him from a black-and-white Tim Burton prop.

URSULA: Where's Zooey?

ADRIAN: Sleeping.

*(Pause.)*

URSULA: Can I sleep with her?

A bullet shell snapped under Kimrean's shoe.

Adrian rounded on the rickety little kid on the bed, her size 5 feet swinging in the air.

"Are you—you— *What the fuck?!*" he settled with in the end. "What's the deal with girls and bad boys anyway?"

"Am I the bad boy there?" said Ursula, amused by his anger. "It's no big deal; I just want to snuggle."

"Yes, it is a big deal, and no, you can't!"

"Why not?"

"For a million reasons!"

"I'll take one."

"Because— You little— Oh, God," Adrian struggled, clutching his scalp, trying to sort through the million reasons for one that was remotely close to a PG-13 rating. "Because, for fuck's sake—don't they teach you anything in school?! 'Don't talk to strangers' and shit like that?!"

"But I know Zooey."

"Obviously not enough!" he terminated. "So no, you can't snuggle with her. It's wrong, it's inappropriate, it's gross."

With that he turned around, taking the argument with him, and Ursula just sat frustrated, appalled that this would count as a dialectic victory for the grown-up.

"What the hell is wrong with you," she said, lowering her head. *(Turns around again, louder.)* "What the hell is wrong with *me*?! I'm the one—"

"No, not you," Ursula said, blocking off his rant with hardly a whisper. "I know what's wrong with you: you're a jerk. I meant, what's wrong with *you people*."

A gentle thunder underscored that perfect comeback.

Then there was silence. Silence from the broken ceiling fan, from the harbor, from the deactivated private eye, frozen in mid-charge.

"You all make me feel like I'm growing into a monster," the eleven-year-old girl said. "I don't know what it is. Well, I guess it's the boobs," she added, checking a fold on her T-shirt. She confronted Kimrean. "Is that why you hide yours?"

Adrian, craning over the kid, his rage defused, looked into her eyes if only to avoid looking anywhere else—on her body or his.

Ursula went on, like an unstoppable storm of soft little-girl voice: "It's not just that they don't want me in my father's swimming pool—which is unfair enough, but whatever. It's the same in the Caymans. I used to be everyone's favorite; the staff, the bodyguards, everyone complimented me. Now I show them a new outfit, they stare at the ground. I'm supposed to be proud of all the new things going on in my body, but if I talk tampons, everyone's embarrassed. I cuddle with my friends, everyone stares; I bump against my PE teacher, he jolts like I'm toxic. Everyone's all happy I'm turning into a woman but freaked out I'm not a child anymore. Like I'm in the gray area, and anything can happen."

She shrugged, her miniature mouth somewhat angled into a timid smile.

"You should've seen my father's men when I arrived for Mikey's funeral the other day. How confused they were when they saw how much I'd grown. Like, 'Should we scorn her because she's a kid? Or should we objectify her because she's a woman? What kind of shit should we make her feel like?'"

She paused, and since no one seemed to challenge her, she added, "Zooey is the only one who acts normal around me."

Adrian, who had stayed in reverential silence, could not help a scoff there. "Yeah, Zooey is the paradigm of normalcy."

The kid frowned at the words but still managed to reply, "You live in an office in ruins with a you-shaped hole opening into the bathroom."

"Zooey doesn't like you because you're her friend, or her bestie, or her shopping buddy," Adrian mocked. "She likes you because she likes everybody! Men, women, young, old—she can't tell the difference!"

"Okay, so she's friendly."

"I don't mean friendly, I mean—"

"I know what you mean, Adrian, *grow up*." She glared back

at the shocked brown eye in front of her. "What? It's funny to joke about me being killed, but saying the word *sex* in my presence, that would be crossing the line? Screw your rating system, man."

She didn't sound spiteful or even loud. Just tired.

"I just want to lie in bed with somebody because I'm cold and alone and I want to feel safe. You're supposed to be the brainy one—is that too hard to grasp?"

"It's hard to grasp that of all people, you pick Zooey," he replied.

"At least she's not condescending. You're just jealous because I choose her over you."

"JEALOUS?!" Adrian cried, leveling up to a new tier of helplessness. "I don't want to be chosen by anyone! I hate people! I hate being touched, I hate sex, I hate that she loves it! I hate being stuck in the middle!"

"Good," the girl said, ever slightly above the whisper threshold. "There's no need to worry then."

And she took Adrian's hand and tugged him toward the bed.

Kimrean looked around, caught unaware by the sudden tension drop. His arm barely pulled back on instinct.

"Worry about what?"

"About this being wrong or inappropriate. Zooey's asleep, and you hate touching people, so . . ."

She gently yanked Kimrean to sit on the bed, and then she prodded their head down all the way to the pillow and hoisted their legs on the mattress, and Kimrean—the mannequin, the marionette, the dummy—could not move a muscle by themselves. Zooey was asleep; Adrian the Left Brain was stunned to have walked into a logic trap.

Ursula crawled over to the far side of the mattress, toed off her Panzer shoes, and pulled the sheets over all three, up to their necks.

She leaned her head on the pillow and didn't close her eyes.

They stayed guessing at each other's shape in the dark, and their mutual hair, and the contours of the sheets, and the sound of their breaths, and the glint in their eyes, while the rain hummed Ani DiFranco songs on the rooftops.

"Which one is her eye?"

Adrian took a while to engage. The question seemed easier than silence anyway.

"Green. The left one. Pretty much everything on the left is hers."

He heard her frowning against their shared pillow.

"You can't move the left side of your body?"

"Yes, I can. We both can move everything. But the left half is hers. Body cells on this side are feminine: XX chromosomes. Gwen has most of it mapped out."

Lying on his right side, he caressed his left shoulder.

"This arm is hers. The navel is hers. We don't know about the legs yet." He stretched his right arm, which was hiding under the pillow. "This one's mine. But the scar tissue on the wrist is hers, strangely."

"What happened?"

"Zooey tried to chop my hand off with a meat cleaver. Kid stuff."

"How old were you?"

"Twenty-five."

Ursula nestled deeper in the bed, shrugged the sheets a little farther up.

Adrian went on with the roll call: "The brain is shared: she's got the right hemisphere; I got the left. Lungs are mine. Kidneys are hers. Liver is mine. Heart is hers."

"I could have guessed."

"You're old enough to know the heart is just a muscle that pumps blood through your veins; it has nothing to do with character."

"Sure."

Ursula's hands were both under the covers. She used neither of them to point at the next question. "Whose is the . . . between your legs?"

Adrian allowed a blank second, free of implications.

"That's kind of shared too."

He counted a few raindrops on the windowsill, then resumed.

"I guess at first they decided I was boy enough, but just in case they still gave me an ambiguous name like Adrian. Afterward, when Gwen identified Zooey, she chose her own name. It's a character from Salinger."

That sounded like a smite.

"Why do you hate her?" Ursula asked.

Some other ambient circumstance or meteorological occurrence that doesn't even deserve to be specified delayed the answer.

"She's my sister," Adrian said. "Siblings hate each other."

"Not always."

"You just lost two in one week and you don't look too broken up."

"Half brothers. And I hardly knew them. But I didn't hate them."

"You didn't because they never interfered with your life." Adrian sat up on his elbows. "Mikey had fifteen years on you. You two never shared a bedroom. He never stole your clothes. He never mistreated your Monster High dolls."

"I don't play with Monster High dolls."

"You don't know what it is. To have a twin. Someone who is always there, in the same room. In the same underpants. Pulling your body, always in the wrong direction."

He shifted, face to the ceiling.

"We've been fighting since before we could speak. No wonder our birth mother just gave up on us; can you picture what we were like as toddlers? When Zooey isn't making a scene in a public place, it's because we didn't agree on going to the place in question. I want to go to the library—Zooey wants to go to the beach. I've got a test tomorrow—Zooey is sniffing glue. I'm taking the test—ooh, time to masturbate. That's every day in my life. So, in answer to your question, 'Why do you hate her?' . . . let us just say that communal living takes a toll."

"But it's her life too. You two are the same person."

"We are *not* the same person," he said, almost raising his voice. "We are as different as it gets. We're each other's antipodes. She's pure right brain—she lives on fantasies and whims, she's like a freight train of emotions, derailed. I am intellect, observation, scientific reasoning. I'm the one doing the detective part of being a detective; she does the smart-ass quipping and heavy-drinking part—with *my* liver, incidentally. I provide for both of us; I take us through school and interviews so we can live outside a psych ward. I want stability; she can't sit still for five minutes. I want harmony and routine; she wants noise and never having sex with the same person twice. I calculate; she guesses. I plan; she improvises. I use logic; she daydreams. I'm rational; she's a wacko."

"She has fun; you're boring," Ursula whispered.

"Oh, you think that makes her fun? Acting on impulse, with no consequence? With no inhibition?"

"That's what you're there for—to stop her before she does something too crazy. You complement each other."

Adrian muffled a macabre laugh. The moon pointed out a vile smirk on his face.

"That's what Gwen told you, isn't it? That we spent the best part of our lives going from hospitals to foster homes and from foster homes to juvenile pens, until she arrived and unraveled our file and finally told us apart. That she took DNA samples and proved before doctors and judges that we were two people, not one schizophrenic who needed to be put away, right? Then tell me why we've been in ten different loony bins since then? Why we were in Claymoore just last week? Oh, right: it's just a rest home."

The whole upper half of his body was speaking now; his left hand seemed to be holding a cigarette, but it wasn't.

"Do you think Zooey is cool? Let me walk you through some highlights of Zooey's life: at age five, Zooey gets sad because Santa didn't bring her a fire truck, so she has one delivered to our foster home by lighting the bed on fire. And right after that, she remembers that Santa won't come unless she's asleep, so she gets *into the bed!* Age seventeen: Zooey's driving to Encino, gets the munchies, decides to drive through a Hard Rock Cafe that didn't have a drive-through! Do you know the Cadillac's rear sticking out of the wall in every Hard Rock Cafe now? We gave them the idea—we considered suing! Age twenty-four: Zooey needs to spend the night sequestered in a hotel room in Raleigh, North Carolina, before testifying in a trial for a case we helped solve. Just to pass the time, she decides she will drink everything in the minibar and refill the bottles with rubbing alcohol; she does that, then she drinks the rubbing alcohol too, and the next morning she testifies *against the judge.* In the wrong courtroom. *In South! Dakota!*"

He refueled oxygen, never looking away from Ursula, never really noticing the panic in her face.

"The truth is," he recapped, "we are not a dangerous schizophrenic who needs to be put away. We are two distinct individuals, one of which is dangerous and needs to be put away."

He rubbed his nose. The room was starting to shiver because of the cold breeze.

"But of course, it's the old conjoined twins problem," he said. "If one of them commits a crime, must we incarcerate him? Or does the good twin's right to freedom prevail? How is it my fault that she's dysfunctional?"

He fell silent after that, the question left behind for the audience to study, like any ancient philosophical problem deserves.

A minute later, Ursula felt she'd mulled over it long enough and sat up too for the rebuttal.

"You are not the good twin. You are just as dysfunctional," she said, enunciating carefully so as not to trip on the word. "If she lacks everything you have, then you must lack everything she has: No sensitivity. No empathy."

"Lacking empathy or sensitivity does not make me unsuited to live in society," Adrian said. "On the contrary, it kinda helps. Most successful people usually skimp on those things."

"Right," the kid said, disgusted. "And they become my father."

"The world is heartless outside your father's business too. You'll find out when you join us in Grown-up Land," Adrian said, standing up like a parent closing the bedtime storybook. "See how far you get without stepping on anyone's toes."

Rain continued its gentle drumroll on the rooftops outside. On the chessboard, the black and white figures glared hatefully at one another, eternally, for reasons long forgotten.

Adrian Kimrean remained just as still, on the rim of the spotlight, fixed on Ursula's feet in her colorful leggings.

"Toes," he repeated.

Ursula released the pillow she'd been squeezing against her chest. "Say what?"

Adrian shook himself out of the trance, then fished back the crumpled check from his shoe and tossed it on the bed.

"Go to the hotel; I need to think."

"What? Now?!"

"Scram."

"It's raining!"

"It was raining when you got here, Columbus is just around the corner."

"But what if they're—"

"They won't."

He wasn't facing her anymore; he had wandered to the center of the room, seeing nothing but concepts, faces, sentences registered in the last two days, replayed in fast motion.

"You really are kicking me out," Ursula said. She didn't bother to append a question mark.

Adrian didn't even roger that.

It was cold out of the bed. Ursula had packed only a hoodie before leaving home. She layered on, put on her shoes, dilating the ritual of tying her shoelaces to give time for a change of heart she knew would not happen. She slung her backpack over her shoulder and walked herself to the door.

On the glass panel she read the vinyl letters, mirrored:

A. KIMREAN

Z. KIMREAN

PRIVATE EYES

"You can't keep me away too long, you know," she told him. "Zooey said I'm the femme fatale of this case."

The machine snapped off.

Adrian strode toward the door, his wake pushing Ursula out onto the landing while he stopped on the threshold. He stuck his mannequin face inches from Ursula's and spewed out the last speech of the night.

"*First*, you are not a femme fatale; you are barely a femme, and if anything, chronologically, you are practically *fétale*, a pun that I assume will go over your head just like the hand of the 'you must be this tall' sign at the teacups ride in Disney World. And *second*, the only archetype you fulfill at this time is that of the damsel in distress—that is a weak, passive, and utterly annoying stock character who is good for nothing but whining while she waits for the hero to come and rescue her, all for the promise of a sexy scene at the end of the story to consummate a romantic plot that the hero will have forgotten about in the next episode, but since in your case the sexy scene won't happen unless we move the show to Saudi Arabia, I don't even see the point of your character staying alive for that long, nor do I see your beloved, micro-attention-spanned Zooey mourning you for more than ten seconds before she moves on to the next sweet-faced, air-headed, dime-a-dozen, stupid useless *bimbo*!"

A bolt of lightning struck a rooftop two blocks away, or in some other county, or in Idaho—who cares. Slowly the air flowed back into the depleted space between both characters, bringing the smell of petrichor.

Thunder boomed. From the lightning before, maybe.

The child on the landing snorted, a tear trailblazing down her cheek.

She said, not allowing her voice to crack, "Do you realize that, since you're so incapable of loving Zooey, she must be the one who loves you?"

There was no answer.

Ursula hurried down the stairs, one hand on the banister, the other holding the backpack over her shoulder, yielding to sobs.

Adrian slammed the office door shut and punched a phone number.

"Danny, where are you?"

"Xander's penthouse." He hadn't been sleeping.

"Spread your troops a little. Send some men back to Villa Leona."

"Why?"

"It just occurred to me—maybe the oldest brother is not in such danger after all."

# 8

Early the next morning, Adrian Kimrean shot the 1969 Camaro back across the Gran South desert, aiming at the viscous pink lava blob of a rising sun ahead—foot grazing the gas pedal, fingers drumming on the steering wheel, train of thoughts traveling way faster than the muscle car. He had not slept, eaten, or drunk since the previous day, nor did he feel an urge to change any of that.

The Prospero Hotel on Palm Avenue was one of many steel-and-glass colossi erected in downtown San Carnal as towering mirrors for the self-contemplation of the city in its evil stepmother magnificence. Additionally, when the sun was low, the outer mirrors served to refract the orange sands into the city, thus imbuing it with the gold-colored light that Hollywood cinematographers believe to be a permanent feature of ancient Greece and present-day Florida. Boasting five stars and three different kinds of salmon in its breakfast buffet, the hotel was owned by one of many companies traceable to the Lyon family, and for that reason Xander Lyon had his usual residence in the penthouse suite—an arrangement that would constitute an exemplary punishment for most hotel owners in the world, but in a few cases it's a treat. The AC never went above 68°F, rooms never went below $500, concierges and bellhops bowed low enough to snog the carpets, and a myriad of employees worked 24/7 to spare the exclusive clientele any contact with people of such indecisive complexion, careless attire, and impetuous body odor as A. Z. Kimrean.

Which is why Adrian chose to sit at a window table in the café across the street, where he had a clear view of the front marquee. Sunlight blasted off the hotel's façade, making the whole building glow like a mythical sword stabbed into a rock.

Danny Mojave joined him minutes later, wearing fresh black clothes and one-day-old circles around his eyes. He skipped the greetings.

"I don't have much time; we're planning security for Frankie's funeral. Xander will have a personal escort of ten in three cars. He'll be riding in the Jaguar with bulletproof glass." He addressed an incoming waitress before she could step within earshot of them. "Coffee, please."

Adrian was about to speak when he noticed that the waitress was not moving.

"I'm fine, thanks," he shooed her away.

She left; Adrian was now noticing Danny's incredulous stare.

"Zooey's asleep," he explained. "By the way—good thing she was, because last night the kid who knows too much sneaked out of Villa Leona and came knocking at my door, doing her Punky Brewster routine."

"Ursula went to San Francisco?"

"Yes! So please congratulate the guards, the dogs, and everyone at home base; they're doing a brilliant job looking after her."

"Well, it was a smart move," Danny reasoned, after some consideration. "There's a fair chance she becomes a target too; maybe she was safer with you. Where is she now?"

"Hotel on Columbus Ave. I guess. Probably. I gave her a check; I don't think they'd let her cash it in anywhere else."

"Oh, cool! Kudos, Mrs. Doubtfire, thank God *you* are looking after her!"

"Well, I'm not the one in charge of security for the Lyon family!" Adrian comebacked. "And since we returned to the subject, why the escort and all the extra padding for Xander at the funeral? It was four days between Mikey and Frankie. Wouldn't you expect at least the same lapse before Xander?"

"I thought so too, but you said the killer is not a planner," Danny explained. "An improviser would have trouble sneaking into the thirty-seventh floor, but he knows of at least one occasion when the elder brother will leave the castle: the middle brother's burial."

Adrian nodded, shyly at first, like one of those slow claps in high school movies. "Nice. We may make a detective out of you yet."

Danny correctly interpreted that as a compliment. He sighed, seemed to relax a notch.

"It's a shame you're completely wrong," Adrian resumed. "Xander is in no danger."

The waitress poured the coffee without Danny or Kimrean acknowledging her existence and left them alone again—two sketchy outlines burned against the glowing window.

"No danger?" Danny complained. "You said after the youngest and the middle brother, the next victim would be the eldest brother. 'Brothers Grimm 101,' you said."

"I know, wrong reference. A hostile takeover is white-collar business; it calls for a highbrow model, not common folktales. Something classic—Aeschylus or Shakespeare. Characters with dark sentiments *and* methodical thinking."

"So you know who the killer is?"

Adrian crossed his legs and stole a lump of sugar. "What walks on four legs in the morning, two at noon, three in the evening?"

Danny quickly reloaded his high school classical history curriculum.

"Man," he answered. "Yeah, a man, I know; I never considered the killer would be a panda. No, wait. Not any man: the third leg is a blind man's cane. The blind man is the guy who solved the riddle without noticing it was about him. Oedipus." *(Frowns.)* "But . . . Oedipus? Who . . . ? Wait, *Xander?*"

Kimrean popped the sugar lump in his mouth. "Good boy."

"Wait, Xander is going to kill his father and marry his mother?"

"Stepmother. One of the drawbacks of marrying someone half your age—suddenly your son starts carrying a saucy pic of Mom in his wallet."

Danny recalled the picture gaffe with Zooey and Xander the day before. "But he called her 'my mother'; how did you know—"

"I know Miss Guatemala is not a blonde. So, hi, Elizabeth Omahira, the British merchant attorney in the Cayman Islands."

"Wait, wait a minute," Danny pleaded. "So Xander just killed his two brothers. In person."

Adrian waived his chance to object, then calmly elaborated: "Focus on the m.o.: someone's dismembering the cartel with surgical precision. He avoids the guards; if he can't avoid them, he takes them out cleanly. Thus far, that could be a hit man. But when it comes to the real targets, the Lyon brothers, he shows cruelty. He engages in fistfights. There's only one person who can inspire that much hatred: a sibling."

Danny sat on that for a while, rubbing his week-old stubble.

"No way," he determined. "Xander and Mikey never got along.

They used to fight a lot, I'll give you that. But breaking into your father's house in the middle of the night to beat your brother to death? That's psychotic."

"Maybe. It's also the mentality of a young Lyon on the rise. Think the '74 Takeover. It's the same cold, ultraviolent streak; it's in his blood. All he needed was a trigger."

"What's the trigger?" Danny asked, and answered himself in the same paragraph: "The shoot-out with the Red Mums."

"The shoot-out at the diner is the first cog, the unmoved mover; the real trigger comes later. Mikey's blunder with the Red Mums causes a crisis. Xander, who was 'abroad attending some meetings,' has to rush back stateside. By the way, when you said he was 'abroad attending some meetings,' you could have just said 'in the Caymans'; I heard Mikey mentioning it in the FBI tape. So 'attending some meetings' *was* a euphemism for 'banging my mistress,' see? Well, more like 'banging my stepmilf.'" He reread that line, omitting Danny's consternation, then appended: "In retrospect, I'd probably hide that under a euphemism too. Anyway, Xander flies back overnight to deal with the aftermath, all the while thinking why is his brother such a douche, and why does he have to split the empire with him. Let that stew for a few hours, top it with an airline breakfast, and it's a matter of time before he snaps."

"Snaps, kills his brother, and blames it on the yakuza? Quite meticulous for a spur of the moment."

"Not really, it's the assassin's trademark: effective attacks despite sloppy preparations. That's why the chrysanthemum is not a chrysanthemum."

He pointed at the window. A delivery van had stopped in front of the hotel; a boy in green overalls was unloading a wreath from the back while a valet in a double-breasted overcoat pointed him toward the reception.

"Chrysanthemums are the emperor's flower in Japan; they stand for power," Adrian recited casually. "Oddly enough, in Europe they are associated with death; they are mostly used in funeral arrangements. That's the view that Hispanics brought to the Americas. For other people, they don't carry that stigma, but still, there's one place where you don't usually find them."

"Hospitals," Danny guessed. "It would send the wrong message." He paused, looked back over that sentence, then slapped his own leg. "The hospital! Hilfiger died in the ER the night of the shooting."

"Everything points at the hospital," Adrian confirmed. "The footprints in Villa Leona contained chlorophenol, a disinfectant agent used in surgery rooms."

"Xander had to go to the hospital morgue to get Hilfiger's items," Danny recalled.

"And that's the trigger, that's when he comes up with the idea: he can try and prevent a war, or he can take out Mikey and chalk it up to the war."

"He walks by the flower shop on his way out of the hospital, orders a red chrysanthemum," Danny followed. "But they don't have any, so he takes any red flower."

"And that night he goes to Villa Leona."

"He knows the north side is the weakest point."

"And the dogs wouldn't snitch on him."

"But he doesn't bring a gun."

"Oh, he does," Adrian countered. "But that handcannon he was toting around the other night? That's a customized Taurus BA-44: made in Brazil, uses very specific ammunition. It's a

signature gun; he knows he can't use it against his own brother.
Maybe he plans to knife him; maybe he knows about the Beretta
Mikey keeps in the pool house and plans to use that. In either
case, Mikey catches him coming in through the window."

"He's the right height."

"And the right shoe size: a little too long for his height. Plus
Latino would have been my second option after Asian. And
Native Alaskan my third, but that's uncommon."

"God, you're obsessed with race."

"Yes, and magical people who don't see race somehow never
win at *Who Is Who?* Anyway, he climbs inside; Mikey catches
him, says, 'You'; a fight ensues. And as in any fraternal fight, it all
pours out: decades of grueling resentment, jealousy, 'I wish you'd
never been born.' Mikey brings in the gun; he loses it; Xander
takes him down . . . Mikey utters, 'Why.' Xander, shivering with
rage, shows him why, then executes him."

He helped himself to another sugar treat. Danny sorted out
his thoughts, not fully convinced.

"And the why is . . . what?" he inquired. "The empire was
virtually his already. The will splits it three ways, but Xander
was to be the new boss, Frankie didn't care, and Mikey was a
lieutenant; nobody argued with that."

"It's not about who's in the will. It's about who isn't."

"Omahira," Danny guessed. "So when Mikey asks why, he
shows him the stepmother's picture."

"The mistress's," Adrian corrected. "Mikey was a textbook
spoiled youngest; to him, Miss Guatemala was the Virgin Mary,
and Omahira is the home-wrecker. After the Lyon dies, if she
marries Xander, she'll get a share of the empire, and Mikey will
not stand for that. Xander knows it. So might as well get rid of
him now."

"Why kill Frankie then? If Xander and Mikey had gone to war over their father's legacy, Frankie would've stayed out of it."

"I know, he's ambivalent. What tipped the balance was bringing me in. Since I'm here to investigate Mikey's murder, Xander fears the flower message wasn't clear enough. So he kills Frankie to underscore the message. Goes into the club, shoots every eyewitness, confronts Frankie, tells him how much he despises him just to gather the courage, then shoots him. Another third of the empire, another red flower, and a clear message: 'Yes, we're at war.'"

The waitress approached with a fresh coffeepot, offering a refill. Adrian shook his head no while Danny held his face in his hands, fingers buried in rapidly graying curls, seriously considering throwing up in his mug. He needed a shower and a joint. Nothing a police detective isn't entitled to after eighteen months undercover as a drug cartel's factotum, really.

He returned from his thoughts the way surviving soldiers used to return from Vietnam.

"What am I supposed to do now, Ade?"

"I take checks," Kimrean said. He was manspread all over his seat, one leg under Danny's chair, the other one threatening to make the waitress trip. "You guys hired me to take the blame off the yakuza. I just did."

"I'm sure the Lyon will be happy to know it was actually his oldest, who incidentally is also banging his wife."

"Do you want me to break it to him?"

Danny met Adrian's trademark peaceful, focused, indifference-born stare.

"I think I'm very good at delivering news," the P.I. said.

"You didn't prove it happened as you say."

"Do I have to?" he moaned like a five-year-old. "It's not like we're taking the case to court."

"The killer took a bullet in the club; Frankie's bodyguard managed to shoot him in the corridor," Danny recalled. "Xander seemed okay when he joined us later."

"A flesh wound. And it took me ninety minutes to drive there—enough for him to patch himself up."

"He still must be patched up now."

"Sure. Can you go and ask him to lift his shirt for a sneak peek? Do you boys have that kind of relationship?"

"No, but I just left him in the penthouse having breakfast and a shower."

"Marc Anthony is in the shower?" Kimrean cried, slamming both hands on the table. "To the Oglemobile!"

Several customers in neighboring booths joined Danny in an admonishing scowl at that reaction.

"I think Zooey is waking up."

"Yup," Adrian confirmed, suddenly gloomy. "Come on, let's wrap this up before she's fully awake."


They jaywalked to the hotel, its glass façade still incandescent under the sun that was rapidly cornering the last puddles of rusty rainwater into the waning shady spots. A temperature drop akin to that experienced at dusk on Mercury welcomed them as they emerged from the revolving doors, Danny in institutional mobster black, Kimrean braving the cold in their tank top and waistcoat, marching side by side through the main lobby.

"Suppose Xander has a fresh wound on his side," Danny weather-talked. "What then?"

"You could tell Lyon Sr., if you trust he won't bite the messenger's head off."

"I don't, but it might help stop a war."

"Xander will stop the war himself; he'll talk to the yakuza, save the alliance, and make his dad proud. Or he may go full Oedipus and kill his dad."

"You would make a terrifying villain."

"I know. I couldn't live with the voice of my conscience, though. There's more than enough voices in here."

At the reception desk, the wreath they had seen arriving had blended into a vast collection of flower arrangements. Frankie being the face of the Lyons' public businesses, it was only to be expected that he would get the most sympathies from the family's influential connections. One of the garlands bore a ribbon with the name Villahermosa—a detail that almost made Adrian chuckle.

An overwhelmed receptionist explained to Danny, "They keep coming, but you ordered us not to send anyone upstairs."

"We'll take them with us to the church, thank you." He turned to Adrian. "Maybe I should go upstairs by myself. I'll call the front desk when I find out."

"Right. Also, Zooey doesn't need the excitement," Kimrean said, green eye deviating from the flowers to the girls in reception. Danny left them and headed for the elevators.

Kimrean turned their back to the desk and scanned the lobby, crawling with businessmen hurrying to random convention events between infidelities and a few tourists who'd been stranded after missing a connecting flight. Xander's men were easy enough to spot—one in the sitting area by the door, one in the chill-out bar, one by the express elevators. They probably weren't even trying to go unnoticed. Out of the corner of their green eye, Kimrean glanced at the receptionist behind them, sorting some envelopes. She noticed, smiled again, almost successfully hiding her surprise at the mismatched eyes, then tried to scurry out of their view behind a bunch of lilies.

And then Adrian noticed the crack.

And watched as this crack slithered across the floor and between his legs, splitting branches, spreading over the lobby, shattering his field of vision, and bringing his whole theory down.

He twirled out of Zooey's flirting posture, lurched to the bunch of lilies. There was no ribbon or card to it. But he'd spotted it, among the ghostly crowd of white lily heads, like a little hooded girl standing against a stream of snowed-on hats: a red rose.

*Erithra lunis.* The red moon.

"Oh shit."

The receptionist meerkated at the cursing; Adrian interrogated her: "Who sent these flowers?"

"These? They're for Mr. Frank Lyon."

"That's not what I asked—*who* brought them?!"

"Er . . . I don't know. Some delivery boy, I think . . . ? I never saw him walk in."

"Did you see him walk out?!"

That was the million-dollar question.

And like most contestants at that stage, the receptionist just stuttered.

By the time the words "I'm not sure" found their way out of her lips, A. Z. Kimrean had already plucked the rose out of the lilies and dashed down the hallway, jumping over the coffee table where one of Lyon's sentrymen was sitting and racing toward the express elevator Mojave was about to enter. The red flower was all the emergency signal he needed.

"Chrysanthemum?" he asked.

"Not a chrys—who gives a fuck!" Adrian confirmed. "How many men are up there?"

"Just Spence, Xander's driver. But he can shoot." He flicked a magnetic card over a scanner, Adrian thumbed the top-floor button two inches into the panel, and the elevator doors closed.

They reopened onto a landing/foyer mediating between the elevator and the single suite on the thirty-seventh floor. A dread-locked 260-pound muscleman in a gray suit standing there had enough reflexes to pull a gun at the mere sight of a red petal in the queer-looking mime's hand.

"He's with me!" Danny said, waiting for him to put the gun down. "Has anyone come up?"

Spence said no and stepped out of the way as Danny and the mime crashed through the penthouse doors.

Kimrean had to close their eyes and peek through shielding fingers: a nuclear blast of adolescent sun flooded in through the wall-to-wall windows opening onto the terrace. It took a while for the darker blotches to define themselves as a sofa with its own tax district, a Narnia-fitting wardrobe, and a TV measurable in acres. The place looked calmer than some European states—and about as large. On the TV, the hosts of *¡Despierta América!* were thrilled to welcome to the studio Golden Globe–nominated actress and star of the upcoming new legal drama *Low Suits* Cameron Diaz.

Xander Lyon emerged from the bathroom, alarmed at the impetus of their entrance, clad only in a towel. A very small one.

"Danny? What the hell is—"

He cut himself off when he noticed Kimrean—or, more precisely, the red rose in their hand.

Danny used up the pause to catch his breath, then checked with A.Z. They were still standing alert, muscles taut, eyes fixed on their naked host, mouth curled back in a snarl to say, "Grr."

"Adrian!" Danny called.

Kimrean shook their head, but didn't take their eyes off the naked man. Perhaps the one adjective nobody would use to describe Xander Lyon's naked torso was *disappointing*.

And yet.

Xander stood still, too deep in confusion to allow anger to take over while the marionette zoomed in, examining his right side, head tilting to appreciate the hidden details. Not an inch of his body betrayed its resemblance to a Renaissance sculpture. Not even the amount of chest hair. Not even the aftershower glow.

Not even the number of fresh wounds: none.

"Danny, what the hell is happening here?" the gangster dared ask, despite having formed his own answer a few seconds ago.

Danny didn't need the close-up to reach the same conclusions.

"We think you're in danger," he said.

Adrian fired a few Gatling rounds:

ADRIAN: How many entrances?

DANNY: One.

ADRIAN: Elevators?

DANNY: No other reaches this floor.

ADRIAN: Stairs?

DANNY: Outside, on the landing.

Kimrean tossed the flower on the sofa and headed for the balcony.

It blazed painfully white. A table and a couple deck chairs

sheltered under the yellow awning. A few rainwater lakes persisted on the table; the ascending sun would evaporate them in a few minutes.

Kimrean leaned over the rail. Thirty-seven floors below, where the parallel lines of the façade converged, miniature cars honked at each other with their cute toy horns. A little closer, a curtain was swinging in the wind. Five floors below.

When they returned inside, Kimrean and the sun spots in their retinas, Danny was still waiting for answers.

"So?"

"He's in the building."

"All your reasoning was wrong," Danny accused. "Every single thing was wrong."

"Not everything," Adrian defended himself, pointing at the gangster. "He's still banging his stepmother."

That effectively killed the dialogue right there. Even the television set glitched.

XANDER: Excus—

"Your toes," Adrian felt compelled to reply, pointing at Xander's feet. "You're a size eight, but you wear an eight and a half, don't you? Shoes in your size cause you discomfort because of your big toe: it's quite shorter than the second. That's called brachydactyly of the hallux, or Morton's toe, and it's a Mendelian trait, caused by a dominant allele. Your father doesn't have it—he was wearing sandals when we met—so you inherited it from Miss Guatemala. But Ursula has it too, and her mother doesn't—you can see her feet in the sarong picture from your wallet. So actually, not only are you banging your stepmother, but you fathered your stepsister."

A few parsecs away, on the TV, the audience of *¡Despierta América!* burst into distant applause.

Someone knocked on the door and opened it without waiting for an answer. Spence stuck his dreadlocks in, tried to read the room, somehow missed all the signs, and spoke anyway: "Uh . . . sorry. Mr. Lyon, the elevator isn't working."

Adrian, at least, reacted to that.

"Close your mouth and secure the room," he ordered Danny. "I need a gun."

Danny pushed his chin up, still dazed, and pulled out his Desert Eagle.

"And your radio, if you're so kind," Adrian solicited Spence, while squeezing the pistol into their pants. Danny nodded at Spence, who grudgingly handed the queer-looking mime his walkie-talkie. "Stay in contact," Kimrean said before his exit.

And they left, evidently not concerned with the aftermath of the bombshell they had just dropped.


A service door blending into the landing led into the stairwell. The *appel du vide* invited A.Z. to stare down the shaft, mercifully too narrow for anyone to fall. A fractal pattern of rails and steps framed the microscopic bottom.

Kimrean ran down to the thirty-sixth floor, opened the door, checked the elevator. It wasn't there.

He checked the thirty-fifth, thirty-fourth, and thirty-third floors. On the thirty-second he found a toilet paper roll wedged under the elevator doors, preventing them from closing. Facing the elevator, a red-carpeted corridor yawned into the east.

The walkie-talkie in their hand crackled: "Adrian?"

Kimrean whispered into the mouthpiece: "Not now."

He tiptoed ahead into the corridor, like a human cannonball

disappearing into the mouth of the barrel. Movement sensors woke up the lamps as they went. Not the flimsiest noise ruined the suspense.

They reached the room at the end—3210. They ducked and felt the crack under the door. A gentle breeze rocking the microfibers of the carpet chilled their fingertips.

A card reader was on sentinel duty. Kimrean offered it the only magnetic card in their wallet: that of the public library. They inserted it between the door and the frame at lock level and pushed with their shoulder. The door clacked open.

They kicked it the rest of the way and barged in, pistol in hand.

A ghostly curtain swayed in and out the open window in the breeze, giggling like a dead little girl's ghost in a Shirley Jackson setting. Kimrean had to shield their eyes from the noisy sunlight to make out the taut vertical nylon rope tied to the radiator.

They ran to the window and gazed up, away from the distant traffic. The sun wouldn't allow them to judge how far up the line reached, but it was an easy bet.

"Danny?" A.Z. radioed. "Check the balcony again."


"Roger."

Danny headed for the screen door, leaving Xander getting dressed and Spence watching the TV, where a prestigious nutritionist was just joining the kitchen set next to Cameron Diaz to debate the benefits of soy milk. Danny's hand instinctively reached into his jacket for the gun Kimrean had borrowed. He regretted that as he slid open the screen door and stepped out onto the scorched terrace.

His sunglasses barely countered the solar outburst. He walked the full length of the balcony, checking under the table and the deck chairs.

Then he saw it, on the far end of the rail: a grappling hook.

He went for the radio when he felt the gentle kiss of a 9mm barrel on the back of his head.

On the thirty-second floor, Kimrean inventoried the room one last time: complimentary candy on the pillows, Do Not Disturb sign hanging from the door handle, late-night snack menus on the dresser. Everything was as it had been left by the cleaning staff.

Except for that key card on the bedside table. That had been left by a guest. One who had left either through the window, or not at all.

Adrian stayed on the balls of his feet, not risking another step while he mentally figured out the room's blueprints and listed all the possible hiding places. Bathroom. Walk-in closet. King bed.

He first skipped toward the bathroom, never entering: translucent shower screen, zero space behind the door. Nowhere to hide.

He then hopped toward the closet.

Coat hangers.

It was then that Zooey realized she had a semiautomatic in her hand.

"Is this thing loaded?"

And much to Adrian's surprise, she fired a round at the ceiling.

And even to Zooey's surprise, a ninja in white camo rolled out from under the bed and slammed them down to the carpet.

—

Standing in front of the panoramic TV, Spence commented, "Man, I gotta start drinking soy milk."

He turned to get an amen and saw Danny out on the balcony, playing human shield to a hooded black figure holding a gun to his head.

Spence almost made it to the first *s* in *boss* before a 9mm round went straight into his frontal lobe.

The 260-pound driver fell like a downed ballista elephant just as Xander Lyon banzai'ed out of the bedroom, firing blindly at the blazing windows in the general direction of the assailant without any previous assessment of the situation.

There was a discrete quantum of time in which Danny Mojave understood, as he caught sight of a lucky Taurus round in midair zooming toward his skull, that no previous assessment from anybody could have spared his life. No matter how well he played his cover, no matter how much the bad guys trusted him, in the end, he would always be a pawn, a disposable extra to someone like Xander Lyon when the latter's life was at stake. In that moment of truth, no loyalty, no honor among gangsters, could stop that bullet for him.

The screen door did. It blocked and deflected the bullet, shattering in the process and offering the killer a clear shot through to send two more rounds unobstructed into Xander Lyon's chest.

Danny seized that extra second of life to make a quick profile of his assailant: five-foot-five, lightweight, small feet.

Wounded.

He elbowed the guy's left side, the shocked gasp betraying he had hit a very tender spot. He squirmed out of the chokehold, grabbed the murderer by the arm, and swung him toward the rail, hitting his head. The killer lost the Beretta to the void.

—

Adrian's brown eye was silently reprimanding Zooey's green one for the earlier gaffe when each of them noticed the other reflected on the shiny twelve-inch steel blade with which Yu Osoisubame, the Phantom Ninja, was about to turn them into his twentieth and twenty-first confirmed kills with one strike. And probably get a bonus score for the combo too.

It was in moments like this—say, lying on the floor of a hotel room with a ninja assassin straddled over them, pressing a knee to their neck and holding a traditional Okinawan stabbing sword over their heart, ready to pin them down like a collectible moth—when the Kimreans were most motivated to put aside their differences and cooperate for the common good. In the tenth of a second before the sword descended, Adrian gained control of their left hand and brought the walkie-talkie over their body so that the blade shish-kebabbed the whole device and barely stung their chest, with the point just jutting through the impaled plastic, the momentum bringing the ninja low enough for Zooey to attempt a headbutt.

And it succeeded. Zooey chortled with delight at the sound of somebody else's nose crunching like something you step on in a movie theater.

The killer in the balaclava seemed to ricochet off the rail and charge again in pain-fueled anger before Danny deflected him with a haymaker that sent the lightweight rival sliding to the right end of the terrace. He ran to finish him, but before he could the enemy had stumbled back up and met Danny halfway. He deserved points for morale.

That was the last noble thought to cross either contender's mind before they crashed into each other and Danny slammed him back to the floor, landing on top—a circumstance the killer used for a very ungentlemanly knee strike to the crotch.

In that lightning of pain, the tables flipped. As did the contenders. They rolled over, bad guy fist-hammering the good guy, and over again, crashing into the rail. Danny caught a glimpse of the miniature life teeming thirty-seven floors below before noticing the actually important element around them that would decide the fight. The killer noticed it a little earlier.

In a lightning-speed movement, the killer unfixed the grappling hook and wrapped the nylon rope around Danny's neck. Strangled, Danny could only attempt another elbow shot at the rival's side, but the rival had learned his lesson—he would not expose his Achilles' heel twice.

Inside, Xander Lyon writhed on the carpet with two bullets cozying up to his vital organs.


Kimrean kickflipped to their feet, tossed the sai-and-walkie-talkie kebab aside, and replaced it with a much better weapon: a rolled-up magazine.

The Phantom Ninja too stood up and upgraded to a katana. A gleam from the yard-long blade momentarily blinded the white-collars in the office building across the street.

KIMREAN: Boy, that escalated quickly.

In the next ten seconds, more things happened than in ten hours' worth of Danish cinema. A.Z. dodged the first swing by bouncing backward and hitting the table behind them; they lay back on the table and spread their legs to avoid the next downstroke; they rolled back on their head to dodge the third slash, off the table and onto the chair at the other end, tipping over the chair and rolling backward again to end up sitting against the wall.

Their hat fell off and landed on their lap. And that was the most crucial event in those ten seconds.

It was Zooey's scattered attention that perceived the single raindrop on the fedora. But it was Adrian who found it relevant.

Rain. When? It had stopped raining when he got in the car this morning. Car. San Carnal. Café. Hotel. Lobby. Elevator. Penthouse. Terrace. Yellow awning. Raindrops on the awning, shaken off by—

KIMREAN: There was somebody hiding on the awning over the terrace!

They pushed against the wall behind them to slide under the table just before the ninja dove in and sank the katana into the floor, then headed off to the minibar. They opened the door to block off the fifth thrust, which cleanly split halfway through the refrigerator door before the sword got stuck just six inches short of slicing the whole thing in two. Zooey seized the chance to grab a few cans of beer and started playing the maracas with them, stepping back for some playroom.

With a scream that even a professional anime voice actor would condemn as overacted, the ninja managed to tear the katana out of the fridge door, just in time to fend off the can of beer that the P.I. had hurled at his face. The blade sliced the can in two, spraying foam all over the battlefield.

"Good idea, Max—let's play Fizzball!"

They threw another two cans with a .5-second interval; the ninja lobbed away the first but only managed to bat the second; it hit the floor and immediately glided toward the opposite wall, propelled by the jet of beer gushing out of a fissure.

"Whoa! Time bomb! We got a time bomb!"

Zooey jumped out of the path of the can as it ricocheted off the corner, tunneled under the bed, bounced off the bedside table, and rocketed toward the ninja, who this time managed to slice it in two.

Which was the distraction Adrian was waiting for to step in and bash the ninja's head in with an ashtray. Zooey retrieved the katana, Adrian went for the key card, and both of them left the room. The ninja could wait.

The corridor lights lit up again as they zoomed toward the elevator, flinging the katana down the laundry chute on their way.

Danny's consciousness was beginning to flicker away. His blood-smeared, bloodless fingers were losing their grip on the nylon rope squeezing his larynx. His vision was tunneling. He had not an ounce of fight left in him. Maybe half an ounce.

Which he decided to stow away for the moment, until his attacker had finished dragging him back against the rail and tying the cord around his neck to one of the posts.

In the penthouse, Spence was already cruising the Styx. Xander lay bleeding at the foot of the sofa, a desperate hand trying to lure the rounds out of his abdomen.

The red rose snoozed on a cushion. In the blissful realm of morning TV, the perennial grin of Cameron Diaz brightened the world as the hosts and nutritionist continued to sing the praises of soy milk.

Xander's Taurus BA-44 waited for someone to remember it and pick it up.

And the killer obliged.

Gun in hand, the hooded figure tipped Xander's face up with a punt to the ribs before peeling the balaclava away. Xander squinted through sweat beads, trying to distinguish the sun-haloed face over the gun barrel.

With difficulty, the unfocused picture began to resolve into black hair, electric-blue eyes.

"Y . . . Y-you . . ."

And he scowled. And his bloodied lips blurted out:

"Who the fuck are you?"

The last vivid sensation he enjoyed was the weight of an innocent flower gently landing on his once unblemished Renaissance chest.

The bullet through the brain a second later, he didn't notice.

But it did wake up Danny. At a perfect time to cash in that half ounce.


Back in the stairwell, Kimrean, incidentally wondering about the fate of that Desert Eagle they'd borrowed from Danny, heard the gunshot. They voted against the door-bashing, time-stopping, pants-soaking entrance they were envisioning and instead tiptoed up to the penthouse door. The foyer was empty. The pause allowed them to consider how the killer had sneaked into the room. His first plan must have been to bring the flowers himself, but the receptionist barred him, so he'd left the flowers downstairs, taken another elevator and then the stairs to the rooftop, and dropped from the rooftop to the awning over Xander's terrace. Meanwhile, Kimrean had brought the rose upstairs for him.

It made Zooey feel used. And it scandalized Adrian: so many things could have gone wrong with that plan. There could have been guards on the rooftop. Any sentryman could have spotted the rose and stopped him. He had bravado, but he wasn't doing bad in sheer luck either.

That notion conflicted Zooey as well: it transgressed her own brand of logic—that of aesthetics. Why would the killer be so lucky? Villains don't rely on luck; fortune favors the heroes. It's a principle as sacred as the femme/thug alternation.

Adrian swatted that ridiculous thought off their mind and listened at the door.


The killer pulled the balaclava back down and glanced at the terrace: Danny was staying put like a good boy against the rail, rope keeping his head up, eyes closed.

He pocketed Xander's handcannon and proceeded to search the body of the dreadlocked giant. He had fallen facedown; it would prove tricky to reach the gun under his jacket, but a more accessible pocket in his pants hid a better jackpot: a key card to the hotel's parking and some car keys. With a Jaguar emblem.

He took everything and headed for the door, which just opened by itself.

"Hi!" Zooey greeted.

Before she could utter another syllable, she was staring into the barrel of the Taurus. Adrian peeked over it, tried to make out the little portions of a face that the balaclava exposed. Dark skin. Dark hair. Cyan eyes, scintillating with rage.

And some more movement beyond, way in the back. A black blob stirring on the terrace.

Oh, he looked good. *For someone who's been undercover for*

*eighteen months, carries a gun under his jacket and another one on his ankle.*

Danny Mojave, micromanaging every molecule of air squeezed into his lungs, pulled the gun from his ankle holster and aimed through the broken screen door at the killer. A most commendable sense of sportsmanship made him give a warning call before shooting someone in the back.

"Hey!"

That was truly a waste of a second.

Because it was the one second somebody five floors below chose to grab the other end of the rope wrapped around Danny's neck, put his full weight on it, and start climbing.

The nylon dug into Danny's throat with 140 pounds' worth of deadweight, pulled him back against the rail, and severed any new attempt to shout.

Xander's killer and A.Z. checked each other's eyes—brown-green asymmetry on one side, lightning blue on the other. There was little to discuss: the killer was holding every ace: the gun, the car keys, a finished job, and the certainty of not being Kimrean's priority. That was the end of the negotiations.

The killer darted out for the stairs, and Kimrean sprinted to the terrace where Danny, his face going from red to purple, squirming for a chance to scream, strove for a grip on the rope sinking into his flesh, well aware that this time around he would not be strangled: he would be decapitated.

Kimrean leaned out from the balcony in time to see the ninja hanging by the rope and instinctively moved their head away at the first glimpse of him flinging something shiny upward. The shuriken swished by their right ear and bored into the concrete ledge above.

Kimrean glared back at the enemy, left hand smearing a warm trickle of blood oozing out of the gash in their cheekbone.

KIMREAN: *(Softly.)* Mouthbreather.

Zooey retaliated by grabbing a large flowerpot bunking a ficus and flinging it over the rail.

She didn't hit him. Instead, the ninja checked his suit for the most recent addition to his exotic arsenal: the Desert Eagle.

"Oh," Zooey said. "There it was."

They fell back from the rail to dodge the bullets, all while Danny sat against it, immobilized, fingers bleeding under the rope's pressure only to stop it from slicing his jugular. He was starting to look like Arnold Schwarzenegger when his helmet breaks on the surface of Mars.

Kimrean scanned the terrace for more projectiles: Deck chairs. Table. Broken glass. Broken glass!

They grabbed a large shard of what had been the screen door and tried to saw the nylon rope. A bullet flew past, then another, millimeters away from their hand and Danny's skull.

And then they saw it: another forgotten element sitting on a planter box some floors below.

Adrian writhed to unpocket his cigarette pack, retrieved the Detective Kit™ inside, picked out the magnifying lens, and held it at an angle while his other hand held up the shard of glass against the sun. All that was left was to cheer for solar energy, keeping their pulse as steady as they could, funneling all the heat off the glass and through the lens into one single point.

The assassin averted his eyes from the gleam, then squinted to follow the beam falling vertically a few feet to his right, on another balcony. On a planter box on the balcony. On an alien object in the planter box on the balcony.

On a 9mm Beretta in a planter box on the balcony, glowing under the spotlight, the concentrated heat piercing through the grip and into the magazine, heating it up to 100°C. 150°C. 200°C.

And then it exploded.

A dozen bullets were shot at once, in every direction, chopping plants, piercing glass, splashing concrete.

The ninja clung to his rope, curled up like a caterpillar for a few seconds, before he dared open his eyes.

He felt his legs, torso, and head.

Not one.

Not a single bullet had grazed him.

He looked up.

A nutritionist pouring soy milk into Cameron Diaz's latte approached him at 200 m/s.


On street level, the valet in the double-breasted overcoat, while fending off the rubberneckers from the death scene of a suicidal ficus in front of the hotel door, was lucky enough to have a front-row view of the meteorite composed of plasma TV and ninja assassin blasting through the marquee and smashing into the solid ground, sending chunks of glass and cement flying across the avenue.

Kimrean had to settle with a cheap thirty-seventh-floor seat.

"Ah, kids. Always glued to the TV."

They dropped next to Danny as he got rid of the rope, swallowing air before someone or something else curtailed his right to oxygen.

"Who . . ." he wheezed. "Who the fuck was that?"

"That? That was Yu Osoisubame, the Phantom Ninja," Kim-rean answered, panting as well from hauling the TV all the way to the terrace. "Turns out the yakuza *did* declare war on you after the shoot-out. They tried to kill off your major pieces too, but somehow they were always late." Adrian took notice of Xander's body inside, gore censored by the sofa blocking that angle. "Someone got to them before him."

"No kidding. Who?"

"I don't know. I know your men downstairs won't get him. He had the Jaguar keys on him when he left."

Neither of them could speak except between deep, coarse breaths. Zooey touched their cheekbone: hopefully the gash wouldn't need stitches.

"Someone really good. And with beautiful eyes," she added. *(Checking Danny's profile.)* "Did you almost die asphyxiated, or are you happy to see me?"

Danny laughed, sputtering a little blood and saliva. "I'm *very* happy to see you, Zooey."

Zooey kissed his lips and leaned her head on his shoulder. The howling of police sirens came up from the avenue.

# 9

"A fucking mess!" plot-summarized Deputy Chief Carlyle, banging the desk hard enough to make the diplomas on the wall shudder.

Greggs, Demoines, and A. Z. Kimrean lowered their heads and weathered the storm. Kimrean had just driven back from San Carnal, checked into headquarters, and reported on the events of the last forty-eight hours with the other two detectives removing the pictures of cartel actors from the case board as Kimrean pronounced them dead. All that while, Carlyle, leaning on a radiator and chomping on his cigar, had been hoarding energy for the expletive-rich monologue at the end of the scene. It was his big moment, and he was giving it everything he had.

"Two years we've been working this case! Eighteen months Mojave's been undercover, and for what?! For one goddamned loose cannon to undo everything in one week! And you! *(Pointing at Kimrean.)* Is there anything you do well, apart from dropping people off buildings?"

Adrian recognized the question as rhetorical, but Zooey answered: "Well, I'm a decent pianist."

"A fucking mess!" Carlyle rounded off, finally knocking out Greggs's desk with the last hammer-punch.

After that, the storm subsided. Timidly the voices of fax machines and typewriters from the bullpen ebbed in again. Kimrean swept the commissioner's spittle off the rim of their hat.

"Heartbroken though I am for the futility of your efforts, am I the only one who is kinda okay with a drug cartel being annihilated?"

"Who cares about the cartel!" Carlyle grunted in a tantrum like an earthquake aftershock.

"We need a big shot alive to help bring down the badapple-troika," Greggs explained. "If the cartel just dies out, another will take its place. Villahermosa is already in line. As long as they keep the badges and the gavels happy, nothing will change. And there's no reason to think the killer will stop until he reaches the guy at the top, Victor Lyon himself."

"There is one, actually," Kimrean commented. "He's been to Villa Leona already; he could have killed two Lyons then, and he didn't."

"Not a very solid point," Carlyle judged.

"Yeah, I think so too," said Adrian.

"My point is, we should try and salvage what we can," Greggs resumed. "Danny, for instance. We should pull him out yesterday."

"After the Lyon has lost his three sons, you want Danny to vanish?" Demoines objected. "You know how that will look?"

"Who cares about appearances—the Lyon will be dead in a week."

"Suppose he isn't. Suppose he's spared. Then what's left of the cartel will hunt down Danny like a dog."

"How do we help him then?"

"Cast the net," Kimrean said. They read the room, then continued, chin-pointing at Carlyle: "You said it, the case is coming undone. After two years coordinating, eighteen months undercover, you gotta have something. Just raid in, bring them to court, take all you can. Victor will cooperate now; he has barely anything to lose, and he wants something you can offer: protection."

"The question is, protection from whom?" Carlyle cued.

Kimrean scowled, biting a colorless lip.

"Shit, you love to hear me say it, don't you?" Adrian jeered. "You all want me to say it."

They stood up, extended their arms, and delivered the crowd-pleaser:

"Well, rejoice: *I. Don't. Know.*"

Then they put their hat on and walked out of the room.

A few curious heads hatching out of their cubicles followed them to the elevator and watched the doors close. Then they turned back to Greggs's office.

The detectives remained seated, waiting for instructions. It was their way to commemorate the rare occasions when they didn't have any better ideas.

Carlyle blew a couple consonants in smoke signals and squished his cigar in an ashtray.

"Call state, the feds, and the rest: they have sixteen hours. We're wrapping this up first thing tomorrow."


Right at that point along the plot, in other offices in other novels, different detectives sat facing their own case walls covered in pictures of their dramatis personae connected with wool thread. Police inspectors smoked, P.I.s drank and smoked. House, MD, balanced a ball on the end of his cane. In 1890s London, Sherlock Holmes lay interred on his own sofa under a toxic cloud of pipe tobacco and tried to pluck some music out of a twenty-ounce bottle of morphine after having shot his own violin up his cubital vein. Meanwhile, behind the door with the glass panel and the fresh shiny vinyl letters, A. Z. Kimrean kept wearing out the floorboards in their apartment, up and down the pool of light from the window like a Brechtian actor, chewing on hypotheses and spitting them on the floor. Every now and then, one of their hands hovered over the chessboard and prodded a piece. That was their thing.

"Who."

They peeked through the blinds hanging loosely over the broken window. Their right hand rubbed their eyes, cheeks, and chin.

"Who?"

The left hand moved some piece on the board.

Then the whole body bent backward:

"WHOOOOO?!"

The scream faded out with the flapping of a dozen seagulls scampering away from the docks.

"*Who is it?!* Who the hell breaks into a drug lord's fortress, a crowded club, and a thirty-seventh floor penthouse without planning ahead? Why does he do it, how's he so reckless, what's the point?!"

"Check."

Adrian Kimrean froze in midstep.

With an audible whiplash he spun around and looked at the chessboard for the first time in hours. Maybe days. He played in his head; he didn't need the visual aid of the pieces.

A black pawn and a knight in row one had the white king cornered.

"What the fuck is that knight doing there?"

"I promoted."

"Pawns are promoted to queens!"

"Not necessarily. You're allowed to promote to knight. Check."

Adrian closed up on the game. Without too much consideration, just like someone pushing the reset button, he had his king personally execute the black pawn.

His left hand immediately lifted the black knight and replaced the white king's rook.

"Check."

Adrian opened his mouth really wide. He didn't yell, but the next line came out of tune anyway.

"How did you— Did you even know what you were doing when you promoted to knight?"

"Not really. The pawn just wanted to be a knight."

"Nobody wants to be a knight! Everyone promotes to queen because it's the best piece!"

"It's my pawn; he can be whatever he wants as long as he's happy. And I'm winning thanks to him. Hey, this is the second time I beat you at chess!"

"You never beat me at chess before; you cheated! You took my queen with He-Man! And no one, *no one in their right mind* promotes to knight!"

By the end of that speech he was hunching menacingly over the board, his shadow's spidery fingers on the wall curled into evil claws above the round wooden heads of his embarrassed troops.

Outside, seagulls were warily returning to their posts on the crane.

When he looked back up, Adrian had spotted the key phrase.

"No one in their right mind."

Stripes of midmorning illuminated their right profile.

"That's it. He's all right brain," said Adrian in awe. "No reason—only passion. It's not business at all, it's not about justice.

He's not seeking balance. All he wants is to hurt. But to hurt . . . *(Mimes a gun with a hand.)* . . . by just killing people? No, of course not! He's hurting the father! It's not about murder, it's torture! He wants the father to suffer by killing his offspring!"

"Whoa—all of his offspring?" Zooey inserted. "Then we better warn Ursula before—"

The green eye summoned a frown over both.

The rest of the body attempted to move; Zooey prevented it by fastening her left foot to the floor.

"Wait. Ursula . . . was here?"

She focused on the door with the glass panel and the fresh shiny vinyl letters. Then her sight line shifted to the bed. Then to the guitar next to the bed. Then to the pillows, beyond her own raised hand, petrified like a wait cursor.

*(In a whisper.)* "What did you . . ."

Her green eye, fixed on the penumbra region by the bed, watched last night's movie replay. The bed scene. The toes. The check. The door.

The farewell speech.

Zooey winced.

Their knees bent, slouching away from the light. Her words rose like the last bubbles of breath from a drowning victim.

"What . . . How could you say that to her?"

Adrian pulled themselves together, stiffened up, commanded their chin to attention.

"I had to." *(Moves for the kitchen.)* "This was wrong—you know very well it was wrong." *(Opens a Pop-Tarts sachet, moves toward the toaster.)* "She's infatuated and you're enabling her. Someone had to slap some sense into her, so I did—without the actual slapping, by the way."

*(Inserts the Pop-Tarts into the slots, pushes down the lever. Then*

shoves their right hand into the slot, all the way down, scraping off the skin against the red-hot wire grill, and the left hand holds the right by the wrist, and the right arm wriggles and jolts while the left arm and shoulder and hip and leg lock it there and let the rest of the body shriek at the feeling of skin vaporizing into grilled-chicken smoke and the red flesh below simmering in its own blood for a whole second, two seconds, three seconds, four seconds, before a final jolt throws the toaster across the room, pulling the plug, and the whole body falls to the floor, gaping at their mutilated hand.)

(And then the unharmed left hand punches the skull into the floor.)

"How could you tell her that, you soulless monster?! She's a child! *She's only a child!!*"

(Adrian doesn't answer, all his strength focused on dodging the left fist's jabs while his own hand, in flesh and blood, lies palm-up on the floor twitching like a dying tarantula, and the feet fight each other, memories of the previous night still downloading for Zooey to see, now reaching Ursula's last line before Adrian slammed the door with the glass panel and the fresh shiny vinyl letters: "Zooey does love you.")

"NO, I DON'T!" Zooey yelled through both her and his tears. *"I DON'T LOVE YOU! I HATE YOU! I HATE YOU AND I HATE MYSELF, BECAUSE YOU DESERVE TO DIE ALONE AND I'LL BE STUCK HERE WITH YOU!!"*

(But Adrian isn't looking for excuses; he channels what little strength he still has to his elbow, the right one, as it pitifully tries to tug the whole body across the room, toward the desk, and Zooey's left hand is clawing at his side of the face as his right one pulls the top drawer off the desk, and the case with the syringes comes tumbling out, and Adrian manages to grab a syringe and stab her shoulder down to the bone, and then another syringe, and then another, and another, until the left arm has gone numb, jerking in spasms like a wounded snake, and even then he stabs the last syringe again and again and

*again and again die die die until the shoulder cramps and the muscles
beneath turn into jelly.)*

*(And then the cramp unexpectedly crawls up toward the neck, and
for one sudden, terrifying second his windpipe is paralyzed, but then as
though someone cut the noose it relaxes and his chest muscles liquefy and
the cramp marches on to the right side of the body and flows into the
arm, toward the elbow and the forearm and the charred, bloodied hand
pining for it, begging it to smother its frenzied nerves, and finally the
shock wave reaches the wrist and the thumb and splits into each of
the four phalanxes up to the roasted fingertips and it disconnects all
the alarms, every system inside the brain, every standby light, and the
orange-brown eye looks in to check all systems are off and yields to the
weight of its own eyelid and shuts down.)*

*(And Kimrean fades to black.)*

# 10

The lightspill from the window was lime colored, as though the sun had been hitchhiking in the rain and splashed by mud from a pickup truck and then three rednecks had jumped off the truck and beat him and left him bleeding in the ditch, and the sun was really angry about the whole incident.

The first thing Kimrean felt, long before seeing it, was their right hand, bloodied and grill-marked and polka-dotted with patches of exposed flesh.

They scrambled up, hissing, shielding the wound from floating particles.

"Ow! Pain! Pain pain pain pain pain."

With the help of what could pass for a clean piece of cloth, they improvised a bandage. There was not any liquor in the house (liquor having a life span of minutes whenever it entered the house), so they finally decided that their natural blood alcohol level would probably be enough to prevent infection. They swallowed a couple painkillers, washed them down with tap water, and finally scanned the tiger-striped office: living area, desk, chessboard.

"Right. Right!" shouted Zooey, stumbling back to her corner, fists up. "Okay, what were we fighting about again? I'm gonna kick your ass so far your turds will have jet lag."

She completed a full spin around their axis—a full day on planet Kimrean.

"Adrian?"

She stopped. Then she described a full circle again, counterclockwise, *without looking outside.*

"Ade?"

*(She stops, tilts her head.)*

"Adie Adie Adie?" *(Beat.)* "Dickhead?"

Something cracked under her sole when she stepped forward. She lifted her foot. It had been a syringe.

She touched her left shoulder. The pain in her right hand had pushed the mildly annoying needlestings way to the back, but the spots where the syringes had stabbed her arm stood out in plain sight. Five, six, seven of them.

Her green eye glinted and nudged the brown one to follow.

"Oh, you poor thing—you never knew how to do drugs. You overdosed on Diarctorol!"

She hollered at the ceiling, stretching her arms like someone seizing a double bed all for themself.

"Ooooh, yeah, baby! This calls for celebration! *(Takes a bottle of whiskey from the waste bin, confirms it's empty enough to belong there, tosses it again.)* Sleep tight, little boy. Mama will come home late tonight, oh yeah she will!"

She Hammer-timed all the way to the coat stand for her hat and waistcoat, put her business/party accessories on, and skipped back to the chessboard, where the remaining black pieces stood witness to the astonishing resurrection of their commander in chief.

"Ding-dong, motherfuckers. The witch is dead." *(Knocks down the white king; it crashes with an echoing boom among its jaw-dropped soldiers.)* "And I didn't need no He-Man this time. Tough luck, bro."

She cavorted out, grabbed the door handle, smiling at the fresh shiny vinyl letters, and stopped.

"Oooh. Wait."

*(Right hand raised, because, you know—wait!)*

"There was something else. A case. A mystery killer. 'No reason. Only passion.' A right-brainer. *(Strikes out a word on an imaginary blackboard.)* No executions. *(Circles one.)* Torture! He tortures the father. Kills his offspring. Offspring. 'And all the girls say I'm pretty fly, for a rabbi.' Ha! No, wait, that was Yankovic's take. Another prime example of a cover improving on the original. This could be a theme for a mix tape! *(Runs to the desk for paper and pencil, stops after two strides.)* No, wait wait wait wait. Right-brainer. Someone irrational. Someone sadistic. Someone unbalanced, taking on the whole cartel. Not business. Personal. Someone aggravated. A casual victim. Collateral damage."

She stared at the wall, arms akimbo, like a quantum physicist at a buzzing blackboard. Only the wall featured nothing but bullet holes.

*(Scoff.)* "Gosh, collateral damage from a drug cartel? That could be anyone. I mean, it could be—"

Every trace of a smirk left the building.

Outside the window, the universe stopped expanding.

"Holy Gandolfini."

The left hand clutched the skull, tried to squeeze it. Inside, Matrix source code was spilling in an avalanche of data.

"Oh, fuckity-fuck. *Ursula!*"

She dashed outside and forgot to close the door.

The corpse of the white king rolled off the chessboard and fell to the floor as Zooey's steps vanished down the stairwell.

Hotel Bohème was a ten-minute walk from A.Z.'s office or a three-minute sprint: Zooey ran all the way down Columbus Avenue, barely dodging the street musicians and tourists waiting for the trolley, and veered sharply into the narrow front door under the marquee. The air over the Bay Area was heavy with the apocalyptic gloom of any given Sunday evening.

She galloped up the red-carpeted stairs and hesitated on the landing, just long enough for a Michael Caine–type receptionist to pop out.

"Oh, Adrian! Is your friend in 210 staying another night?"

"No! She's checking out!"

She ran up another flight of stairs and bounced off two corridor corners. The lock on room 210 stopped her for good; she pounded on the door.

"Ursula! Ursula! Ursula! Ursula! Ursula! Ursula! Ursula!"

She had to wait almost a full second, pondering whether kicking down the door would put much of a strain on her friendship with the Michael Caine–type receptionist, before she heard the bolt click.

The door opened an inch, enough for Zooey to crash through, grab the child, and drag her like a football to the goal line.

"Ursy! I solved it! I think I solved it—maybe not for sure but let's say ninety percent with a fifty percent error margin or something but you gotta come with me you're in danger!"

Ursula processed the message, mentally adding the missing punctuation. She was wearing her second T-shirt and cradled a Kerouac book in her arms. The exiguous contents of her backpack and a couple shopping bags were spread over the quilt—paperbacks and enough soft drinks and snacks to kill a type-1 diabetic from long range. By the time Kimrean had taken in all those atmospheric details, the child was still reading into her eyes.

"Where's Adrian?" she asked.

"Dead. Or sleeping. Maybe. Doesn't matter. Come on, we gotta go."

She grabbed her arm; Ursula gaped at the ugly, badly dressed burns.

"Oh my God, Zooey, your hand!"

"Not my hand, don't worry; come on!"

She tugged again, but Ursula resisted. In fact, Zooey realized, Ursula did not seem overjoyed to see her. That was inconceivable.

"Is something wrong?"

The gap before the next line of dialogue immediately nodded: *There is.* A gossamer rustle from the bed canopy shushed down the room.

Ursula, an eleven-year-old in her own check-paid hotel room, lowered her head and said, "What do you care."

San Francisco had somehow gone silent.

Zooey knelt down, craned to make eye contact. "Of course I care. How could I not care? You're the femme fatale, remember?"

"No, I am not a femme fatale!" Ursula objected. "Adrian was right; I do nothing but wait around for my rescuer to save me, and then what? They'll take my parents, I'll have nothing left, but I guess it's okay because somehow you and I will just live happily ever after?"

She allowed a gap for snarky replies, knowing that she would get none.

"I'm just the girl. *A* girl. And as soon as you solve the case you'll discard me and forget all about me. You might as well drop me off now."

Zooey listened intently, brain visibly accommodating to follow the logic of the argument.

ZOOEY: Couldn't you just hold on a bit longer? 'Cause it's gonna be tricky to replace you now that the third act started; I could always ask Demoines, but—

URSULA: No, *I don't want to be replaced!*

ZOOEY: Then what do you want?!

"I just—" she false-started, and then she looked away, pressing Kerouac against her chest, and said, "I want a happy ending! I want to not be left on the curb by the end! I want to mean something to you, but I'm stuck in this role, and I hate being the girl!"

"Ursula, *I am* a girl!" Zooey proclaimed, pointing at herself, challenging anything in the room to contest her. "I am a girl, and I'm the detective! I have my office and my hat and my vinyl letters on the door, and I'm solving the shit out of this case! You can be anything you want—not the girl, not the femme fatale—anything! Besides, femme fatale is a bullshit cliché—it's a plot device that male genre writers use to ultimately blame all the violence and conflict on some outside force, because somehow in their manly mind-set it's more forgivable to make stupid decisions for the sake of a beautiful woman."

Ursula almost felt the pain of that offhand slam.

"You never said that the other day."

"I know," Zooey admitted. "I would never tear down something while you like it."

She closed up, one knee still on the carpet, lipless mouth in a sweet angle of a smile.

"Listen, I know you feel like a kite in a storm now. That's not because you're the girl, it's because you're a kid, and that's what being a kid is. But it gets better. You will take the reins. You'll write your own story. And I wouldn't miss it for the world, okay? I'm not leaving you on the curb. I am hooked. I care."

Ursula snorted, made sure not to sound weak when she ordered, "Promise."

"I promise," Zooey said, like it was the easiest dare in the world. "Right now I'm just trying to keep you alive long enough, okay?"

The hotel room held a respectful silence, and then waited to watch the kid's reaction.

Jack Kerouac on the back of the book against Ursula's chest breathed a little easier.

"Okay," she whispered, drying the last tear. "Good."

"Good," Zooey said, standing back up. "Fine."

She puffed out, glanced around the room, satisfied with her point.

And then she said, "Come on—my car is parked around the corner!" and clasped the off-guard kid's wrist and pulled her off her feet and out of the room like a flying kite.

The book fell on the carpet and Jack Kerouac heard them disappear down the corridor, Ursula yelling, "Zooey, wait! *You* are driving?!"


She was driving indeed, since there was no guarantee that Ursula could do it any better and it was actually likely she would not reach the pedals, but the trip was fairly uneventful. Perhaps one or two little life-before-your-eyes flashes while Steve McQueening down Nob Hill, and during a couple shortcuts through roads under construction where there weren't any workers anyway, but once they rushed through the last yellow lights out of the metro area, it was a smooth ride. Except for that tiny near-brush with that biker gang on the highway, of course, but that was really their fault for hogging all the lanes and for being such douchebags, as Zooey made sure to point out to each and every one of them while leaning out her window and replacing -*bag* with another suffix for each member. And that was pretty much it. It would be difficult to fit any more remarkable incidents into the thirty minutes it took Zooey to drive eighty miles, really.

It was still a long way to San Carnal when Zooey steered left like a heat-seeking ICBM, leaped off a curb that barely lifted the pony car six feet off the ground, and landed it onto the parking lot of a diner. *The* diner.

Zooey jumped out while Ursula, tangled in her seat belt, struggled to sit back upside up. Behind the diner's double doors, the few truckers ruminating in front of their coffee didn't have time to appreciate the dramatic fedoraed silhouette framed by the western sky; it strode in right away and confronted the violet-haired waitress who was mopping the floor.

"You, Frenchy! The girl you're filling in for, where is she?"

The woman with the name Cecilia embroidered on her uniform didn't seem to recognize her.

Zooey expanded: "I was here on Friday, asked you about the girl you're replacing. You said the surgery had gone well. She was shot. A stray bullet through that window hit her in the boob— I'm seeing the darn in your uniform right now. Where is Cecilia?"

"Wh-what?" she stammered. "Who are you?"

"Yeah, that happened," another waitress assisted from the counter. "One of the Lyon kids was here; they met with some Japanese gang outside and started shooting each other." She pointed at the brand-new panoramic window.

"Where is she now?"

"I guess she's still in the hospital."

"Right," Zooey said, asking over her shoulder on her way out, "Who responds to 911 calls from here—San Carnal Medical?"

"Yes, but she didn't take an ambulance—what's-her-name took her. Her girlfriend."

"Girlfriend?!"

"Yeah, she was here when it happened, saw the whole thing. She wouldn't wait for the ambulance—carried Cecilia to her van and they drove off."

"A flower delivery van?" Zooey guessed, turning back to the doors that Ursula was just coming through. "Thanks!"

And she snatched the child by the collar and tugged her back to the car.

Half an hour and seventeen serious violations later, the Camaro parked in front of the emergency entrance of San Carnal Medical Center on 12th Street under the Palm Expressway. This time around, Ursula was quick enough to jump out of the car, close both doors, and follow Zooey into the main building only ten seconds behind her. They raced past the waiting room filled with ghostly eyed citizens passing the evening there, all holding alien objects lodged inside their bodies or having accidentally run into bullets too fast, and Zooey flashed her badge in the general direction of the admissions desk.

"I'm looking for a patient, name Cecilia, came in Monday night with a bullet wound."

The avian clerk put the glasses on her beak and started typing away with annoying meticulousness, but another girl who was just leaving the nurses' station with a coat and handbag was faster. "Cecilia the redhead? Are you family?"

"Am I?" Zooey gaped, consulting with Ursula. "Wow, that would be some twist, wouldn't it? Well, a little too forced maybe. Let's say no."

"They released her about an hour ago," the nurse said. She was Latina, around thirty, with thirty-five-year-old eye bags—the kind of professional whose attitude says, *I am a very nice person but also the one who decides where to give you your injections, so don't try me.* "We told her to stay another day, but she insisted on leaving."

"Do you know where?"

"No. But they left some stuff in the room."

"Number?"

"You can't go in outside visiting hours," the avian clerk nagged.

"Can you show me?" Zooey rephrased.

The nurse sighed and started taking off her coat.


They exited the elevator on the seventh floor, the nurse leading the way, followed by Zooey, followed by Ursula. Zooey caught the scent of chlorophenol as soon as she stepped on the corridor.

"We couldn't reach her family," the nurse narrated. "Only the girl who brought her came to see her. More like never left, really. You don't see that often."

"You mean, between friends?" Zooey queried.

"'Friends,'" she repeated, amused. "More like between humans. You see devout wives, desperate mothers . . . but this girl . . . God forgive me, she was like a dog. You know, that kind of purely instinctive loyalty? She stood outside the surgery room while they removed the bullet. She lived here on this floor all week. She washed the patient, she helped her to the toilet, she barely spoke to anyone else. And every time she popped downstairs, even for a half hour, she always came back running out of breath and bringing a gift. We all thought it was weird—like psychological abuse or something."

"Did you report it?"

"No. I did bring it up to the patient, though, once. She waved it away. In fact said she'd do the same for her."

"This friend, did she leave Monday night?"

"Uh . . . yes, that was after the surgery; patient was in ICU, so they kicked her out."

"Friday night?"

"Yes."

"How about this morning, eight to ten?"

"Yes! Maybe she went to work; she drove a delivery van."

"Did she look okay after Friday, or more like she'd been grazed by a bullet to the ribs?" The nurse seemed taken aback by the slightly loaded question, but Zooey found the answer on her own. "Yeah, right—and she had bandages and painkillers readily available, so . . . Did you catch her name?"

"Yeah," the nurse searched. "Something with *J* . . . Joanne . . . No, Juno!"

"Five-five, light build? Could she pass for an Asian boy?"

"Yes, totally. Except for the blue eyes. Actually, I think she was Asian, like, Siberian, you know? Like an Eskimo."

"*Eskimo!*" Zooey yowled, startling both Ursula and a woman pushing a cart of linen. "Damn, Native Alaskan was my third option!"

"Right, Cecilia mentioned her family was back in Alaska. Anyway, here, this is it." She pushed the door numbered 714 and waved them in. "I'm glad I'm back, actually. I meant to take a picture before they clean it out."

Zooey stepped in, absorbed the atmosphere, and felt almost like she could cry with joy at the sight of the glowing red room.

Roses. Roses on the bedside table. Roses on the windowsill. Roses concealing the armchair and smothering the oxygen supply. Roses haloing the headboard and spilling over the pillows, slithering along the rails and swooning off the foot of the mattress like a flowery waterfall; roses climbing over the switchboards and creeping up the tubes; three out of four walls colonized by roses. Roses bleeding out of the bathroom; roses stamping on roses; roses raped by roses. An orgy of roses, a biblical plague of roses, the Wars of the Roses of roses. Every scar-textured, blood-colored petal glaring at the temple raiders from every corolla in every bunch in a hive-minded swarm of roses.

An unmitigated, unreproducible curse word came out of Ursula's mouth.

Zooey, clutching her head in amazement, green and brown eyes gleaming with bliss, could utter nothing but a sportive, honestly admiring, one-mad-person-to-another chuckle.


After a new ellipsis, Zooey and Ursula were back on the road, testing the indulgence of traffic laws in downtown San Carnal.

"I knew it!" Zooey chanted, banging on the wheel. "She's the perfect match! Introverted, invisible, cut off from mankind except for one person, one soulmate that she can communicate with and goes on to fill every role: sister, friend, lover—her only mediator with the outside world. I tell you, I've seen guys like this before;

there's one in every nuthouse. They usually end up smothering their mediators or killing them out of jealousy, but these two—oh, they make the perfect storm! Just picture Juno: young gay native girl raised in a rural godforsaken state? The amount of shit she must have taken, the anger she's holding inside! But this Cecilia knows how to tame her! Did you hear the nurse? Didn't that strike you as very zen? 'Someone shot me in the tit, my girlfriend's going crazy, but it's okay?' That's a chillingly cool head. *(Understanding.)* That is Juno's left brain, right there. And Mikey and his men almost removed it from her."

"I don't get it," said Ursula, trying to ignore the speed at which they were stealing off the expressway, under an ovation of eighteen-wheelers. "So she killed Mikey because he shot her girlfriend by mistake? Why did she kill the others?"

"Because one body's not enough!" Zooey raved over the roar of a fire truck they were overtaking. "You and I would kill Mikey and move on—we're easygoing like that. But for Juno, it doesn't equate. It's not a life for a life, because Cecilia is not just a person, she's her voice of reason, her god! Did you see that room? That wasn't a room; it was a shrine! And Mikey is nothing, he's less than a person; to Juno, he's a by-product. Her own past determines her view of the problem: it's not just Mikey, it's the system that made Mikey, it's the communities that raise bullies, it's Victor Lyon's fault! So she takes out the spawn first, just to show him, and then she'll kill him last!" She continued to slap the steering wheel like she would a horse, ignoring the Camaro's pleas for clemency. "Oh, it's so good! Everyone was thinking of cartels and power struggles, they thought we were in a Mafia movie, but we're not! We're in a one-woman-against-the-world movie—it's a crossover! She's Kevin Bacon in *Death Sentence*!

Denzel Washington in *The Equalizer*! Liam Neeson in *Taken*! But you had to think in genre principles to see the pattern, see? That was me! Remember this: Adrian didn't solve this one— I did! I detected this one!"

URSULA: Wait a minute—so now that she's done with my brothers, she's gonna take out my father?

ZOOEY: Sure, now that Cecilia's safely home? I bet she's heading to Villa Leona right now!

URSULA: And you're driving *me* there?!

*(Zooey's mouth vanishes from her face in the blink of an eye.)*

*(Pause.)*

ZOOEY: Okay. See? This is the kind of thing that Adrian *is* good at.

Too few minutes later, the screeching Camaro swerved out of Palm Drive at a speed never seen outside the *Fast & Furious* franchise, bowling through a set of poorly placed trash cans, and revved onto a dirt road that stretched through a modest grove of inbred pines and then a corrugated desert flanked by cacti, heading for the tender cyan shadow of yet another moody Sunday night.

Danny Mojave, sitting atop the sentry booth in Villa Leona, registered the incoming yellow-striped blue car through his binoculars. He put them down and gazed naked-eyed at the sunset. He felt the angst of Sunday evening in his bones. The undone top buttons in his shirt exposed a crimson mark around his neck, where a nylon rope had almost choked him to death that morning. The day might die, but this souvenir from it was a stayer.

Tiredly, he stood up and signaled the sentries to open the

gate. The blockade of gangsters wielding $250K worth of black market military-grade weaponry moved aside to allow Kimrean and Ursula into the last bastion of the Lyon family.

Zooey drove up the slope to the garage, but veered off the first curve and ruined some thirty yards of lawn and two flocks of petunias before pulling up near the outer brick wall, behind a hedge and a small kiosk, hidden from both the front gate and the main building. She keyed off the engine, exited the vehicle, and pointed a dictatorial finger at Ursula before she could follow.

"Get in the backseat, lie down, and whatever happens, do not leave the car. Ever. You're trying to stay off the clichés, so don't become the child who leaves the shelter to stroll right into the epicenter of the disaster, because that's the absolute worst."

"How do you know the killer won't come for my father, then steal this car to escape and take me along?" Ursula asked.

Zooey granted the scenario a full second, then answered: "Because now that you said it aloud, it's unlikely to happen."

She slammed the driver's door and ran back to the front gate, where the soldiers had retaken their positions, watchful of the bleeding western horizon.

"Okay, listen everybody," Zooey called. "Bad news is it's not the yakuza—it's something worse. Good news is . . . *(Thinks.)* Sorry, there is no good news. I was just trying to give positive reinforcement."

The few soldiers who had seemed to care resumed their duties while Zooey nodded to herself reassuringly: "Good pep talk."

Danny came to join her in the back lines.

"You know who it is?"

"Yes. Remember the civilian Mikey shot in the diner in neutral land? Congrats, you angered a lesbian in love. It's okay—it's a common mistake."

Danny frowned.

"What are you talking about?"

"The waitress whose tit you blew off on Monday? Her name is Cecilia. It's her girlfriend, Juno."

"What . . . How's she connected to this?!"

Zooey paused, considered reordering the words. "She's Cecilia's girlfriend."

"You said this was personal!"

"It is. You guys shot Cecilia."

"And the girlfriend happens to be a trained assassin?!"

"No, nothing that interesting. She's from Alaska."

"Are you telling me a random woman just waltzed into Villa Leona to kill Mikey Lyon?"

"No, you showed her the way in," Zooey said. "Every time you need to make a private call or smoke one of your hand-rolled specials, instead of the Newports you smoke when you're in business mode, you go to the north side of the fence, because it's private and has phone signal. How many times did you go there the day after the shooting? All she had to do was watch: you showed her the safest route in and out."

Danny listened, took a minute to gain control of his mouth again for the follow-up: "What about the cameras at the club?"

"She passed two out of four in rotation. Her odds were good: she had a . . . 56.25 percent chance of missing both. *(Shakes her head.)* Oh, wow. Is this what the left brain is for? *(Checks again.)* Holy shit. Math is fun!"

"But what about the chrysanthemum?!"

"It's a rose! She delivers flowers and she likes those roses a lot. It was a coincidence; this was all about revenge."

"Revenge?!" cried Danny. "She gunned down six men because one stray bullet killed her girlfriend?!"

"Oh, no, it didn't kill her—she was just released from the hospital."

Danny wandered away from the conversation, rubbing his forehead, his mien like that of a man who is ready to walk out of the theater and ask for his money back.

"But . . ." he tried, turning to give the narrator a last chance. "I mean, now she's gonna come and kill the crime lord of Southern California because some asshole shot her girlfriend?"

"Yes," Zooey said. She was perfectly at peace with the simplicity of the whole plot. "I mean, she came here once already, and she's better equipped this time, so . . . I don't know, it's what I would do."

"All right," Danny puffed. "Tell me, what can we do to stop her?"

"Well, it's a little late to send her chocolates and a get well card, so—"

"Zooey, shut up! Adrian, what can we do?"

"Uh . . . Adrian's not home. Care to leave him a message?"

"What . . . what do you mean 'not home'?"

"Yeah, we had a fight, and . . . I won!"

"Zooey, *where is Adrian?*"

"I'm glad you asked, because the answer calls for many beautiful, symbol-rich analogies: remember that episode from *Buffy the Vampire Slayer* where Buffy goes catatonic or something and Willow has to get inside her head and in her memories Buffy is just placing the same book on a shelf over and over again? Okay, well, it's not like that at all."

"ZOOEY!"

"Listen, we don't need Adrian, okay?" Zooey appeased him. "I found out who the killer is, I know how she thinks, and I'm the one who knows what she's going to do next. So, where is the Lyon?"

"In the mansion, with four other men and two more by the door."

"Move him to the pool house. This time she's taking the mansion."

"How? I thought she only brought what weapons she found from the previous scene."

"Yeah, that's my point: in the previous scene she got a tank."

She pointed west, right before the sentries spotted the lone white dot against the purple farewell of the day. The camera shot off Kimrean's index finger and zoomed across .74 miles of desert into Xander's bulletproof Jaguar in the middle of the dirt road, just as the driver in a balaclava rolled back her electric-blue eyes with the last scent from the *Erithra lunis* caressing her nose, then tossed the flower on the seat to her right, next to the Taurus BA-44, cracked her knuckles, gripped the steering wheel, and floored the gas.

A Tokyo-razing roar burst from the engine and the tires kicked up a ballpark's worth of dirt in dust-cloud form the second before the 1.7-ton luxury missile gunned straight into Villa Leona.

"Go!" shouted Zooey, bumping Danny off the front row, over the chorus of clicking guns and gritting teeth. "Get the kingpin out of there, now!"

Among the horde of the badly shaved, badly suited, sunglassed men forming the army, a late '70s beach bully with sideburns and in brown corduroys, acting as second-in-command, stepped in as soon as Danny left running for the mansion and barked a commendably simple order: "Stop that car!"

A cloud of parrots scampered off the palm trees at the break of thunder: every rock, every pebble, every grain of sand of the desert shook with the rumbling orchestra of machine guns being fired at the one-woman cavalry half a mile ahead and incoming, like a louder, meaner version of the credits shot for *Knight Rider*. Just as fast. Just as fearless. Just as symbolic of the end of all things.

"My money's on the car," Zooey confided to Sideburns. "No offense."

"None taken," the commander answered, before he shouted over his shoulder: "Bring the jalapeños!"

The back row of the blockade gave way to a big, long-haired goon with the kind of mustache that automatically bans you from working within five hundred feet of a school, dragging a large khaki suitcase with Cyrillic characters stenciled on it. Kimrean could not contain an excited "ooh" and some clapping when she identified the Russian RPG-7 the grunt was now bringing into the battle. Two other men helped him support the six-foot rocket launcher between the bars of the front gate, while Big 'Stache loaded an anti-tank grenade and propped himself on one knee, ready to fire.

Juno, flying against the bulletstorm clinking off the Jaguar's bodywork like horizontal hail, shifted to fifth and lowered her side window. The thunderous noise of the 140 mph desert wind flooded in.

"On my signal," Sideburns ordered. "Hold it . . ."

Juno pulled the key out of the starter.

"Hold it . . . !"

She stuck her hand out the window, 7.6-caliber rounds whizzing by her exposed, skinny arm.

"Hold . . . !"

Even at that rapidly abridging distance, Zooey could tell she wasn't holding a gun.

That point was confirmed when an unattended green LED flared up on the security gate's control board, and the hinges clacked and squeaked to life.

". . . Fffffuck!"

Sideburns aborted the order as the gates swung inward, forcing the gunmen to move back, dragging the rocket launcher stuck between the bars, causing the operator to tip off-balance and sway the weapon to aim into friendly lines. Lyon's troops scattered, bumping against the moving gates and surrendering to chaos.

Zooey checked the car again, which she had averted her eyes from for exactly one second. It had come so much closer!

An instinct she'd forgotten she possessed made her scram instead of staying in the first row.

Amid Sideburns's hysteric cries as he stood right in the RPG's line of fire, Big 'Stache was still struggling to pry the weapon from the moving gate, until with a final teeth-gritting yank he pulled it out, and in the same movement fell on his ass, and the weapon discharged.

With a basilisk hiss, the rocket launcher spat a grenade in a perfect vertical, followed by a twirling trail of blue smoke that Sideburns watched ascend and disappear into the remote twilight sky.

And just as he looked back to ground level, the Jaguar knocked him into the stratosphere. Juno hardly caught a glimpse of him flying way above the hood like a bumped mailbox as she swerved up the slope to the main building, not even dreaming of tapping the brake.

The rest of the scattered sentries regrouped and resumed firing at the car's tail, while the artillery guy, lying faceup on the ground, wiped the gravel from his eyes and scrutinized the sky.

Up there, in the starry silence above the gunfire, the rocket-propelled grenade coughed up the last fumes of fuel, reached the zenith of its trajectory—wings spread out, tail still smoking—and came to a glorious stop at the top of its parabola. Then it gracefully bowed back, gently rotating around its axis, and let gravity pull it back to earth, hardly a couple yards from its takeoff point—actually very close to the khaki army case where it came from and the remaining grenades waiting for their turn, which, incidentally, would never come.

The explosion swallowed and regurgitated in the same hundredth of a second the gate and the entry booth, much of the fence, two lime trees, and fourteen people.

From the mansion, the view of the west side of the villa going up in a Superdome of flames, hurling chunks of fence out of the state, made the sight of the Jaguar swerving off the garden path and charging at the building almost pale in comparison.

The guards at the front door barely had time to appreciate the homicidal maniac's cyan eyes before a reflex act, as symptomatic of their inclement childhoods on the streets as it was stupid in practice, made them fire instead of jumping out of the luxury tank's path.

Look up from this page and imagine a car in the room where you are right now. Imagine how close to the ceiling it would stand. Picture it in frontal view (a big, boastful, midlife-crisis-palliating luxury sedan), try to frame it in the doorway, and imagine the technical difficulties that simply allowing that monstrosity into the room would pose and how little space you would have left.

And now imagine it moving. Imagine it coming through that inconvenient, non-customized door, at the speed you reach when overtaking a trailer truck on the highway. Imagine the momentum of that steel-and-aluminum mammoth entering the room where you are, whether there's a doorway or not.

That happened in Villa Leona.

And it took the house three whole partitions to stop it.

In its wake lay a razed foyer, the living room from Chapter 3, ten hunting trophies, a minibar, a full bar, a dining room for twenty people, four people, and the best part of a $200,000 titanium kitchen.

The dust had not even considered settling, and in fact boulders of concrete were still flumping from the ceiling onto the hood of the vehicle, when Juno popped through the sunroof, shot the thug taking shelter in the meeting room, fired several rounds toward the spiral stairs (which were not typically visible from there) until she hit the kneecaps of a second thug she'd heard coming, then spun at the noise of cracking glass behind her to find a maid stumbling out of the ruins of a pantry and shouted her own trigger finger to stay put.

She puffed—more like gasped—then stayed there, every single muscle tensed, panting like she'd just washed up on the beaches of Normandy, a similar landscape of ruin and destruction surrounding her brittle figure sticking out the top of the tank. She shook the adrenaline and the mortar from her shoulders and shooed the maid away like a fly off a cake. The woman scuttled away through what was left of the service door.

Another figure crashed in through the devastated dining room, gun in hand, catching the assailant unaware.

"FREEZE!"

Juno turned anyway. Kimrean was coming around the car,

pointing a gun at her while skipping between fragments of ceiling. Suddenly, she seemed to notice the semiautomatic she had borrowed from one of the corpses outside. She peeped down inside the barrel.

"Is this loaded?"

She pulled the trigger; there was a click.

"Okay." She tossed the weapon and grinned at the astonished enemy. "Imagine if I didn't check and found out it's empty when I meant to fire—I'd feel pretty stupid then, right?"

Juno hopped out of the car, shoved Zooey against a pillar, and inserted three inches of Brazilian gun barrel into her mouth. Zooey could feel the burning steel tip grazing her uvula as she stared into the same electric-blue eyes she had confronted earlier in Xander's penthouse. Her balaclava needed fixing; Juno chose to tear it off altogether. The eyes matched a clay-colored, indecisive face, spectacularly young. Short oil-black hair. Five-foot-five—considerably shorter than A.Z. Her feet did look small.

"Who are you?" she inquired.

"Eyheekiwea," Zooey tried, before standing on her toes to distance herself from the gun. "I said A. Z. Kimrean, private eyes. You can call me Zooey."

"I will." She pushed the gun half an inch farther up her throat: "Where's Victor Lyon, Zooey?"

Zooey humbly requested some room for phonation, gagged out some spit, then answered.

"Okay, first off, let me tell you I'm super impressed with your m.o.; you—" She aborted the praise when Juno pressed the barrel tip against her lower jaw. "Right, right, okay, look, I'm usually not this easygoing but you caught me on a particularly positive day, and since I see you and I are a lot alike, I thought maybe we could agree to solve this peacefully if I tell you that Mr. Lyon is hiding in the pool h—"

Juno cut her off again, this time by striking her with the butt of the gun. Kimrean dropped knocked out on the ruins.

Then the killer gazed through the shattered windows, toward the swimming pool and the little path that led to the bungalow. Some ninety yards away, she reckoned.

Better take the car.


From the pool house, a box hedge partially blocked the view of the mansion. The last thing they had clearly spied from there was the explosion at the gates; the rising pyrocumulus was probably visible from Nevada. News of the Jaguar sodomizing the main building they had inferred only from a humongous dust cloud from that direction—accompanied by a similar sound to that of Genghis Khan riding into Samarkand.

They were three people listening, technically hiding: Victor Lyon, Danny Mojave, and a bodyguard who does not merit a name because he will most likely be dead in the next page.

Victor sat in a dull armchair, a gun on his lap and his sight wandering around a bowl of fruit. A pear stared back at him.

"Where is my daughter?" he asked softly.

Danny, on the lookout by the north window wielding a submachine gun, was caught unprepared by the tone of his voice: still solemn, but nonetheless surrendering.

"She's safe," he answered.

The Lyon sighed, pitifully. "Do you think there will be anything left to leave her?"

Danny bit his tongue: he was just remembering a minor plot

twist in the penthouse, minutes before Xander was shot. The distant revving of the Jaguar beyond the double glass doors absolved him from answering.

"Are they coming?"

Danny tried the radio again. "Mendes. What's your status?"

The hedge was blocking the garden path, but he heard again the sound of debris stirring and a car pulling back.

"Mendes?" he insisted. "Somebody! What is happening out there?"

There was no answer. No other noise from the outside.

But then, beneath the pregnant silence, Danny felt a timid trepidation, like the first warning tremor household pets sense before a big earthquake.

The car purred again, far away. Danny turned and faced the bodyguard standing in front of the fireplace. He saw the mirror over the mantelpiece. He saw his reflection's weapon, aiming at him. He saw, in the line of fire, Mikey's red rose trembling in its vase on the mantelpiece.

He saw the rose and the vase and the mirror and the fireplace and the bodyguard blown into smithereens, and while the shock wave slapped him off his feet and toward the bedroom, he even caught sight of the Jaguar that had just appeared in the middle of the room.

Victor Lyon was gripping his pistol at that moment, but the entrance had caught him by surprise anyway: he stumbled up so fast he didn't hear his spine reminding him to grab his cane. He gripped his pistol at the same exact moment that Juno squiggled through the sunroof and pointed her Taurus at him, shouting at the top of her lungs. "Put it down!"

"You put it down!"

"I'll fucking kill you!"

"Do you think I give a fuck anymore?!"

"Do you think I *ever* did?!"

Danny groaned up to his feet, found himself in the middle of the standoff with way too many fucks to give. His weapon was lost to the ruins like a five-year-old in a mall. He timidly raised his hands.

A breeze came in through the newly opened hole, sweeping the brick dust to the whistling of an Ennio Morricone tune.

Juno, holding the Taurus with one hand, reached inside the car, retrieved something from the dashboard and lifted it to her face for the audience to see. The red petals exalted the blue of her Neptune eyes.

The Lyon's gun didn't quiver. His mouth did. To Danny, the legendary Victor Lyon, the man behind the '74 Takeover, looked like a plain old man—another pink, Bismarck-mustached senior citizen from Florida in a Panama hat and unforgivable shirt, miscast in a gangster role.

He pronounced one word, painfully close to a whimper: "Why?"

The girl scoffed with something that didn't remotely pass for amusement.

"Why, you ask? 'Oh, why did this happen to me?'" she mocked, with the flimsy voice of a coal-smudged orphan in Dickens's London. "'I worked so hard to get here. Fought so long to build this. How can my story of struggle and success end this way?'" She snorted. "You think it's unfair, don't you?"

She was breathing faster now; she noticed and steadied the gun with both hands.

"Do you want a real story? I met . . ."

False start. She swallowed, started again.

"I met Cecilia when we were eleven. I was a dirty commie

immigrant to a Christian community in Alaska. She was the reverend's daughter. The second we locked eyes, we knew the rest of the universe was context. I endured their daily insults, for her. I stopped punching back, for her. I left my family for her. They caught us kissing in a barn. I was beaten. By teenagers. She was flown to North Carolina and put in a torture chamber masquerading as a Christian boarding school for deviant children. I rose from my ashes for her. I set their farms on fire for her. I hiked across the winter tundra for her. I lost toes for her! The day I rescued her and she made love to me, I knew neither of us would ever long for anything else, that we could live without warmth and food and air as long as we had each other. I worked a strip club for her. I wrestled hobos for her. I have crawled coast to coast through the sewers of this kingdom of bigots, bullies, and bipedal maggots, this place you anuses call the land of opportunity, to carry her in my arms to San Francisco, so we could be left alone. And we made it.

"And then one night, after my twelve-hour shift carrying dirt in a garden center, I drive to the diner where she works to give her a rose and drive her home, as I always do . . . and out of nowhere comes this coked-up punk. He orders a hamburger, insults her, points a gun at me, and then leaves, and ten minutes later he starts shooting at the diner from the parking lot like it's a stall in a carnival. They gun her down! Just like that! And no one even notices! They don't give a shit! Not him, not any of your spoiled children, not you! Do you think your business is the main plot of the universe, and the rest of us are just sitting here like disposable extras to add a splash of color when you blow off our heads?! Well, I'M FUCKING NOT!! You, and your family of amoral cunts, are accessories in *my* story, and I'm weeding you out! Do you hear me?! I killed all three shitstains that were your sons! I shot them down like the damaged animals they were! *I razed in one week what it took you a life to build, so weep! Weep like a man for what a woman stole from you, you weak, disgusting, laughable old shit!*"

A stone that was, against all odds, still sitting on top of another one tumbled down, announcing a new entrance.

ZOOEY: Okay! I heard enough!

Kimrean, a blue-purple bruise blooming around her left cheekbone, stepped in through the front door, preceded by a new gun to join the standoff. She chose a nice unobstructed spot, equidistant to the other two weapons and close to Danny, who asked her, "How long have you been here?"

"Awhile," she answered, keeping Juno in her crosshairs. "She was at the bit with the kiss in the barn when I arrived, so I stood by in case the story got saucy."

JUNO: *(Smiles.)* Hey, Zooey. Did you check the gun this time?

ZOOEY: No. I realized it's stupid to waste a round to check, so from now on I'll just trust my luck.

DANNY: *(At the top of his lungs.)* But why don't you just release the magazine and look?!

*(Pause.)*

ZOOEY: Oh. Okay, I'll try that next time. *(To Juno.)* Easy there, honey. You still need to look after Cecilia.

Juno had not yet had the courtesy to aim back at Kimrean, although she was showing definite interest now.

"How did you find me?" she asked.

"I used my imagination," Zooey replied. "The little things just fit. Like the fact that Mikey recognized you when you climbed through his window. Or the fact that you hesitated when you were running out of the club after Frankie, because your instinct was to stand in line for the ladies' room. By the way, the lost toes thing?" she said, aside to Danny. "That explains the shoe being too big for her foot size."

"Yeah, I got that, thank you."

"Okay. Just making sure." She returned to Juno. "It was a nice puzzle, all in all. But since you're so adamant on giving your stories a happy ending, you ought to know that the good guys must always win."

"These people aren't the good guys."

"The old one isn't." She head-signaled at Danny. "This one is."

That line made a couple guns waver and a few eyebrows rise. Juno's Taurus slowly shifted toward the unarmed man with the curly hair.

"I know him," Juno said, not bothering to hide the quiver in her voice anymore. "He was there, in the diner. He was with that asshole while he harassed Cecilia."

"You might remember I was trying to calm him down," Danny tried.

"Not fucking hard enough!" Juno yelled. "You are all the same scum!"

"Actually, he's nothing like them," Zooey said. "He's a cop."

She took a moment then to watch the reactions. Juno said nothing. Danny said nothing. Victor Lyon said nothing. But the Jaguar with its Rocky-at-the-end-of-each-movie countenance seemed to gape at the revelation.

"What?" said Juno in a soft voice.

"What?" Victor echoed, very loudly.

Danny whispered, "Zooey, why don't you go to sleep?"

"I'm serious," Zooey resumed. "He's been undercover for eighteen months!"

"San Carnal cops are no better than the mob," Juno retorted, gun dangerously shivering in her hands.

"He's not with San Carnal. He's from San Francisco. Just like you girls."

That line, for some strange reason, made the Lyon boil up.

"YOU!" His gun had swerved ninety degrees and was aiming at Danny's skull—if shoving two inches of barrel into the target's hair counts as aiming.

DANNY: Zooey . . .

ZOOEY: C'mon, we were stuck! Let's stir it up a little more, see where it takes us.

VICTOR: *(Shouting, into Danny's ear.)* I trusted you with my son's life! You traitor!

JUNO: You are both lying!

"Juno," Zooey called. "Listen to me. They've been working the Lyon family for a year. They're purging San Carnal too. But they need the old man alive, so you can't kill him. And Danny is a good guy, so you can't kill him either."

"You're lying!"

"I don't lie. Even this room is bugged."

VICTOR: WHAT?!

Zooey ignored him, her attention and her gun on the girl atop the car. "I'm serious. You can check yourself. There's a framed portrait under your front left tire; there's a hidden mike in it. The FBI's listening right now from a paint store on 10th Street. Good agents, Marlow and Dawes. They must be on their way right now, if they're not too busy making passionate love on the desk. *(Shouting at the portrait on the floor.)* And if you are, I'm so happy for you guys, but come here anyway!"

Juno swallowed something the size of a golf ball.

"Show me," she ordered.

Zooey lowered her gun, picked up the picture of nine-year-old Mikey and his mom, and took some pleasure in carelessly smashing the glass against the car hood. From behind the photograph she scraped off a black plastic circle, half an inch across, and showed it to the audience. No one needed any more clues.

There is a first time for everything: Zooey was, unbelievably, the coolest head in the room at that moment.

Danny, on the other hand, could feel a zero Kelvin drop of sweat freeze his spine. Victor's hands as he gripped his own gun showed symptoms of imminent heart failure. Juno had trouble breathing again. Her breast heaved with every intake of air. Tears were building up in her eyes. She compelled herself to take a deep breath—and hold it. Her pulse steadied.

Then she turned the gun ten degrees to the right and shot Victor Lyon.

By the time the drug lord fell to the floor, everyone in the room had comprehended the strategy behind that move: the shot wasn't lethal, but it would be in a few minutes. She had avoided the vital organs, but not the main arteries; he would bleed to death.

Juno then aimed at Zooey, blue irises sparkling, brimming with pride, a demented smile distorting her gentle traits.

"You need him alive? Then *run!*"

Zooey didn't argue; she tossed the gun and ran to attend to the old man. The cleanness of the wound didn't stop it from hurting like hell; the Lyon had not ceased yelping since he'd hit the floor. It intensified when Zooey used a tablecloth lying around to apply a tourniquet.

The next move was a little harder to follow but still masterful: Juno got off the car and shot Danny in the leg.

Danny screamed only once, more out of surprise than actual pain, and fell down as Juno rushed to grab him and put the gun to his temple. Zooey lurched for Victor's gun, but Juno uh-uh-uh'ed her out of it.

"Just kick it away," Juno ordered.

Zooey obeyed, staring with renewed admiration. The hostage—were he able to stand—had at least ten inches on his kidnapper. The difference showed even now. Juno noticed it; she thought it was funny.

"Since there are real cops after me now, I'll have to hold on to this one until we're in the clear," she explained. Her eyes shone free of any trace of caution.

"Seems fair," Zooey said.

Juno helped/dragged Danny to the Jaguar and kicked him onto the backseat.

"On the floor, facedown!"

Zooey nodded in acknowledgment: he would be as good as hogtied trapped there on the floorboard between the seats. Juno slammed his door, climbed in front, and as she sat down at the wheel she remembered about the present she was bringing.

She leaned out the window and tossed the last *Erithra lunis*. It landed gently on Victor Lyon's stomach.

"Pleasure meeting you, Zooey."

"Same here," said Zooey. She meant it.

The engine wheezed through the first two tries of the ignition key, but on the third it finally harrumphed to a triumphant start. Juno smiled through the chickenpoxed windscreen, winking at Kimrean like, *Hey, fuck plausibility, right?*

Zooey gave her an admiring thumbs-up.

The car reversed into the garden like a stuffed elephant head on a wall would, leaving an astonishing gaping hole opening onto the starry night. It pulled a U-turn on the lawn, ruining the azaleas, and it rolled away, speeding down the garden path toward the beautiful smoking wildfire in the general area of what had once been the front gate.

The aroma of blood made Zooey pop back from her amazement to more pressing matters: she tightened the tourniquet around Victor's shoulder, whose screaming had long ago remitted into a raspy gasp. A large red stain mitigated his Hawaiian shirt.

"FBI will get here in ten minutes. Try and hang in there," Zooey told him. "I know I should stay, but I really like Danny better than you."

She showed the courtesy of leaving properly through the front door and disappeared.

Lying on the ashes of his empire, the Lyon reined in his breathing. He attempted some movement: his right arm was out of discussion. And he would definitely require the strength of both arms to sit up.

His left one, scanning the rubble, bumped into a gun. The one the crazy P.I. girl had carried in.

That feeling, the loyal touch of steel, granted him some peace.

There wasn't much left to deliberate. The FBI was on its way. A soft melody of fires crackling and crickets singing between the azaleas would serve as background to the curtain fall.

Victor Lyon thanked the moment with a tear.

He put the gun to his mouth, and squeezed the trigger.

Zooey popped her head back in through the hole in the west wall.

"Oh, by the way—I can tell whether a gun's empty by its weight. I'm not stupid, you know."

And she scurried off.

Victor dropped the gun by his side a few seconds later and stared at the remains of the ceiling. A teeming firmament spied between the roof beams, following the whole story that was developing down on Earth, and as the stars looked at the old man lying there in the wrecked pool house, they said, *Look at that extra.*

Kimrean reached the front gate in time to catch a glimpse of a single red taillight shrinking into the western horizon. That was far beyond the warped metal and stumps of pillars that constituted the gate proper, dotted here and there with burning bodies.

Kimrean ran on toward the dark end of the garden, hopped inside the parked Camaro, and keyed the engine to life. Ursula jack-in-the-boxed between the front seats:

"What happened?"

*"Shit!"* Zooey jolted. "The fuck are you doing here?!"

"You told me to stay!"

"Right. I knew that." She reversed the car onto the driveway, offering Ursula her first view of what she'd had only red glows and booming sounds to hint at.

"Oh my God, what happened here?" she cried at the sight of the desolation. "Why is everything on fire?! What happened to my dad?!"

"Oh, don't worry, he'll live. *(Shifts gears.)* In prison, that is."

And she gunned the car down the slope, rolling over debris that had probably been alive some minutes ago.

They hit the desert, and in far less time than the car manufacturer claimed they were doing 120 on the dirt road toward downtown San Carnal. By the time Ursula had fastened her seat belt, they were back on asphalt, traversing a residential neighborhood and flowing onto a neon avenue, causing much sensation among the bystanders and the many other vehicles that swiftly made room for them by climbing onto the sidewalks and headbutting the parked cars. At that point, feeling at ease on the wide, well-paved roads of downtown, Zooey deemed it safe to speed up.

Ursula didn't see much of the race through her own fingers, but she was confident she would read about it in tomorrow's newspapers anyway, provided she still had the ability to read. Zooey drove considerably well for someone who kept one hand on the horn all the time, and she even seized a tranquil stretch between unanimously red lights to check the radio for a decent station, although she desisted when she had to steer left for the expressway so hard that she goaled a newspaper vending box right into a bar and grill. After that, it was just a minute's worth of dangerous overtakes and a couple of chain collisions on the junction before leaving behind the last skyscraper and hurtling onto the empty road to the coast.

Far ahead, where the dark earth and the last blue sigh of yesterday met, Zooey saw the single red taillight again.

"Do you have Danny's number?"

"Yes," Ursula uttered.

"Call him."

Ursula glanced through her hands, found some reassurance in the scarcity of objects with which they could collide head-on in the desert, and pulled out her cell phone.

—

In the Jaguar, Danny, wedged facedown on the backseat floor, felt a new kind of vibration on his chest, besides that of the 464-horsepower engine reverberating through the chassis directly beneath him. The tune to *Dora the Explorer* also came out of his breast pocket.

"Is that you?" Juno asked, distractedly aiming the pistol at him while she steered with her left. "Please, pick it up. No problem."

It took him a while to roll over on his injured leg, but the caller did not desist before he was able to draw a hand to his pocket and take the call.

"Yeah?"

"Hi!" Zooey greeted. "Put me on speaker."

Danny obeyed and strained to prop the cell phone in the drink compartment.

"Juno!"

"Zooey!" the killer answered. "I'm driving, talking to you, and aiming a gun at this guy's brain. Try and make it quick."

"Let me take some of your load: give me Danny."

"No way." Juno queried her mirror. "In fact, I might shoot his other leg if you don't keep your distance."

"We can make a deal."

"I don't make deals."

"Come on, not even with your old friend Zooey? I'm as nuts as you."

"I'm not nuts. I'm thorough."

"Not that much. You missed a spot."

"What are you talking about?"

"You were trying to get rid of the spawn of Victor Lyon, weren't you? Well, you forgot one. There's a tween Lyon. She's adorable! Say hi, Ursy."

URSULA: What are you doing?

"Good girl. So, what do you think, Jay? My hostage for yours?"

Juno, frowning, checked with her hostage. Danny looked just as confused.

"Is that really a kid there with you?" Juno wondered. "Where did she come from?"

"Glad you asked! Theoretically, she's Victor's daughter from his second wife, but actually she's Xander's daughter."

URSULA: I'm *what*?!

"Shit. Sorry, I meant to tell you in private. Whatever. The thing is, Juno Mars, she's a pure-blooded Lyon."

DANNY: Zooey, what the fuck?!

"That can't be true," Juno said. "You're playing me. There's no little girl."

"Oh, don't be silly—just look at your phone screen."

Juno let go of the gun or the steering wheel (both options were considerably reckless) and picked up the cell phone.

A little girl in a Bulbasaur costume grinned at her from a profile picture above the name: *Ursula Lyon*.

Juno floored the brake into the ninth circle of hell. The Jaguar skidded a full U-turn after one O-turn along a hundred-yard stretch, ripping flames off the tarmac.


In the Camaro, Zooey saw the lonely red light far ahead become two whites and pulled up.

"She's here with me, Juno," she lured into Ursula's phone. "Come and get her."

Then she hung up.

She turned to the terrified little girl in the backseat. "Right side, seat belt, head between your knees."

The kid stared back, black teary eyes undecided between brown and green, like a broken compass. Her mind ached with a thousand thoughts put on hold; too many things had happened in the last five minutes.

"Ursy, look *at me*," Zooey ordered.

Ursula's eyes found hers, startled. Zooey's unusual gravitas garnered the attention of the purring car and the desert itself.

"I know what I'm doing. I can play this game. Better than Adrian. But you have to do exactly as I say: right side, seat belt, head between your knees. Now."

Ursula breathed in and out twice, then tightened up her seat belt and pulled her legs up.

Juno studied the Jaguar's steering wheel, concluded that if her entrance in Villa Leona had not caused the airbags to deploy it was surely because there were none, sighed, and then casually glanced at Danny.

"You might want to hold on to something."

The tires scraped another inch-thick layer of asphalt before firing the luxury sedan from 0 to 60 in 5.6 seconds.

Zooey made out the other car's lights approaching and dedicated Juno a smug smirk.

"Right-brainer."

She gripped the wheel, pressed the accelerator, and let the needle on the speedometer get acquainted with the right end of the dial.

—

Juno shifted two gears up at a time, the engine's roar wandering out of tune due to the excitement.

Kimrean shifted to third, fixed her waistcoat, smoothed her tank top, pursed her lips at the mirror, shifted to fourth.

A dung beetle roaming in the middle of the road suddenly became aware of the air pressure on both sides rising slightly, foreshadowing the confluence of two four-wheeled horizontal rockets at jet fighter speed.

Gritted teeth.

White knuckles turned whiter.

Electric-blue eyes charging up.

Brown and green ones' pupils shrinking under the opposing lights.

Two racing hearts counting the thousandths of a second available for the sudden steer that spares both from the impending catastrophe, and Zooey glances out her side window.

"Oh, look! Roadrunner!"

—

The crash sent a circular shock wave rippling across the tarmac, undulating the road and the desert like the surface of a pond after the drop of a meteor. The momentum was way too much for either car to stop the other: the vintage muscle car simply bounced over the larger, heavier sedan like it was a speed bump, made a full corkscrew in the air, and landed far away in the ditch.

A. Z. Kimrean stayed on the road, though. They flew straight through the Camaro's windscreen on impact, glided some fifty yards through the air, then skidded fifty more on the coarse pavement.

They stopped, eventually, at the end of a trail of blood and glass powder parallel to the yellow dashed line.

The wind carried their tattered fedora a few seconds later.


Some minutes of unsuspected quietude followed.

Inside the yellow-striped blue wreck, Ursula regained consciousness to the sound of someone struggling with the warped door to her right. The seat belt had held her, at the cost of a burning red abrasion on her neck and a painful whiplash. She smelled blood in her nose from booping against the front seat. She couldn't see anything: the stars had flicked off.

In fact, it took her quite a while to notice she was upside down.

The door opened, or came clanking off its hinges, and Ursula caught the gleam of a moonlit gun.

Juno, covered in glittery bulletproof glass, a broken arm hanging dead by her side with a piece of ulna sticking out to stargaze, allowed the desert night to adumbrate the face of the surviving child. Ursula never made out the killer's features against the full moon.

Their breathing was heavy again, but not frantic. Juno's hand was steady.

She murmured over the handcannon: "You could have just gotten out of the car, you know."

Ursula thought about it. It had never occurred to her.

Or to Zooey.

She felt a tear blossom in her eye and roll down her forehead.

"That would have meant leaving me on the curb," she whispered.

The killer clicked the gun's safety off.

Or maybe on.

"I know a little girl in love when I see one," she said.

And that was all.

She pocketed the gun and left on foot, heading west. The diner and the parking lot could not be that far.


Danny, wrapped inside a luxury twisted steel-and-aluminum cocoon, was already grazing his phone with his fingertip when he heard the first sirens.

A beautiful post-traumatic sun shone over the Bay Area, despite the new low-pressure front drifting in from Southern California. Meanwhile, a state government staffer had apologized for his unfortunate remarks on Armenian American citizens, BART was promising the renovation of its trolleybus fleet, and California Democrats had just announced their candidate for the Fifty-Fourth District—Gran South County. Hollywood rejoiced with the first photographs of a popular star couple's second adopted child, and the Sacramento Kings had eked out an unlikely victory over the Lakers, 92–89. As for the weather, a beautiful sun was shining over the Bay Area.

Adrian squirmed to escape the nightmare of the infinite news loop, but dull, firm, multitudinous pain reined him in. White light and gamma rays jumped on his retinas like the infected on Milla Jovovich in the *Resident Evil* movies. Or like Zooey on Milla Jovovich that day they ran into her in a Wendy's. He lowered his eyelids, breathed once for courage, and lifted them a crack. He saw dust specks flying like distant whip-poor-wills in a sunray and the green hillscape of his EEG. He made out a balcony in the far back and the inconsiderately white day.

In front he saw his sheets, a doorway, and a hallway in that bland pistachio green that is widely believed to soothe patients, thanks to psychiatrists who persistently ignore the evidence that homicidal mania feeds on pastel hues. To his right sat a retro wooden radio, its voice pushed into the background by the noisy morning light.

He asked the pain permission to prop himself up and sat on his elbows. He caressed the many slashes across his arms, all shiny red. His right hand sported a clean bandage. Beneath the impractical hospital gown he felt more bandages constricting his chest, substituting the elastic band he used to wear for the same reason. He touched another bandage around his head; a swollen cheekbone too. He counted his teeth, then checked his nose, broken and realigned again. That was twice in one weekend.

"Well, there's another unlikely story for you," he said, and closed his eyes.

After a second he opened them again. Intrigued, he checked the inside of his skull.

"Zooey."

In a delicate close-up shot, the brown and green irises shuddered with the opening and slamming of doors behind them.

"Zooey?"

The Kings had beaten the Lakers 92–89 and a beautiful sun was shining over the Bay Area.

Kimrean's left hand scratched that side's ear.

"Oh shit. I need a cigarette."

A mischievous smile came to haunt their face.

"Breathe, nerd. Who would beat your ass at chess if I wasn't here?"

—

Danny Mojave, or some Danny Mojave from a parallel universe with a bruised face and one leg in a splint and his sexiness lost to another polka-dotted gown, yet retaining the sunglasses from this dimension, limped in through the balcony door, a Newport hanging off his lips.

"Well, hello. How many children are up?"

"All of them," Kimrean puffed, letting the fluffy pillow swallow them back like the Cure's Robert Smith in that music video with the spider. "I saved your ass again, didn't I?"

"Yes, you did. As neatly and with as much regard for public and private property as is your trademark," Danny said. "You've been in and out for two days. Let's call your doctor."

"I'm thirsty."

"Coming." He pressed the call button and went on to fill a Dixie cup. "You lucky bastards got the room with a terrace."

"Is that whiskey?"

"No, it's water. Remember water? The thing you wash yourself with?"

"I want whiskey," Zooey spoke like a toddler, but she still pulled the cup to their lips and drank it up. Then she gently held on to the cop's wrist. "Danny."

"Yes?"

"Your car."

"What about it?"

"It's not in Pristina."

Danny laughed as hard as his broken ribs could bear.

"I know, you stupid bitch. Who gives a damn."


The doctor joined in a few seconds later, stood arms akimbo before the bed.

"Do you know how much it upsets me every time I get a phone call and it's about you?"

"Gwe-e-e-e-en!" Zooey sang, spreading her arms to the maximum width allowed by the tubes.

Gwen hugged Kimrean, and seeing the opportunity, she also read their pulse and checked their pupil reflex. She was wearing the compulsory white coat on top of street clothes. She then slapped Danny on the side; he bent in pain.

"You been smoking."

"Aw, fuck! You too!"

"I'm a doctor, I do what I want."

KIMREAN: I saved his life!

GWEN: *(Reading the EEG.)* I know.

DANNY: Yes, you did.

"Is Ursula okay?" Zooey wondered, concerned.

"She is; she was released yesterday," Danny told. "And Victor Lyon will live too. He's already trying to cut a deal. I talked to Demoines—he's singing enough names to reset San Carnal to the pioneers' age. They're talking promotions all around."

"Wow, I'm good," Kimrean said, leaning back again. "Juno?"

"She escaped. Stole a car from the diner; the next day it was found on the Mexican border. No sign of the waitress either."

"Damn. Almost a perfect ten."

"That's not important. You were hired to get me out alive and stop a gang war. You did that and made my time undercover worth it." Danny raised his sunglasses, exposing some more bruises around the eyes, and clasped Kimrean's left wrist. "To me, you outdid yourself. Selves."

Adrian noticed the nuance. "To you. So, what did I miss?"

DANNY: Nothing.

GWEN: Well . . .

KIMREAN: What?

The radio cared to fill the pause by reminding everyone of how sunny it was outside.

"Well, some people resent how Juno and Cecilia were allowed to escape," Danny said. "I mean, no one questions your allegiance, but there are some concerns from the brass about your methods. Because, you know, you've been linked to several instances of reckless driving in San Francisco and San Carnal . . . and then there's the part where you brought a minor to a gunfight and played chicken with another car with said minor in your backseat, which kind of constitutes child endangerment."

"I wasn't putting her in danger," Zooey protested. "I was looking after her."

"Zooey," Gwen intervened, "did you notice that she was safer in San Francisco before you took her back into the combat zone?"

Zooey gave the question a fair amount of thought.

"Well, I see it *now*," she said.

"Look," Danny resumed, "Demoines and Greggs and even Chief Carlyle—they all support you. But some people in the security bureau suggested to temporarily suspend your P.I. license. Which is expired, as it turns out."

Kimrean blinked. Twice.

"I was planning on renewing it any day now."

"The head of the bureau said you could have it back," Gwen chimed in, "provided that you first . . . submit to some psychological evaluation. For a few days. In a suitable institution."

She and Danny stood by while the patients digested that information.

"They can't lock me up again," Kimrean said. "I've only been out for a week."

"Well, you gotta admit it's been an intense week," Danny remarked.

"No. Fuck you—where have you been all my life? This was a pretty smooth week. Bumpy, at most."

Gwen tried to push them back to bed: "Listen, we'll cross that bridge when we get there; first you two have to get better and—"

"No way," Kimrean declared, flipping off the sheets. "I'm not gonna lie around for the orderlies to get me."

GWEN: Ayzee—

KIMREAN: Aw, soothe your saggy bags, Mom! I'll be fine, just give me— *(Falls facefirst to the floor.)*

Danny and Gwen stayed put, the former too hurt to help, the latter too surprised, while Kimrean, welcoming the smell of chlorophenol on their nostrils, muttered: "Okay. There might be a problem."


Two more days elapsed in the same ward, whose pastel-green walls went from inefficiently soothing to frankly annoying.

The second day was going off like a cigarette in an ashtray. Greggs and Demoines and Danny Mojave were present, all passing the X-rays around and pretending to interpret them, while Dr. Gwen Temperance Quain, in the same white coat from two days ago and the same street clothes below, leafed through the results of the tests performed on A. Z. Kimrean—the ones sitting in the wheelchair.

"The legs are fine," she said. "And the X-rays show no injury to your medulla, so the problem has to be in your head. That's what got the worst of the trauma; the swelling when you were brought in might have pressed too hard on your brain, constricting the blood flow in your psychosomatic system. It would explain why you retain sensitivity in both legs, but no mobility in the right one."

Kimrean said nothing. They weren't looking. Nobody was. Gwen skipped a page of her notes. She had slept about four hours out of the last forty-eight.

"It's difficult to establish a prognosis; brain traumas are already unpredictable, but in your case they're worse. The asymmetry of the lesion is very infrequent. Your left leg is responding quite well, but the right one . . . in layman terms, your brain knows it's there, but can't talk to it."

Greggs alighted a hand on Kimrean's shoulder, white-skinned and bare under the gown. Kimrean swatted it off like a horsefly.

"We can try rehab," Gwen continued. "If your left leg improves, you can switch to a crutch. As for the right one . . . I don't think there's much we can do."

Kimrean's mouth barely moved to ask, "Whose leg is it?"

"That's irrelevant; you are both—"

"Whose leg?"

The doctor sighed. She pretended to search for the answer on a different page, but she knew it without a doubt. It was not irrelevant; she had performed the DNA tests herself.

"It's Adrian's."

Gwen lowered her clipboard shield and confronted her patients.

Their reaction was undetectable. Barely a minimal pursing of the already inconspicuous lips, nothing else. Whereas the cops surrounding them rubbed their jaws, clicked their tongues, swayed away from the blow, Kimrean never flinched, never took their eyes off the same spot on the floor tiles beyond their bare feet propped on the footrests. The hands did not shift; the chest did not heave; the brow remained taut like a lying sphinx's. The eyes didn't blink; the brown and green irises didn't glint, or dim, or show a glimpse of what was happening behind. Nothing in that mouthless, colorless mannequin mien moved—and yet, after a minute, the whole meaning of that expression had changed.

And by the time the lips reappeared, the only thing to come out of Kimrean's lips was "I'm sorry."

Those were their last words for another two days.

Visits ceased. Danny was released the morning after, and even though he considered staying, rightfully guessing that somebody might need him close, he also guessed that somebody else, like a dog guarding its turf, would bark him away. He didn't need to ask, because he feared the barks.

In the end, he gave priority to Adrian's explicit will over Zooey's unspoken wish, and he took a cab home. Half an hour later, he arrived at the apartment he had not stepped into for eighteen months. He removed his black jacket and shirt, as fast as his injuries allowed, and put on an old campy tee. After that, no other indulgence seemed urgent—not his music, not the TV, not a drink, not even a cigarette. He sat down in a shrouded armchair by the window and pondered the full meaning of the phrase "permanent condition."

On the third day, a psychiatrist was due to visit Kimrean to evaluate their state and recommend their transfer to a different hospital. The patients' left leg had improved remarkably, perhaps upon realizing that its fitness was the only thing now separating the Kimreans from a full-time caretaker. That was a scenario that Adrian would simply not consent to. Two is already a crowd. Three is a prologue to homicide.

Gwen had respected Kimrean's muteness for the first day, she had tried to break it on the second, and she was still mad about the results on the third, when she rapped on their door.

"Got a visitor."

Kimrean lay on the bed, facing the balcony, their left side buried in the pillow. The visitor was smart enough not to block their line of sight; she approached them from behind instead.

Adrian had recognized her well before she entered the room: by her gait, by the rustle of her clothes, by her smell. In all fairness, the scent of marijuana had disappeared.

"Gwen told me about your leg," Ursula said. "How are you?"

There was no answer.

"How are you, Zooey?"

Adrian spoke into the pillow. "Zooey's grounded."

Ursula didn't dare go around the bed. Her arm was still in a sling—the only memento of the car crash she kept.

"I wanted to explain to everyone that you did what you had to do, but no one listens to me. They arrested my mom in the Caymans. They're going to send me to a foster home. Just like you."

The parallels did not stir any sympathy.

"Can I speak to Zooey, please?"

"Get lost."

A seagull landed clumsily on the balcony's stone rail. Ursula checked her hands: they were trembling. She immediately knew that this realization would trigger all the other symptoms, like an avalanche; next would be the lump in her throat and the tears in her eyes. She hurried to speak her mind before it happened.

"It wasn't her fault, you know that. You injected yourself with the medicine; you were trying to block her out. You overdosed, and she had to take the wheel. She did the best she could."

"Hoo-fucking-ray."

"She solved the case."

"She showed up for the climax."

"She saved my life," Ursula whimpered right before the sob.

Kimrean went off, rolling over, their face red with anger:

"She traded it for *my* fucking leg!! Had anyone asked for my opinion, I would have said it was a shit deal!! *And so would she!!*"

Gwen, from the nurses' station outside, saw the child dart out of the room, tears running freely down her cheeks. Ursula fended off the social services worker who'd accompanied her and crashed through the restroom door.

The social services worker, a sweet lady in her thirties who had allowed Ursula to do most of the talking to Gwen, locked eyes with the doctor and then, looking helpless, sat back down.

A messenger was coming up the hallway now, carrying a bunch of flowers. He stopped by the counter and showed Gwen the card. She read it; in her face gleamed a private smile. She tipped the messenger and took the flowers to Kimrean's room, without knocking.

"You can punish her as much as you want, Adrian. She'll always have more fans than you."

She tossed the flowers on the bedside table behind the patient and left.

The perfume reached Kimrean's nose a second later. They turned over. *Erithra lunis.* A dozen red roses.

The outside of the card bore only two initials, *Z.K.* On the inside, there was a small home-printed picture and a frugal message. The picture—a selfie—described two girls on a boardwalk by the beach. Juno, eyes the color of a lagoon in the Pacific, held the camera with her left arm, which was in a cast, while kissing the other girl's cheek. Cecilia, the former waitress, had red hair, gray eyes, and a round face with many freckles and a candid, small-toothed smile.

Kimrean stayed on her for a minute, and resolved: "Well, she wasn't that great."

The handwritten message read, *Well played.*

Adrian lowered the card and confronted the big toe at the end of his right leg wiggling at him.

"What the . . . Are you doing that?"

"Yup. Can't you?"

The toe stopped moving. Adrian focused on it, ordered it to twitch. He tried shaking his whole leg: the response stopped at his hip; the rest only jolted with inertia.

Then Zooey tried again. All five toes waved hello.

"This can't be. We share a somatic system."

"I don't think this was the trauma after all. I think it was the overdose," Zooey said. "You got brain damage. *You* lost your leg. I didn't."

Adrian stuttered, but Zooey cut him off:

"Don't fret—I'll treat it as if it were mine."

Running on crutches is not particularly difficult if circumstances demand it; stealth mode on crutches is something more of a challenge. Kimrean poked their head out into the hallway and took a census of the waiting room and the nurses' station beyond. Nurses, doctors, a social worker cracking the *USA Today* sudoku, and Gwen browsing Kimrean's clinical history. It was easy to spot—it was the only file that came in two volumes.

Kimrean hopped across to the neighboring room, yanked the monitoring sensors from the mortal coil of an old man who had been dozing there for two weeks, and returned to their own room as soon as the alarms went amok, summoning all medical personnel next door. Kimrean scurried along the empty hallway behind them.

Gwen, in her role as guest doctor, had not joined the others, but she leaned into the hallway anyway. Bewildered though she was to see Kimrean moving around, a natural and long-tested inclination to secrecy when it came to her star patients' life prevailed. She just mouthed, *Your legs!* to which Zooey cartoonishly mimed, *I know, right?* while Adrian signaled at the waiting area outside.

She did not require any more instructions: she breathed in, put on her best unambitious doctor smile, said something friendly yet professional to the social worker, and pointed at the file as if she wanted to share something under the window light. Her own body stance subtly forced the woman to turn her back to Kimrean as they stole the few yards to the ladies' room.

They hurried past the stalls and checked the window. It was a short jump to the balcony, and then a fire ladder down to the ambulance parking lot. In Kimrean's rating system of medical institutions based on breakout convenience, the SF General had always been a solid 8. Exhilarated, Zooey couldn't refrain from singing the "Best of Buddies" theme from *Snoopy, Come Home* while she hopped onto the sill and helped their legs up:

*Me and you,*
*A two-man crew*

"Zooey?"

A door banged and Ursula emerged from a stall, her face tear-stroked.

"Zooey, is it you?"

"Heeeey, Ursy!"

She considered the safest way to hop back to the floor, but before she could the child was hugging her legs, asking, "Where are you going? You can walk?! Where are you going?!"

"I'll walk fine in a few days, but I need to disappear for a while. There's people intent on putting a jacket on me, and you know I hate business attire."

"Well, I'll go with you!"

Zooey repressed a quip, as though she had been given the wrong cue. She gazed down into Ursula's starry black eyes.

"I will," the child insisted. "I'm a fugitive too! They want to put me in a foster home, we can hide together, I . . . It's what I want to do," she said, stiffening up, making sure she looked composed enough. "It's the role I want. I want to be the girl."

Kimrean stayed frozen, perched on the windowsill, through a soft, snowy silence.

Slowly an honest yet crooked smirk appeared on their face.

"Ursy, I'm so sorry. You can't."

The air around them was still and crystal clear, like a beautiful sunny day atop Mount Everest.

"But—but they're going to take me away," Ursula stuttered. "They'll put me in a foster home! I can't go to a foster home! I—"

"I know, I know it's tough, but . . . Look, some foster families are fine, and where I'm going—"

"I can go!" Ursula cut her off. "I can look after myself!"

"Yes, you can. But you can't look after me."

The mannequin face looked disarmingly calm, the smirk never fading away. Her whisper could stop a charging army.

"And I need to be looked after," she resumed. "I do. The jerk is right sometimes. I can't just block him out. It's dangerous."

"But they're gonna take me away, and they'll make me change

schools, and—and you promised! You promised!" Ursula rapid-fired, burning through every argument, just because she feared that any words now could be the last words, and none of them would matter, and she was sobbing, and she could only hold Zooey with one hand because the other one was in the stupid sling, and there was no way this could be the end because they were so close now, face-to-face.

"Ursy, I promised I cared," Zooey said. "And I do. You're too young, and I'm wanted in too many states now." She shrugged, pointing at the gap between them. "This is me caring about you."

"No, it's not!" Ursula countered, punching their leg in anger. "This is you discarding me, like you promised you wouldn't do! It's typical male writer bullshit—kicking the girl out when she opens her heart! So what—*now* I'm too young?! So the right thing to do all along was to kick me out into the street? You're telling me Adrian did the right thing?!"

Zooey fell silent, choosing the next words really carefully. There was, at some point, a jerk toward the window, like a reflex, but she contained it. The smirk was gone.

"No, he didn't do the right thing. He was only trying to spare himself this."

She slid off the windowsill as gracefully as she could, and for a moment it seemed their bad leg was yielding, but it wasn't. It was Zooey taking a knee, mismatched eyes level with Ursula's, delivering the final speech point-blank at her face.

"I've seen your routine. You're a tattered child raised in crime-paid luxury into whom life has smacked too many lessons too quickly, forcing you to grow a carapace of protective sass under which a soft heart yearns for love, and that's a cliché grown-ups find annoying because deep down they wish they were like you.

They wish—we wish we had that ingenuity, that resilience, that capacity for love, because we lost it long ago. You keep something precious under your carapace while people who look down on you are just empty shells, beaten by lives not necessarily harder than yours, grown cynical and materialistic since they decided it was easier to fling shit back at the world than try to stay clean, and now here you are, dazzling them. And they skulk through life clinging to Adrian's doctrine, forgoing empathy and sensitivity, being hard-boiled and tweeting hate while they vampire the light from people like you, claiming that somebody will do it anyway, that you're too good a thing to last. Because adults are fucked up: we are so toxic that we ruin good things just by thinking of them, so nihilistic we wouldn't know what to do with your kindness, so hypocritical we think the right move is to kick you out into the street, to throw you to the wolves before someone thinks we are wolves ourselves. But nothing they do, Ursula Lyon, will wither you. On the contrary, you will thrive on their bullshit, like flowers do, and you'll light up everything you touch; you will improve everyone's story just by being there, whatever role you play, like you improved mine. You are smart, you are tough, you are honorable, and you are so kind you can see me through Adrian's abuse and you can see Adrian through my insanity, and I can count on *my hand* the people who can do that, so there is no way I am ever discarding you. I will see you again, many times, and I will never let anyone push you out of my life. In fact, I would totally hug and kiss you right now if Adrian were not holding me with everything he has."

Ursula chuckled at the last sentence, and she wiped a tear. It was the chuckle of ultimate truth, the smile of an actress right after the director says cut, the intimate joy of seeing the other's soul naked and acknowledging yours is naked too.

They looked at each other, and they knew they would never be alone.

"Also, you know what?" Zooey said. "I think Danny was the femme fatale all along, because all he did was get in trouble and have me save his hot Mark Ruffalo ass all the . . . what?"

She saw Ursula's eyes widen in shock.

URSULA: *(Pointing.)* There! Roadrunner!

ZOOEY: Oh my God where, WHERE?!

The second she turned, Ursula lurched forth and hugged her like a tiny sumo wrestler in love.

And that was it. Ursula squeezed all that temporary power and made sure that her last words were *I love you I love you I love you I love you* whispered a million times into Kimrean's left ear. Then she planted a kiss on their cheek, let them go, and added: "Sorry, Adrian. Good-bye."

Adrian stared at her blankly, the smirk and the mouth all gone. He sighed, nodded millimetrically to acknowledge the apology, and hoisted themselves up, flamingoing on the leg he could use. Zooey was too drunk to pilot. He hopped back onto the windowsill, opened the window, chucked out the crutches first, and jumped out.

They landed on the fire escape, and their legs failed to hold them up and they fell on the metal grille, but that held them up just a few seconds before standing straight again, tossing the crutches over the rail, releasing the ladder, and descending to street level.

Inside an open ambulance they found a neon-yellow vest, a shirt, and some boots. They put it all on over their gown; they were missing some pants, but from the waist up they could pass without being looked at thrice. They limped around the vehicle and climbed into the driver's seat, quarreling between their teeth:

"Remember, perv—I drive. You hear me?"

"Okay."

"I drive!"

"Okay."

As they were torquing the key in the ignition, the shotgun door opened and a fat paramedic puffed on board, reading from a clipboard.

"Mission and 24th, motorbike crash, one nonresponsive— better step on it."

He looked up from his orders right then. There was a second's worth of silence, spruced up by the idle engine.

"You're new, aren't you?" He offered a hand; Kimrean accepted it. "Robert. Fancy, fifteen years on the job, never had a girl driver. Come on, show me what you can do."

A smile like the San Andreas Fault split Kimrean's face the second before flooring the gas.

# About the Author

Edgar Cantero is a writer and cartoonist who was born in Barcelona in 1981. *This Body's Not Big Enough for Both of Us* is his fifth novel and the third in English, after *Meddling Kids* and *The Supernatural Enhancements*.